Kick the Bouquet

A Flower Shop Mystery

Kate Collins

Kick the Bouquet
A Flower Shop Mystery
Copyright © 2022 Linda Tsoutsouris
All rights reserved.

ISBN: 9798366535403

Cover design by Arash Jahani

CONTENTS

"When solving problems, dig at the roots instead of just hacking at the leaves."

-Anthony J. D'Angelo

PROLOGUE

Wednesday, November 16th

Attorney Dave Hammond cleared his throat and began to read, "I, Arthur McMahon, of Port County, Indiana, declare this to be my Last Will, revoking all previous Wills and Codicils."

The attorney glanced around at the faces in the room before continuing. Arthur McMahon's oldest son, Rowell, wearing an unbuttoned navy suit jacket and a crisp white dress shirt that fit too snugly over his bulging belly, sat forward in his chair with an eager gleam in his eye. His brown hair was short but curly on top. His once stubbled double chin had been freshly shaven, and Dave could still see the angry, red razor burns.

In the corner behind Rowell sat his younger brother, Birch, dressed in a ragged-looking tan blazer, a brown t-shirt, and jeans with holes in the knees. This was the first time Dave had seen Arthur McMahon's youngest son. He had long dirty-blond hair tucked behind his ears making him look more like a rock star than a mechanic. With a nervous twitch in his left eye, Birch focused not on Dave, but on each of his siblings. There was also a noticeable smell of body odor and motor oil coming from the corner where Birch sat. Dave wrinkled his nose and looked down at the papers in his hand.

"Can we hurry this along, please? I have an appointment across town in fifteen minutes."

Dave looked over at McMahon's only daughter, who tapped her diamond-encrusted wristwatch. A woman in her early thirties, Crystal looked the most put together of the group, with an off-the-shoulder red top and tight black skirt. She had large brown eyes layered in mascara, with exceedingly long eyelashes. She was rail thin yet remarkably voluptuous, leaving Dave to wonder whether her curves were as fake as her lashes.

Behind them stood Grant Starling, McMahon's business partner, a tall, older gentleman with bright blue eyes and thick gray hair who was well known around town for his winning personality and charity work. He made a show of checking his watch as well, and once he had Dave's attention, he recrossed his arms and nodded his head, encouraging Dave to proceed.

Attorney Hammond cleared his throat. Everyone was listening with rapt attention, all waiting to hear what they had received. He read through the standard language of Item I, directing that all bills be paid first, and then paused again. "Any questions so far?"

Head shakes all around except for Birch, who seemed unsure of what was going on.

"Item two," the attorney continued. "At the time of signing this, my Last Will and Testament, I have attached hereto and made a part hereof, a specific listing of certain items of personal and household effects and designating to whom those items are to be distributed. I incorporate by reference this listing and direct that my Personal Representative will distribute those items to the person or persons so designated to receive them."

Each person sat forward expectantly, waiting to see who the personal representative would be. No one seemed the least bit aggrieved by the sudden, tragic loss of this man. Not that Dave could blame them. Arthur McMahon had been a real piece of work, a loud, self-centered sociopath, but a genius when it came to making money. Dave wondered what kind of father Arthur had been. Or business partner, for that matter.

"Item three," the attorney read. "I constitute and appoint my son Rowell to act as my Personal Representative of this Will."

Crystal pouted. Grant Starling didn't seem surprised. Birch's clueless expression remained the same.

"Item four," the attorney read. "To my son Rowell, I leave the downtown building known as Five Franklin Street, my real estate properties, and one third of my estate."

Rowell folded his hands across his expansive belly, looking pleased.

"To my son Birch, I leave my Lamborghini and one third of my estate."

Birch sat back, his eyes widening.

"To my daughter Crystal, I leave the house and one third of my estate."

Crystal smiled, studying her long polished fingernails.

"To my business partner Grant Starling, I leave the business known as McMahon and Starling Realty together with all office equipment and furniture."

Starling didn't bat an eye.

Fifteen minutes later, the attorney put down the document and removed his reading glasses to rub the bridge of his nose. It was done and everyone looked content. But then McMahon had been exceptionally generous, more generous than he should've been by the stories McMahon had told him.

That thought made the attorney pause. The hungry looks in the eyes before him made Dave feel uncomfortable, as if they were a pack of jackals waiting to pick the carcass of the freshly deceased.

Before Dave could say anything further, however, Rowell stood and wiped the sweat from his wide brow. "Thank you, Mr. Hammond. That will be all." He strode to the door and turned to say, "We won't be needing your services anymore. Have the paperwork sent to my father's office" -he cast a good-humored, if not somewhat sardonic, glance at McMahon's business partner- "or should I say, Grant's office."

At that, Crystal stood, smoothing the wrinkles from her skirt before following Rowell through the door. Grant Starling followed behind, leaving Birch still sitting by himself in the corner. He raised his hand, as if out of habit, then put it down and asked, "When do I get the car?"

Dave answered his question and waited until Birch had gone before closing the file. Had McMahon really been killed by an intruder, Dave wondered, or had the true murderer been sitting in this room?

CHAPTER ONE

Sunday, November 13th
   Three days earlier . . .

Marco opened the door that led from the garage into the house, and we stepped into the hallway, setting down our suitcases with tired sighs. No three-legged mutt hobbled up to greet us. No Russian Blue cat wound around our legs.

Marco and I removed our shoes in eerie silence.

"The house feels so empty," I said.

"Don't worry. It won't be empty for long." He pulled me close to him.

At five-foot-two, I had to stand on tiptoe to kiss him. My handsome husband, Marco Salvare, a former Army Ranger, with his manly swagger, his dark hair that waved down over one eye, and sexy five o'clock shadow, still made my heartbeat quicken, even after almost two years of marriage.

He bent down for another kiss and said, "I had a great time."

"Me too," I told him.

He picked up both suitcases and headed off to the bedroom. "Let's get unpacked before we call Theda."

Marco wasn't just my husband, however. He was also my best friend, my hero. We'd met just after I'd bought Bloomers Flower Shop, when my beloved vintage Corvette had been hit by a hit-and-run driver who had ended up being a suspect in a murder case. Marco had come down the street from his bar, Down the Hatch, to see what the ruckus was about and had ended up helping me solve the case. We'd been a twosome ever since.

I shook off thoughts of the past, realizing that goosebumps had risen on my arms. "Something feels off," I said, traipsing after him.

Marco had already emptied his suitcase onto the bed and was in the process of tossing his clothes into the laundry basket. "What feels off?"

"I don't know. I just have a funny feeling that something's about to go wrong."

"Why? Because you just had the most amazing, unscheduled, unblemished vacation, and now you feel the universe is going to retaliate?"

How did he know? "Don't make fun of me."

"I know you, Abby Knight Salvare. I know how your mind works. Nothing bad is going to happen to you. You'll be fine once you see the pets and get back into your routine."

I could only hope he was right. I shook off another shudder and opened my suitcase. Inside were the summer clothes I'd taken to Key West, where we'd gone to get away for a needed break after a grueling murder investigation. We'd left our animals with our next-door neighbor Theda Coros, a sixty-something woman who'd become an invaluable friend. We'd known they'd be in good hands. Why did I feel apprehensive now?

I put a load of laundry into the washing machine and pushed the button. Nothing happened. I lifted the lid and peered inside, but no water filled the tub. "I knew it!" I called. "I knew something was going to go wrong. Marco, the washer isn't working."

"I'll take care of it," he called. "I shut the water off is all."

I heaved a sigh of relief and headed to the kitchen, to the island in the middle where Theda had stacked the mail. Once again, I had that funny feeling and began to shuffle through the envelopes looking for bad news, like an overdue notice of a bill I'd forgotten to pay.

"Hello!" I heard Theda call, and then she stuck her head inside the door. "We're here!"

Little Seedy came loping into the kitchen first, her long bushy tail wagging excitedly as I bent to scratch her head. Seedy was a rescue, a sorrier sight I'd never laid eyes on, with a missing hind leg, patchy brown and white fur, an underbite, and a bristly muzzle. But she'd won me over with her big, loving brown eyes and sweet personality.

Considered unadoptable, Seedy had been at the top of the list to be euthanized when I'd found her at the animal shelter. I'd worked hard to find her a home, thinking that Marco wouldn't want to start married life with a new pet. But in the nick of time, Marco had swept in and rescued her.

Rescuing Seedy had been the second-best decision we'd ever made. The first, naturally, had been to marry each other.

Theda appeared next, a tall, imposing woman with the strong profile of her Greek heritage. "I hope I didn't bring them back too soon."

"Not at all," I said, and then felt Smoke rub against my legs. I bent down to run my hand down Smoke's back, and he purred in satisfaction. Months ago, Theda had been fostering the big, silver-blue cat when Smoke came to my rescue during a struggle with a murderer. I knew right then that we'd have to adopt him, too.

"How was your vacation?" Theda asked.

"Wonderful," I said. "We went parasailing, swam in the ocean, ate delicious meals-"

"I even got her out in a kayak," Marco said as he joined us. "We went through the mangroves and saw some enormous sea turtles."

"And a manatee," I added. "It was just the break we needed. Thank you so much for taking care of Seedy and Smoke."

"It was my pleasure," Theda said. "You know these two are my grandbabies."

Theda had no children and had been a widow for ten years. She didn't want pets of her own because of all the traveling she did, so we knew she appreciated the company. I'd long suspected that Theda had once worked for the CIA, or some other secret governmental agency based on the knowledge she'd shared on a previous murder investigation, but she would never admit to it.

"I do have some bad news to tell you," she warned.

I held my breath, waiting.

"The homeowners' association will be raising our dues in three months. You've got a notice in your pile of mail there."

I exhaled. That wasn't so bad. In fact, we'd been expecting it.

"Would you like some tea?" I asked her.

"No, no. I'm not going to keep you. I'm sure you have lots to do." She walked to the door and stooped to pet Seedy, who'd followed her. "Be a good girl now and come visit me soon." She straightened and smiled. And with that, she was gone.

"What do you say we take Seedy for a walk and stretch our legs," Marco said. "After that plane ride, I'm in need of some exercise."

We leashed Seedy, put on our jackets, and went out through the garage, closing it behind us. As we strolled down the sidewalk, I pulled my jacket closer against the chilly November breeze.

"Are you feeling better now?" Marco asked.

"I still have the feeling that something is going to go wrong."

Marco sighed heavily. "Nothing bad is going to happen to you."

He was such an optimist.

"Abby!" I heard and glanced across the street to see our neighbor Gayla come hurrying over. "Hi, Marco. Hey, you two, how was your trip?"

In this neighborhood, everyone knew everyone's business.

"Great," Marco and I said together.

"I just wanted to be the one to break some horrible news to you," Gayla said. She grimaced to emphasize the gravity of her information.

"We know about the homeowner's fees," Marco told her.

"No," Gayla demanded. "It's much worse than that."

I inhaled sharply. Here it came.

"Our mail delivery is going from ten-thirty in the morning to four-thirty in the afternoon. It'll take all day before we get our mail!"

I exhaled. That was hardly worth the excitement.

"Thanks for letting us know," Marco said.

As soon as Gayla had trotted back across the street Marco looked at me with a raised eyebrow. "Are you okay?"

"I am now. I honestly thought she had bad news."

Marco put his arm around my shoulders, "Babe, what's going on? We just had the most wonderful, stress-free vacation. Why are you so nervous?"

"I think that's exactly why I'm nervous. Everything has gone so well that I keep expecting the proverbial shoe to drop."

"I'll tell you what," Marco said. "Why don't we worry about the bad things when they happen, not before."

I suppressed the feeling and gave him a smile. "You're right. Let's talk about dinner instead. What do you say we order out?"

"Sounds like the perfect end to a perfect vacation."

Monday, November 14th

I loved Mondays. They were like doors opening up onto brand new vistas, an artist's canvas that had yet to be painted, brushes and paints at the ready. That Monday was no exception – with one exception. I still had the feeling that something was going to go wrong, and I couldn't figure out why. I'd fallen asleep in the arms of my loving husband, with our dog at my side and the cat at our feet. But then I'd awakened with that same feeling; Bad news was coming, and I had to prepare myself for it.

After a quick cup of coffee with Marco, I applied some blush and a light coat of lipstick, combed through my fiery red bob, grabbed my purse, jacket, and cell phone, and was out the door. Marco stayed behind. He didn't have to be at his bar, Down the Hatch, until mid-morning.

This November day was beautiful but too chilly to put down the top of my 1960 Corvette. Instead, I turned up the radio and sang along with a Beatles song. I'd rescued the vintage car after my assistant Lottie's nephew, a car repairman, found it abandoned in an old barn. The car had been rusty, and the leather seats torn, but because I'd bought it for a song, I'd been able to have the seats refurbished and the car repainted to my favorite color, yellow.

I parked in a public lot a block away from my shop and walked over to Franklin Street, where both Bloomers Flower Shop and Down the Hatch Bar and Grill were located. Franklin was one of four streets that formed a square around the old, imposing limestone courthouse and its wide expanse of lawn. Concerts were held there in the summer and people congregated at the park benches scattered around the perimeter.

Around the square were quaint gift shops, a women's boutique, a deli, a jewelry store, a shoe shop, three restaurants, several law offices, including that of Dave Hammond, my former boss, and much more, all housed in two-and three-story brick buildings built around 1900. I felt fortunate to have a shop on the town square.

I paused outside Bloomers to take it all in – the bright yellow frame door centered between two big bay windows filled with pots of blooming flowers, the red brick exterior that had been standing since the early nineteen-hundreds, and of course the sign over the door that read, *BLOOMERS FLOWER SHOP. Abby Knight, Prop.*

I still hadn't had the sign repainted to reflect my married name. It was Abby Knight Salvare now.

I stood for a moment gazing at the three-story redbrick building that housed Bloomers. The shop occupied the first floor, with the display room up front, a coffee-and-tea parlor off to one side, the workroom in the middle, and a small bathroom and kitchen across the back. A heavy fireproof door opened onto the alley and a steep staircase near the back door led to the basement. We kept larger supplies and huge flowerpots down there, along with pieces of my mom's art that we were too embarrassed to display in the shop.

I opened the door and walked inside, where the aroma of fresh flowers and freshly brewed coffee wafted around me.

"Welcome back!" Lottie called, coming out from behind the cash counter to hug me. "How was your vacation? No, no, don't tell me now. Wait until we get everyone together, so you only have to tell it once."

"Sounds like a plan," I said, then crossed my fingers and asked, "How's everything been going?"

"Running like a well-oiled machine," Lottie said. *Whew.*

Lottie Dombowski was a large Kentucky woman with curly red-orange hair and a proclivity for wearing pink. Today she had on a pink T-shirt and pink sneakers with jeans. Over her T-shirt, she wore the yellow bib apron with BLOOMERS printed on the front.

The mother of quadruplet teenage boys, Lottie had originally owned Bloomers. When I'd flunked out of law school, I'd come back to the flower shop where I'd worked summers hoping to find employment. What I'd found was a career. Lottie had taken me in and taught me everything she knew. And when her husband's medical bills had threatened to send them into bankruptcy, I'd come to her rescue, using the rest of my grandfather's college trust fund to buy the mortgage for the flower shop.

"Here's our girl," Grace called, sailing out of the coffee and tea parlor with a mug in her hands. "I figured you'd be needing a jolt of java to get you going this morning."

"Thanks, Grace. You've got that right." I took the cup from her and took a drink, closing my eyes as I savored the delicious hints of pumpkin spice and cloves. "Heaven," I said on a breath.

Grace Bingham, a slender, silver-haired woman in her sixties, was wearing her usual sweater set and skirt, this set in gray and blue floral with a gray skirt. She had been born and raised in the UK. She ran our coffee and tea parlor, a feature I'd created out of a storage room when I'd first bought the flower shop. It had proved to be a huge draw to shoppers on the square and the many employees at the courthouse. Grace brewed the best coffee in town.

"We're all excited to hear about your holiday," she said in her crisp British accent. "Unfortunately, you'll have to wait a bit. Rosa isn't here yet. She's had a mishap."

"I knew it," I exclaimed. "I knew something bad was going to happen."

"She's fine," Grace said. "Her son forgot his homework, so she had to go back home to get it."

Okay, so that wasn't it. I let out a sigh of relief.

Lottie folded her arms across her Bloomers smock. "But we do have some bad news," she said.

"What's wrong?"

"We've lost us another longtime customer," Lottie explained. "That's three this month we've lost to that new discount garden center."

"That is bad news," I said.

"But all is not lost," Grace beamed. "The coffee and tea parlor is picking up the slack. My scones are bringing in more customers every day."

Lottie patted Grace on the shoulder. "Word got out on Friday that Grace had made her crazy popular pumpkin scones, and suddenly there was a mad rush to get inside. Grace had to go home and make more scones."

"'Twas a madhouse," Grace said.

19

A madhouse I could handle. What I couldn't handle was more grim news about the new floral shop in the nearby city of Maraville, Dora's Discount Flower and Garden Center. Dora's occupied a huge former warehouse and ordered everything in bulk. Arrangements were pre-made and ready-to-go, drawing many New Chapel residents and former customers of ours. My small shop was no match.

Fortunately, Down the Hatch was pulling in a decent profit, and our private eye business was adding even more money to the nest egg. A slowdown at Bloomers wouldn't be the end of the world as far as our finances went. We still had a big group of loyal customers who would keep us going until the busy holiday season.

Then again, I'd noticed a few of our loyal customers hadn't come back either. Lottie had tried to calm my nerves, insisting that she'd seen many flower shops come and go, reminding me that we'd managed hard times before and would again. And although her words registered, the question remained, what if business never picked back up?

"Hola!" Rosa called as she came through the front door. She had on a shiny silver blouse and stretchy black slacks which showed off her voluptuous curves, and as always, a pair of high heels to match her outfit. "Welcome back, Abby! We've missed you."

"We were waiting for you, Rosa," Lottie said, "so Abby could tell us all about her trip."

"*Lo siento mucho*," Rosa said. "I'm so sorry. But please tell us now. We still have half an hour until we open."

Rosa Marisol Katarina Marin was a relatively new addition to the Bloomers family. Originally from Columbia, Rosa had come into our lives when Marco and I investigated her husband's death. Her nickname was *Relámpago*, which meant 'lightning.' Her husband had

20

called her that because she'd lit up his life like a flash of light. Bereft from the loss of her husband, Rosa had started hanging out at Bloomers and eventually began working on arrangements, revealing an innate talent for floral design. I'd hired her soon after.

We proceeded into the coffee parlor and pulled out chairs at one of the white, wrought iron ice cream-style tables. In the center of each table was a small vase filled with yellow, pink, and white mums. With its yellow walls and white curtains at the big bay window, it was a bright, cheery room. That is, until one of the fluorescent lights above my head began to flicker.

"Don't worry," Lottie assured. "Just an old bulb. Go on. How was your vacation?"

I had just finished my tale when there was a banging on the front door. Lottie checked her watch. "We don't open for another ten minutes."

I walked out of the parlor to see an attractive young woman with her hands cupped around her eyes, peering into the shop. She had on a bright blue silk shirt and black jeans, with black flats, and a black purse dangling from her shoulder.

"We open in ten minutes," I called through the door.

"I've got questions about wedding flowers and I have to be at work soon. Could we talk for a few minutes?"

I glanced back at Lottie, who shrugged. "It's up to you, sweetie."

Wedding flowers were always lucrative, so I made the decision to open the shop, especially now that Dora's Discount Flowers was stealing away my wedding business. I held open the door and she stepped inside, turning in a slow circle at the center of the showroom, taking in the floral arrangements all around her, some on the floor, some on the antique round oak table near where she stood, some on the big armoire against the inside wall, and some filling the glass case on the back wall.

She turned back to me with a smile. "You do small weddings, don't you?"

"Of course," I said.

"Great. Can I see some wedding arrangements?"

"Why don't you have a seat in the coffee parlor? I'll grab the wedding book and be right there."

Now that was how to start a Monday.

Once I had finished with the bride-to-be, I headed back to the workroom, parting the purple curtain and stepping into my paradise. It was a windowless room but the scents of all the flowers combined with the wreaths that hung on the walls, the arrangements in the process of being completed, the big stainless coolers, the large slate worktable in the middle covered with uncut stems - everything combined to make it a delightful place to create.

I put my purse under the computer desk on one side of the room, plucked an order from the spindle, and set to work.

"Hey, sweetie," Lottie said, sliding through the purple curtain that separated the workroom from the sales floor, "you've got a wedding consultation this afternoon at two. Woman by the name of Honey Chen. Sounds like she's planning something big."

"Fantastic." *Another wedding!* My fears had been for naught. Everything was going remarkably well.

The rest of the day flew by. Orders came in, Rosa and I made them, and Lottie delivered them. Customers came and went. The coffee parlor filled and emptied, and then it was two o'clock, time to meet with Honey Chen.

The parlor was fairly empty at that time of day, so I sat down with Honey in the corner near the front window. Honey was a very pretty Asian American with long jet-black hair pulled back in a loose bun with diamond earrings dangling at her ears. She was wearing what appeared to be a Chanel suit in powder blue, matching Ferragamo heels, and carrying what I was sure was a Dolce and Gabbana purse. Clearly, the woman had money.

"We're going to have a Christmas wedding," Honey said. "It's my fiancé's wish. And we want to have it at the New Chapel Country Club, in the banquet room. It's going to be epic, so I'll need lots of floral arrangements. Will you be able to come up with a plan? Price is really no concern to us."

I swallowed my excitement and kept a straight face. "I can do that. Why don't we go over some of your options, so I have an idea of what you're looking for?"

I spent the next hour with Honey as she poured over floral arrangements from our wedding catalogs and selected what she liked. She seemed very pleased with the plan, and I promised to have a quote for her by four o'clock the next day.

"This wedding is going to be huge," I told the ladies afterward. "If we get her business, it'll mean all hands on deck. I'll have to ask Jillian and Marco's mom to come in and help."

"Did I hear Honey say that it would be held at the country club?" Grace asked.

"Yes," I said. "Wedding and reception."

"We've never done a wedding at the country club before. We're bound to get more business from it," Lottie said.

Could the day get any better?

The next time I glanced at the clock, it was three-thirty on a Monday afternoon. That meant it was time for my mother to make her weekly appearance.

Maureen "Mad Mo" Knight was a kindergarten teacher who spent her weekends on various art projects, a different one each week, which she then brought down to Bloomers for us to sell. And she had made many –

from feather-covered picture frames whose colorful dyes had run all over the frames, to sea glass studded sunglasses that were so heavy it gave wearers headaches, to footstools whose legs looked like actual human feet, to bat mobiles, with actual hanging plastic bats – and too many more to mention.

We'd done our best to sell them, and rather than disappoint her, had toted what hadn't sold down to the basement, to a storage shelf that she'd never see. Now I waited to see what she'd bring in today, preparing for the worst. Maybe this was what I'd been dreading.

"Hi, ho," I heard from the other side of the curtain, and then it parted, and in came my mother, dressed today in her standard teacher outfit of a pair of beige slacks and a brown pullover sweater. She wore her light brown hair in a bob like mine but with bangs. She carried a tote bag that looked heavy.

"Hi, Mom. You look very nice today." I gave her a kiss on the cheek and went back to the roses I was cutting.

"Thank you, honey." She set the tote bag on the worktable and took a seat. "How was your vacation?"

"It was perfect," I said. "Exactly what we needed." I finished cutting the stems and placed them into a white ceramic vase, highlighting the deep red of the roses and the delicate white of the spider lilies. "My only problem is that I keep getting this strange feeling that something bad is going to happen. We had such a great time in Key West, too. No worries. No problems. But then I get back to New Chapel and something just feels wrong. I don't know how to explain it."

My mom smiled. "No need to explain. I know exactly how you feel."

"You do?"

"Oh, yes. I used to get that same feeling. It runs in the family, you know."

"What does?"

"Agoraphobia."

I put the shears down and focused on my mother's expression. She was completely sincere. "I don't have a fear of leaving the house, mom. I'm claustrophobic, not agoraphobic."

"Agoraphobia can manifest in many ways, Abigail." She almost always used my given name.

I scoffed and refocused my attention on the flower arrangement. "It's not manifested through me. I can promise you that."

My mother watched as I spun the vase, finessing the dainty white stems of the spider lilies. "Your aunt had it. Did you know that? Diagnosed and everything."

"She did?"

"As she got older, she became a shut-in."

"I remember that. She was afraid to leave the house."

"It wasn't that she was afraid to leave. As she grew older, her eyesight failed, and she was no longer allowed to drive. Your aunt simply refused to allow anyone to drive her around. She couldn't bring herself to relinquish control. That was her fear, and I believe that's what runs in the family, a fear of losing control."

I didn't want to believe I had agoraphobia, and yet there was something to her theory about losing control. "What about you?" I asked her. "You said you used to get the same feeling."

"Oh. Yes. It started when I went away to college. Nothing seemed familiar anymore and it scared me. The structure of my old life had seemingly vanished, and it was causing anxiety attacks. I had to see a specialist to learn techniques for dealing with that fear."

"Wow, Mom. I had no idea."

"Finally, I found something that helped, which is a wonderful segue into why I've stopped by today. I have something new to show you."

She reached into the tote bag, pulled out a piece of polished wood about five by eight inches in size, and set it on the worktable. "Inspirational plaques."

She pulled out several more and lined them up for me to see. She had written in pretty lettering a familiar saying on each one and then made a little design to go with it out of small flat stones. *Take time to smell the flowers*, said the first one. The quote was accompanied by a sketch of three daisies, filled in with yellow paint, with flat gray stones at their centers.

Change the world by being yourself showed a sketch of a child's face smelling a big yellow daisy, a round black stone at its center.

Every ending is a fresh beginning was a sketch of colorful flowers whose petals were made of oblong stones.

They actually weren't bad. "Nice job, Mom," I said, holding one up to admire it.

"Thank you, Abigail."

"This is what helped you deal with your fear, your art projects?"

Mom arranged the plaques on the worktable. "It was a suitable distraction. Whenever I felt my anxiety creeping up, I would think about my next project, taking inspiration from my surroundings instead of fearing them. And that's why I believe you work so hard to solve other people's problems. It's a form of control. When you're away on vacation, and things are going well, something seems off. When there's no problem to solve, your mind tries to invent one." She reached out to lay her hands on mine. "Maybe you should try pottery."

I held in a laugh. "I don't really have time to make pottery, Mom, but I get it. Thanks for talking it out with me."

"Any time, Abigail. Now, getting back to my plaques, what do you think we can sell them for?"

That was always the question I hated. Although I thought the plaques would sell, I had no idea what to ask for them. "Have you seen anything similar around town?"

"No. Mine are originals."

"How much do they cost to make?"

"The frames are ten ninety-nine. I have the paint, and the stones were free," she said.

I turned the frame over to examine it. "How about nineteen dollars and ninety-nine cents?"

"If you think that's a fair price," she said with a smile, "let's go for it."

Grace brought in cups of tea for both of us and stopped to admire Mom's work. "How creative, Maureen. I'm sure they'll be a hit."

Rosa walked into the backroom with a new order. I saw several more orders on the spindle and had to excuse myself to get back to work.

"I'll let you get busy," my mom said. "But don't forget, we have dinner at the country club on Friday." After a quick hug, she sailed through the curtain and was gone.

By five o'clock we had cleared off the spindle as well as the orders that had come in online and were cleaning up for the day. I breathed in the floral aromas and sighed in contentment. As much as I'd enjoyed our trip, it felt good to be back at Bloomers doing what I loved best. And nothing bad had happened all day.

A weight lifted from my shoulders. I'd worried for nothing. I thought back to what my mom had said. Maybe my anxiety was simply a fear of losing control. And maybe the flower shop was my comfort zone. Nothing made me feel better and more relaxed than arranging the perfect bouquet. Lesson learned.

I drove home singing happily, the setting sun glowing orange and pink on the western horizon. At home, I stepped into the house and was instantly greeted by my loving little dog and big, furry cat, both of whom wanted their suppers. Soon I'd be joined by my handsome hubby, and life would be perfect.

My phone rang and Marco's name appeared on the screen. I answered with a cheery, "What'cha doing? I thought you'd be home by now."

"Abby."

His solemn tone frightened me. My stomach contracted. "What happened?"

"It's about Down the Hatch." He drew a breath. "I'm being evicted."

CHAPTER TWO

"What? Evicted! Why?"

Marco let out a sharp sigh. "I don't know. It didn't say on the notice – which came the day after we left for Key West, by the way. My brother decided not to tell me about it. Can you believe that?"

"Why didn't he want to tell you?"

"He said he didn't want to ruin our vacation. I was so mad when he told me that I sent him home. I think I upset him."

"I'm sure Rafe didn't mean any harm by it."

"No harm? I had sixty days to vacate the premises. Now I have a week less to relocate."

"Wait a minute. When did Rafe tell you about the notice?"

"When I got here this morning."

"And you waited all day to call me?"

"I didn't want to ruin your first day back . . . and I see what you're saying."

"It must run in the family. What are we going to do?"

He let out a slow exhale. "I don't know."

I could picture him sitting at his desk, holding the phone to his ear, the other hand smoothing back his thick hair, which is what he did when he was worried.

"Have you talked to the building owner?" I asked.

"Arthur McMahon? Not in detail. I asked him to stop by the bar this evening, but he's got a dinner with his family and who knows what else going on. He said he would try to make it around seven-thirty –" Marco let out another long exhale – "but who knows?"

I didn't often hear Marco talk like that. He was always so positive. "Isn't McMahon's office right next door? Just go talk to him."

"He's not there. I just checked. His business partner, Grant Starling, is there. I suppose I could go talk to him, see what he knows."

I smiled. "There you go. That's a start. Will you be able to get away for dinner?"

"Rafe is at home, so I'll be closing the bar tonight. Why don't you come down here? I'll have the kitchen make us some comfort food."

"I need to walk Seedy first." I checked my watch. "I should be able to make it by six-thirty. In the meantime, go talk to Grant Starling and you can fill me in at dinner."

"Good enough. See you then."

❧ ❦

I had just returned from walking Seedy when Marco's mother, Francesca Salvare, phoned. Francesca was a stunning woman of Italian heritage, looking very much like Sophia Loren. She had raised four children on her own – her husband had died young – and was a very independent, strong-willed woman.

"What is going on with my sons?" she asked. "Rafe came home early and said he and Marco had gotten into a fight. He's been moping around ever since."

"I think you should talk to Marco about it," I said.

"Is Marco being evicted or not?"

Oh, boy. Rafe must've told her. I cleared my throat. "He got a notice while we were on vacation. And I really think you need to talk to Marco about it. Why don't I have him call you after dinner tonight?"

She took the hint and let it go. I'd have to give Marco a heads-up. Poor guy, it was one more thing he'd have to deal with.

My thoughts were spinning with worries as I drove back downtown and parked. I walked into the bar and glanced around, my eyes adjusting to the dim light. Marco was behind the bar, pouring wine into two glasses while the other bartender, Chris, was filling a beer mug. It was such a familiar sight; I couldn't imagine the bar not being there.

Down the Hatch Bar and Grill was an institution in New Chapel, well known for its loyal customers, including the attorneys and courthouse staff from across the street, a group of active senior citizens, and college kids from New Chapel University. Decorated in a corny fishing theme - complete with a fake carp mounted above the long, dark wood bar, a bright blue plastic anchor on the wall above the row of booths opposite the bar, a big brass bell near the cash register, and a fisherman's net hanging from the beamed ceiling -- it screamed for a rehab. I'd encouraged Marco to redecorate but he insisted that the customers would revolt.

I scanned the booths that lined the right side of the long, narrow space. All were filled except for the last one. More customers sat at the L-shaped polished wood bar that occupied the left side of the room, watching the two TVs hanging above each end of the bar.

"Hey, babe," Marco said, coming out from behind the bar. He was carrying two glasses of red wine. "We've got our usual booth."

I led the way to the last booth, which the staff had dubbed "the Salvare seat." I slid across the orange vinyl cushion and Marco set the wine glasses down before sliding in opposite me.

"Can you believe this?" He unfolded a piece of paper and handed it to me.

Notice of Eviction was printed in thick black letters across the top. I read the document and handed it back. "I can't believe it. This bar makes good money. Why would Arthur McMahon want to put it out of business?"

"It's not just the bar, Abby. There are other tenants in the building – two renters for the second and third-floor apartments, both of whom are going to lose their homes."

"Did Grant Starling say why McMahon is emptying out the building?"

"He said he preferred for me to speak to McMahon about it."

"What about the McMahon and Starling Realty? Is Arthur evicting his own business?"

"Nope. Not according to Grant. But I talked to the two renters just before you got here. They're both very upset. If I can arrange a meeting with McMahon, they want to be there." Marco glanced at his watch. "I asked Arthur to meet me here in half an hour. We should have time for dinner before he gets here – if he comes at all." He lifted his hand to signal Gert, the waitress.

"By the way," I said, "your mom called. Rafe told her about the eviction notice and now she's worried. She wants to talk to you. I said you'd call her this evening. I hope that was okay."

"Rafe." Marco heaved a sigh. "It's okay. She would've found out sooner or later. I'll give her a call after I meet with McMahon."

"Have you talked to Rafe this evening?"

"I haven't had time."

"Maybe you should call him tonight, too. Apologize."

"Maybe I should."

Gert came bustling over to the table. "What'll you kids have?" she asked in her gravelly voice. A tiny, thin woman who looked to be in her early seventies, Gert had been a waitress at the bar for thirty-some years. She knew the menu by heart and knew what her regulars liked to order.

"I think I'll have the grilled ham and cheese sandwich tonight," I said.

"Same for me," Marco said.

"Well, how 'bout that? I already put in the orders."

"That's why you're the best," I told her.

"Oh, go on," she said with a wink.

As soon as Gert was gone, Marco lifted his wine glass to mine. "Let's forget about the eviction for the moment. Here's to my beautiful wife."

"And to my gorgeous husband."

"I'll drink to that."

As we sipped our wine, I told him about my day. "Two weddings! Can you believe it? That's going to help our slump. And you'll never believe this. My mom actually made some sellable art. She calls them her inspirational plaques."

"Good for you. And good for Maureen." Marco forced a smile. "See, I told you nothing bad was going to happen to you."

I reached for his hand, threading my fingers through his. "I'm sorry, sweetheart. This is not what either of us expected."

"It's okay," he said. "We'll figure something out."

"By the way, my mom did some figuring out, too. She came up with an explanation for my fear that something bad was going to happen. She said it's agoraphobia and it runs in our family."

"Agoraphobia? She can't be serious."

"Mom says it can manifest as a fear of losing control. Supposedly that's why I'm always looking for problems to solve. Is something wrong with me?"

Marco laughed, breaking our somber mood. I could see the smile lines return on the sides of his eyes. "You don't have agoraphobia," he said. "You're just a problem solver."

"Thank you!" I squeezed his hand. "We're a good team, Marco, and we're going to fight this eviction somehow."

"You can't fight an eviction when the building is owned privately. But thank you for your support, Sunshine." Marco glanced up. "And here comes our food."

"Ham and cheese for the boss and his squeeze." Gert placed the dishes on the table. "I also have a couple waters here for you, and I brought the bottle of wine." She looked at me. "He's had a rough day."

"Thanks, Gert."

We continued our conversation over dinner and when we'd finished, Marco checked his watch. "McMahon should be stopping by any minute." He looked up. "And here he is now, right on time."

I turned to glance over my shoulder and saw a smartly dressed, attractive older man walk up to the end of the bar and slide onto a stool. He had a thick head of white hair that brushed his forehead, a tan complexion, and a strong jawline. He wore a white shirt with a dark red tie and charcoal gray slacks. He greeted the others at the bar as though he knew them well.

"I'm going over to talk to him," Marco said.

"Wait a minute. What are you going to say?"

"I'm going to ask for a meeting, that's all."

"What if he says no?"

"I know Arthur. He's all business. I'm sure he'll agree to a meeting. Considering what he's doing to us, it's the least he can do."

Marco walked over to Arthur McMahon, had a brief conversation, and returned to the booth. "He's willing to meet with the tenants at eight-thirty tonight. I don't know how this meeting's going to go, but I have to find out why we're being evicted and see if there's any room for negotiation."

"Do you want me to stick around?"

"No, it's okay. Why don't you go home and relax? I'll be closing up tonight, so I'll talk to you tomorrow."

Relax? With the bar's future in question? Not possible. I grabbed my purse and jacket and slid to the end of the booth. "I'll wait up for you. Good luck. And call your brother." I gave him a kiss and headed out.

Sometime after ten o'clock that night I fell asleep on the sofa and was awakened later by the door closing. I sat up and saw Marco walking quietly past the kitchen at the other end of our large, open living room.

"You're home late," I said with a yawn.

"Sorry I didn't call. I figured you'd be asleep. We were jammed at the bar, so I stayed longer than I'd planned."

"No problem. How was the meeting?"

"Unproductive." Marco sat down on the end of the sofa. "McMahon is going to turn the building into a boutique hotel. He also said his realty company can help his tenants find new accommodations."

"That was big of him."

"Tell me about it."

We got ready for bed and climbed in between the sheets. Marco put his arm around me, and I laid my head on his shoulder as Seedy began her usual trial runs. Because she was missing a hind leg, it took some encouragement to get her up to speed, even with a small step stool to help her. Finally, she leaped onto the bed and began digging around in the sheets by our feet until Smoke jumped up and forced him to Marco's side. I was tired but had the feeling sleep would be elusive.

I sighed. "Then you'll have to move the bar?"

He stroked Seedy as she snuggled in closer to him. "Or close it."

"Marco, you love the bar."

"So does everyone else. Rafe is already pestering me about finding a new location, but I can't imagine Down the Hatch anywhere else. I could just close it and focus on our private investigation business instead."

"Think about it," I said. "You don't need to decide anything tonight."

"You're right. My thoughts are all over the place." He leaned toward me to give me a kiss. "Let's call it a night."

Easier said than done.

Tuesday, November 15th

I awoke the next morning to an empty bed. A note on the kitchen counter said Marco had gone out for a run. I pulled on a green T-shirt and a pair of khakis, applied some blush and a light coat of lipstick, ran a brush through my red bob, and went to the kitchen for my favorite breakfast of almond butter on toast - and still Marco hadn't returned. I scooped out the kitty litter, walked Seedy around the block, and waited as long as I could before finally leaving him a note wishing him a good morning. As I drove to Bloomers, he called.

"Sorry I missed you, Sunshine. I needed time to think."

"Did you make a decision?"

"No. There are a lot of different options and they're all expensive. I'm going to call our accountant and set up an appointment to go over the financials. I'll talk to you about it later."

"Okay, Marco. Try not to worry. We'll work this out."

"Thanks, babe. Have a good day."

But that was harder than it sounded. As I sat at one of the white tables in the coffee parlor going over the day's schedule with Grace and Rosa, I felt gloomy, causing a pall to fall over the room. Lottie hadn't arrived yet. She'd had an early dentist appointment.

"Abby, dear," Grace said at last, "far be it for me to pry, but I can't help but feel that something is weighing heavily on your mind."

I took a sip of coffee, but even Grace's gourmet blend didn't help my mood. "Marco got an eviction notice for the bar."

"An eviction notice!" Grace exclaimed.

"*Madre de Dios,*" Rosa whispered.

"The landlord intends to put in a boutique hotel." I explained, "And Marco isn't sure whether he'll open the bar someplace else or simply close it down for good."

"This is all too sudden for him to absorb," Grace said. "Once he's had time to consider, I'm sure he'll decide to relocate." She grasped the edges of her cardigan and lifted her chin, going into her lecture pose. "As the Roman poet Horace once said, 'In adversity, remember to keep an even mind.'"

Grace was a walking quotation library, with an endless supply of quotes for every occasion.

"Thank you, Grace."

Rosa clinked her coffee cup against Grace's. "*Muy bien*. And what would the town square be without Down the Hatch?"

"The problem is that there's no real estate to rent on the square that has a kitchen," I said. "I got online this morning and checked."

"Is there any way Marco can purchase the building?" Grace asked.

"He's meeting with the accountant today," I told her. "I'm sure he'll bring it up."

Grace glanced at the clock on the wall. "It's nearly nine o'clock. We should get ready to open."

As we moved out of the coffee parlor, Lottie came in through the curtain in the back of the shop. "I'm here. The dental hygienist took forever" – she tapped her watch – "but I made it." She took stock of our somber faces. "What happened?"

"Marco got an eviction notice for Down the Hatch," I said. "Arthur McMahon wants to turn the building into a boutique hotel. All the tenants got a notice."

"Arthur McMahon?" Lottie repeated in surprise. "From McMahon and Starling Realty?"

"Yes. He's the building's landlord," I said.

Lottie tucked her purse under the cash counter. "Then you haven't heard the news."

"What news?" Grace asked.

"The news about Arthur."

"What news about Arthur?" Rosa asked.

"Arthur McMahon is dead."

I was speechless.

CHAPTER THREE

"I heard the news on the car radio on my way here," Lottie said, as she headed to the coffee parlor to get her morning jolt of java. "McMahon was discovered by his business partner just a short while ago. Take a look outside. There are squad cars up and down Franklin."

I walked over to the bay window in the parlor and saw police cars all along the street, their red and blue lights flashing ominously. "He must've just discovered him because I got here about thirty minutes ago and there were no police."

Rosa joined me at the window. "And now there are so *many* police cars. Why does one man's death need so many police?"

She posed a good question.

Lottie rejoined us holding a steaming hot cup of coffee. Grace stood beside her, and we all watched the activity outside. Across the street from Bloomers was the courthouse, where we could see people in business attire gathered in huddles on the lawn, talking and pointing. Others stood in small groups on the sidewalk, doing much of the same.

"Did you hear any details?" Grace asked.

Lottie took a sip of coffee. "There were no details reported."

I left the group, grabbed my jacket from the tea parlor, and headed for the door. "Then I'll go find out."

A few shop owners were standing outside of their shops watching the activity at the brown brick building down the block. The old building, built around nineteen hundred, housed Down the Hatch on one side of a doorway and the McMahon and Starling Realty on the other side. The doorway in between led to the apartments on the floors above. The blinds to the realty, I noticed, were half closed. Two police officers were taping off the perimeter around the doorway area and two more officers were stationed outside the yellow tape to keep the people back. One of them was my friend Sgt. Sean Reilly.

Sean Reilly was a good-looking man of medium height, about forty-two years old, who displayed an air of confidence without the normal posturing. He had intelligent hazel eyes, good facial structure, and brown hair starting to show a bit of white around the ears. He had trained as a rookie under my dad, Sgt. Jeffrey Knight, now retired, and had gone on to train Marco, who had served only a year on the force. Marco wasn't good at following rules. Perhaps that was what made him a great detective.

"What's the scoop, Reilly?" I asked. "I heard Mr. McMahon was found dead just a while ago."

Reilly hooked his thumbs in his thick black belt and gave me a perturbed glance. "Now how did I know you'd show up here?"

"Come on, Sean. This happened steps away from my door. I know it wasn't just a simple death. There are too many squad cars here."

"McMahon was found dead by his business partner. That's all I can tell you."

"You can't even hint at his manner of death?"

"Maybe you can ask Detective Corbison," Reilly said.

"I would if he were here, but he's not, so I'm asking you."

Reilly smiled. "Will you look at that? Here he comes now."

I watched Al Corbison get out of an unmarked police car and walk toward us. He was a middle-aged man of average height, with brown hair balding on top, and a gut hanging over his belt. Corbison caught sight of me and shook his head. He and I hadn't always been on the best of terms – we'd butted heads over many murder investigations – but because Marco and I had also helped solve many cases, he was finally giving us the respect we'd earned.

"Abby," he said with a nod.

"Detective."

Corbison lifted his collar against a cold breeze and gave me a suspicious once over. "You know anything about this situation here?"

I put my hand to my chest. "Me? No. Why?"

He cleared his throat, an indication I interpreted as disbelief.

"How would I know?" I asked. "I just walked over to find out."

Corbison ignored my question and turned to Reilly. "Someone leaked this to the press. Now I've got the family of the deceased wanting to know why they weren't notified first. You think my job isn't hard enough? If it wasn't Mrs. Detective over here, I have to assume it was one of your boys who leaked it."

"I can assure you it wasn't," Reilly said firmly.

"You can explain that to the family," Corbison said as he lifted the yellow tape and proceeded inside the realty office.

I turned back to Reilly. "Who would've told the press?"

Reilly folded his arms over his chest and looked down at me, raising one eyebrow.

"Wait. Why am I always the first to be blamed?" I asked.

"Maybe it's your reputation."

"Hey, I have a wonderful reputation. You said McMahon's business partner called in the crime. Maybe he leaked it to the press."

"Why would he do that?"

"That's a good question," I said, tapping my chin. "I'd have to know more details."

Reilly glanced at the people standing nearby then said quietly, "I've told you everything I know."

"This is more than a simple death, Reilly. Look at all the police."

"Abby, I agree with you."

"Were there any signs of a break-in?"

"Not that I could see, but apparently there's a security camera in the realty business that should tell more." He put out his hands to stop a heavy-set man in a brown suit from coming any closer. "This area is off-limits, sir."

"I'm Rowell McMahon," the big man said, rudely stepping in front of me, forcing me to the side. "I'd like to know why I had to learn of my father's death on the radio. Who's in charge here?"

"I am." Reilly folded his arms over his navy police jacket and said calmly, "I can't give out any information at this time. We have an active investigation going on."

"An active investigation of my father's death?" Rowell said. "What the hell happened to him?"

Reilly shifted uncomfortably but didn't respond.

Rowell pulled out his cell phone and began to tap in a text. He finished typing and put his phone in his pocket. "When will I be able to find out what happened?"

"I'll let the detective know you're here," Reilly said. "He'll come out to talk to you."

"And he'll know the cause of death?" Rowell called, halting Reilly at the door.

"You'll have to talk to the detective about it," Reilly said and entered the building.

Rowell turned his head to give me a look that said, *What are you looking at?*

Awkward moment.

Rowell McMahon was the manager of several buildings downtown, including Down the Hatch. After Marco and I had uncovered bones under the basement floor, Marco had contacted Rowell about getting the floor replaced, but he'd refused to help. Marco had ended up footing the bill himself. They hadn't been on good terms since.

Not knowing what else to do, I gave Rowell a consoling smile. "Sorry about your father."

He scoffed. "I'm sure you are."

"What is that supposed to mean?"

Reilly exited the building and ducked under the yellow police tape. "The detective is waiting for the coroner to arrive," he told Rowell. "He'll be able to talk to you after the coroner's exam."

Rowell took a deep breath and ran his fingers through his curly brown hair. Looking down at the sidewalk he muttered to himself, "I can't believe this is happening." He looked at Reilly and said incredulously, "I just had dinner with my father last night."

"I'm sorry, sir," Reilly said.

Rowell looked around. "When will I – be able to see my dad?"

"Not until after the autopsy."

Rowell frowned. "Shouldn't an autopsy be the family's call?"

"Not in a situation like this," Reilly said, scanning the crowd that had doubled in size. "That's standard procedure."

"Rowell!" I heard and saw a young man striding up the sidewalk toward him.

"It took you long enough," Rowell said, giving the twenty-something man a harsh once-over.

The thin, shaggy-haired young man, wearing a faded black long-sleeved t-shirt and blue jeans with holes in the knees, looked defiant. "I didn't hear the phone. What happened to dad?"

I was surprised to learn that these two were brothers. They couldn't have looked or acted any more dissimilarly.

"I don't know," Rowell said. "I'm waiting for a detective to talk to me."

"They haven't told you anything?"

Rowell saw me standing there pretending not to listen and said to Reilly, "I thought this area was off-limits. What's she doing here?"

"She's with me," Reilly said.

Rowell gave us both a sordid look and turned to his brother. "Let's go get some breakfast. We can talk in private." He pulled a business card out of his suit coat pocket and handed it to Reilly. "Here's my contact information. Have the detective call me when he's finished inside."

I watched them make their way through the onlookers then cross the street and enter a small deli that had just opened up across the square. I turned towards Bloomers to see Lottie standing outside the shop, no doubt wondering what was taking so long.

"I'll catch you later, Reilly," I said, and turned to walk away. That was when I noticed a man standing behind the police tape who seemed strangely out of place. Kenton Lang was his name and while I'd met him at Marco's bar on several occasions, I'd never actually seen him in the light of day.

Kenton lived above Down the Hatch on the third floor of the building. He was a regular at the bar and had lived in the building for a long time, but surprisingly, I'd never seen him anywhere else in town. Marco believed that he never left his apartment except to come down to the bar.

With long dark hair pulled into a stringy ponytail, and wearing his ever-present green army jacket, Kenton Lang looked exactly as I'd seen him before, except now he wore dark sunglasses and had his collar buttoned up to his chin. Marco had told me stories about Kenton, and from what I remembered, he had a problem with paranoia. With that aside, Kenton had always been kind to me and had a good reputation with the staff at Down the Hatch.

He waved me over to where he stood near the entrance to his doorway, pulled the sunglasses down to the tip of his nose, and said in a whisper, "Abby, it's me, Kenton. What are the cops doing here?"

"Your landlord, Mr. McMahon, passed away in his office earlier this morning. The police are investigating."

Kenton put his sunglasses back on and said quietly, "Do they know how he died?"

"It's still undetermined."

"Hey!" Sgt. Reilly called to Kenton. "You! Stop right there."

Kenton stepped backward, looking ready to flee the scene, but Reilly strode toward him quickly.

"What's your name?" Reilly asked, taking out a slim notebook and pen.

Kenton looked at Reilly as if he had some evil intent. "Why?"

"You're standing inside a crime scene. Now, I'll ask you one more time. What's your name?"

He looked down at the sidewalk. "Kenton Lang."

"Didn't you see the yellow tape, Kenton?" Reilly asked.

Kenton shifted uncomfortably. "I – I just came outside. I live upstairs."

"Is this the first time you've been down here today?"

"Yes. Why?"

"Did you know Arthur McMahon?" Reilly asked.

"Not personally," Kenton answered. "He was my landlord."

"When was the last time you saw him?" Reilly asked.

"At the meeting yesterday evening," Kenton said.

Reilly stopped writing. "What meeting?"

"Tenants' meeting," Kenton answered. "Marco Salvare from Down the Hatch set it up."

"What was the meeting for?" Reilly asked, glancing at me.

"I didn't call the meeting," Kenton began before I could speak, "I just showed up. Mr. McMahon sent out eviction notices to all of the tenants here, so we wanted him to explain why."

Reilly glanced at me again, this time in surprise. "Did Marco get an eviction notice?"

"Yes, he did. He's got less than sixty days to vacate the premises."

"That seems like relevant information," Reilly said. He turned to Kenton. "And you got one, too."

Kenton looked over at the door. "I've lived here for twenty years." His mouth turned down into a frown. "And now I'm being forced out."

"I'm sure that's rough," Reilly said, studying him.

Kenton folded his arms across his chest. He didn't answer.

At that moment, Detective Corbison stepped out of the realty office and walked over to us. "Are you Arthur McMahon's son?" he asked Kenton.

Kenton held up his palms as though Corbison had accused him of a crime. "No way."

The detective glanced over at Reilly. "I thought you said McMahon's son was here."

"He left this for you." Reilly pulled out the business card.

"Where'd he go?" Corbison asked.

Reilly hadn't seen where they went, so I chimed in. "They went to the deli across the square."

"How do you know that?" the burly detective grumbled.

"I watched them."

"And you are?" Corbison said to Kenton.

He dropped his gaze and said nervously, "No one."

"This is Mr. Kenton Lang," Reilly said. "He's one of the tenants in the building. He and the other tenants met with Mr. McMahon yesterday evening about the eviction notices they received. Mr. Lang has lived here twenty years."

Corbison gave the jittery man a scrutinizing glance. "I'd like to talk to you."

Kenton looked up warily. "Why?"

"I just want to get some general information." Corbison glanced around. "Let's go up to your apartment."

"No, sir," Kenton said, backing away. "Not unless you have a warrant."

The detective squinted at him for a long moment, as though he was trying to get Kenton to back down. When Kenton said nothing further, Corbison said, "Then let's step over here."

Kenton followed him some distance down the block and the two men faced each other, Corbison pulling out a small notebook similar to Reilly's, Kenton toying with a button on his jacket, clearly ill at ease.

"So," I said to Reilly, "you made sure Corbison knew Kenton Lang had a motive."

"Potential motive."

"It's pretty obvious that Corbison is conducting a murder investigation."

"It would appear that way."

"You're playing games with me, Reilly."

"You're playing detective, Abby."

I stared him down, but his gaze never wavered. I finally said, "I need to let Marco know what happened."

"Good idea."

I pulled out my cell phone and walked away.

Marco answered his phone on the third ring. "What's up?"

"Where are you?"

"On my way downtown. Why?"

"Arthur McMahon is dead, and it looks like he's been murdered."

"Are you kidding me?"

"Grant Starling found him in the office this morning. I don't have any other details."

"Wow. That's awful. Is there any word on the cause of death?"

"Reilly wouldn't tell me anything else. The coroner hasn't arrived yet, but Detective Corbison is here. He's interviewing Kenton Lang right now. I have to warn you, Corbison knows about the tenants' meeting you held, and the eviction notices, so I'm betting he'll want to talk to you, too."

"I'm sure he will."

"He'd better not think of you as a suspect."

"Let's not get ahead of ourselves, Sunshine. He's just gathering info at this point. I'll be there in five minutes."

48

"Okay, I'm heading back to Bloomers. Keep me in the loop about what's happening."

"Why don't you come down to the bar for lunch?"

"Sounds good to me. See you then."

I was about to open Bloomer's pretty yellow door when I saw Honey Chen walking toward me. I quickly glanced at my watch. It was just after nine o'clock. Hadn't we arranged to meet at four?

"Did I get our meeting time wrong?" I asked her.

Honey's gaze was fixed on the activity behind me, a strange, other-worldly expression on her face. In a wooden voice, she said, "I'm afraid I won't be able to meet with you today."

"Would you like to reschedule?" I asked her.

She said nothing, just continued to walk, passing right by me.

I hurried after her. "Is everything okay?"

"No, Abby," she replied in a quiet voice. "Nothing is okay."

I stopped where I was, watching as she walked up to the yellow tape.

Reilly immediately stepped forward. "You can't go inside, ma'am."

Without even turning her head to look at him she said, "I need to see my fiancé."

"Who is that?" Reilly asked.

"Arthur McMahon."

For the second time that day, I was left speechless.

CHAPTER FOUR

I walked into the flower shop and was met by Lottie, Rosa, and Grace, standing in a semicircle around me. Lottie took one look at my shocked face and said, "Tell us everything."

I gave them a complete rundown of everything I'd learned, including my conversation with Honey Chen.

"How dreadful!" Grace exclaimed. "To think she was planning her wedding just yesterday."

"And now her fiancé is dead," Rosa said. "Just like that" -she snapped her fingers- "he's gone."

"I wonder if something happened after the tenants meeting last night," I said out loud, heading for the workroom. "I wonder if any of Arthur's former clients held a grudge against him. I wonder –" I turned and saw all three women shaking their heads at me. "What?"

"You can't help it, can you?" Lottie asked.

"You've already put on your Sherlock Holmes cap," Grace explained.

"It is in her blood," Rosa told them.

I took a deep breath and blew it out. "Okay. I'm taking off my detective's cap and putting on my florist's apron. Let's get back to work."

I pulled an order off the spindle, dismayed to see that the pile of orders was low. That was due not only to the time of year but also to the new discount flower shop. I hadn't realized until that moment how much I'd been counting on Honey's wedding for some much-needed revenue.

❦ ❧

At noon, I stepped inside Down the Hatch and waited for my eyes to adjust to the dim light. Marco and Rafe were behind the bar, and Marco lifted his hand to acknowledge me then pointed to the last booth, our booth, so I headed there.

I had just slid into my seat when I saw Detective Corbison step into the bar and look around. He spotted Marco at the open end of the bar and started toward him, so I slid out and headed in the same direction.

"What's going on?" I asked as the two men stood together.

"The detective was just saying that he needed to speak with me," Marco replied.

"Look," I said to Corbison, "we know you're conducting a murder investigation, but you can't seriously be thinking Marco had anything to do with it."

"Abby, don't worry," Corbison said. "I just want to ask your husband some questions about his meeting." He turned back to Marco. "Is there somewhere we can talk in private?"

"My office," Marco said.

"Lead the way," Corbison said. "You can come, too, Abby."

That surprised me. Corbison wasn't usually so cooperative.

Marco opened his office door and led the way inside. "Have a seat," he said, indicating one of the two black leather sling-back chairs facing his desk. I took a seat in the chair next to Corbison.

Marco's office could not have been more modern, a sharp contrast to the bar's décor. He had a sleek, black metal desk and matching file cabinet, and modern artwork on the light gray walls. It was very masculine, just like Marco.

"I'm sure you already know that Arthur McMahon was found dead this morning," Corbison began. "According to the coroner's preliminary exam, he was stabbed in the back of the neck sometime yesterday evening. Now, I'm aware of your eviction notices and the tenants' meeting with Mr. McMahon yesterday, so I'm talking to everyone present at that meeting."

"So automatically everyone at the meeting, including my husband, is a suspect," I said to Corbison.

"Don't get a head full of steam, Abby," Corbison said. "Naturally I have to talk to everyone who was there, but I'm not drawing a bullseye on your husband's back, as you like to put it. I'm doing this interview because it's my job. You know I can't rule anyone out until I can."

"We understand," Marco said. "What do you want to know?"

Corbison took out his notebook. "What time did you meet with McMahon?"

"Eight-thirty," Marco replied.

"Who was present at the meeting?"

"Kenton Lang, Devona Esmond, and me. Devona rents an apartment on the second floor. Kenton on the third. McMahon's partner, Grant Starling, didn't make it."

"Where did the meeting take place?" Corbison asked.

"In McMahon's office."

"I know Grant Starling's office is right next door to Arthur McMahon's," Corbison said. "Did Grant come into the building while you were there?"

"Not that I saw."

Corbison jotted it down. "Where was everyone seated?"

"McMahon sat behind his desk," Marco explained, "and Kenton, Devona, and I sat in front of his desk."

"How did the meeting go?"

"It got pretty nasty. Words were said, threats were made – by Kenton Lang in particular."

"Did you make any threats?"

"No."

"What about Devona?"

"She seemed frustrated but didn't make any threats."

"What kind of threats were made by Kenton?"

Marco thought for a moment, then answered, "He said he would come for him. He would find him. Make him pay. Something along those lines."

The detective noted it, then continued. "How well do you know Kenton Lang and Devona Esmond?"

"I know Kenton from the bar. He usually comes down for a beer in the evenings. I know Devona because she lives above the bar. I've also helped her with minor repairs in her apartment. We had a hard time getting Rowell McMahon to get things done."

"Rowell McMahon manages the building?" Corbison asked.

"Right. He's the building superintendent and Arthur's oldest son."

"Did McMahon leave the office when you left?"

"No, he stayed at his desk. I saw him pick up the phone like he was going to make a call."

Corbison finished writing and flipped the notebook closed. "Okay. That should do it for now. I have to review the security camera footage tomorrow and then I may have more questions."

"Listen, Detective," Marco said, "I've got a personal stake in what happened to Mr. McMahon, so I'd appreciate it if you could keep us in the loop – on a professional basis."

Corbison rose and tucked the notebook in his chest pocket. "I figured you'd want to get involved." He looked down at his shoes for a moment, then looked straight at Marco. "Here's my proposition. I'll keep you apprised of our investigation if you'll share with me anything you learn."

Marco gave him a relieved smile. "Consider it done."

I, on the other hand, did not offer a smile. I studied the detective's expression, curious about his newfound interest in our cooperation.

Corbison gave me a wry grin. "Does that meet with your approval?"

"For now," I told him.

As soon as Corbison left the office, I walked around the desk and slipped my arms around Marco's chest. Smiling up at him, I said, "I'm glad you spoke up."

He bent his head to give me a light kiss. "I figured if I didn't, you would."

"You got that right, Salvare. It seems strange that Corbison is suddenly willing to work with us."

He pulled me close. "My little warrior bride, not everything is a fight."

"I don't know, Marco. I have a strange feeling in my gut."

"Me too. It's called hunger. Shall we go have lunch now?"

We ordered burgers and fries, and while we waited, I filled Marco in on the scrapped plans for the Chen-McMahon wedding. "We needed that money, Marco. Dora's Discount Flower and Garden Center is really cutting into our business."

He reached across the table and put his hand over mine. "Business will pick up over the holidays. And don't forget about that giant Christmas order you get from Churchill's department store."

"We've got a way to go before that happens. Right now, we barely have enough orders to keep Rosa busy. I'd hate to have to start cutting shifts." I sipped my iced tea through the straw as my mind wandered back to the murder investigation. "Why would anyone want Arthur McMahon dead?"

"He wasn't well-liked, Abby. There could be any number of suspects, including his tenants. I hope Kenton isn't involved."

"I saw him this morning, just a bit ago. Corbison talked to him."

"I don't think he would do anything," Marco said, "but I did have to cut him off yesterday evening before he got into a fistfight with someone. He left the bar early, and I can only hope that Kenton didn't go back to McMahon's office."

"Hopefully," I said, "the security cameras will catch the killer on video."

"Hopefully," Marco repeated, "because it's also going to catch me."

"What do you mean?"

"Not long after the meeting, I went back to Arthur's office to try to reason with him."

"Why?"

"I thought maybe I could get through to him. But it didn't work, so I gave up and left. What I'm saying is that I may have been the last one to see him alive."

"Why didn't you give that information to the detective?"

Marco smiled. "He didn't ask."

"That's a bold move, Marco, even for you. He's going to see you on the security camera in Arthur's office."

"Honestly, I didn't think about it until now. I'll call Corbison and let him know."

"Now I'm worried."

"Don't be. I have witnesses at the bar who saw me there the rest of the evening. I know they'll vouch for me. And –" He stopped himself, rubbing his hand over his five o'clock shadow.

"What were you about to say?"

Marco looked down for a moment. "I don't mean to sound crass, but this may mean I get to keep the bar."

"Let's worry about you being a suspect first, then we'll think about the bar."

◆ᴥ ᴥ◆

I was late getting back to Bloomers that afternoon, but when I walked in, everything was running smoothly, as it usually was. Grace was in the parlor serving coffee and tea to a large group of women, Lottie was checking a customer out at the cash counter, and Rosa was in the workroom putting together an anniversary bouquet.

Eager to get back to work and get my mind off Marco's situation, I pulled an order from the spindle and went to get the stems from the big cooler. The order was for an arrangement in purple for a fiftieth birthday celebration, so I pulled anemones, parrot tulips, and lilacs, all in shades of purple, with pussy willows and fittonia greens for accent.

"Abby, do you want anything from the parlor?" Rosa asked. "I'm going up front for some tea."

"Not right now, thanks."

I was just trimming the lilacs when the curtain parted, and my cousin Jillian came through lugging a big black case with a long neck. As usual, Jillian had on a chic outfit – a double-breasted tan and burgundy plaid jacket, tan slacks, and burgundy short boots, with a burgundy shoulder bag to match.

"Hi, Abs." She set the case down next to the worktable, tossed her purse on top, and slid onto one of the wooden stools so that she was seated next to where I was standing. "What are all the police cars doing out front?"

"One of the realtors down the street died. Is that a guitar case?"

"Seriously, Abs, you never see that many police cars at one time. Not unless there's a robbery or one of those standoff situations you see on TV." She inhaled as if surprised by her own thoughts. "It's not a standoff, is it? Are there hostages inside?"

"Jillian, there are no hostages. It's not a standoff. No one is in danger. A man died."

"Who?"

"One of the realtors at McMahon and Starling Realty."

Jillian sat up straighter. "Which realtor?"

"Arthur McMahon."

"Oh my God! I know his daughter, Crystal. He and his family belong to the country club."

"That's wonderful. What's in the case?"

Jillian's cell phone rang, and, instead of moving away from the table to talk, she answered it there in front of me.

"What's up, Mom? Yes, I just heard the news." Her eyes widened as she turned to stare at me. "No, I did *not* know he was murdered." She gave me a glare, still listening. "You're one hundred percent correct, Mom. There's nothing holding Crystal back now. Who knows? Maybe she's the one who murdered him.

"Okay, Mom. Gotta run." Jillian made kissing sounds into the phone and hit END. "So," she said, pinning me with her glare, "Arthur McMahon was murdered. Apparently, it's all over the news."

"Sorry. I wasn't sure the police were giving out that information yet."

She huffed as she slid her phone into her purse. "You know you can trust me to keep a secret."

In what universe? I packed wet foam into the white vase. "What did you mean when you said nothing was holding Crystal back now?"

"Her dad was dead set against her getting married. He absolutely forbade it, and he controlled the purse strings in that family." Jillian picked up a lilac and inhaled its scent. "I guess her getting married won't be a problem now."

That was an interesting thought. I filed it away to tell Marco.

"I wonder if I'll get an invitation," she thought out loud.

"Jillian, would you please tell me why you're lugging around that big case?"

She wiggled on the stool, barely able to contain her excitement. "You'll never guess what I've decided to take up."

Space is what I wanted to say. But I held my tongue because I knew the Harvard grad wouldn't get it. Jillian was dense that way.

Jillian Ophelia Knight Osborne was my first cousin. She was a year younger than me, a head taller – but who wasn't? – and about fifteen pounds lighter. Instead of fiery red hair that often defied a comb, she had satiny copper-colored locks, long and straight, with big doe eyes accented with brown eyeshadow. She was a wardrobe consultant and always dressed like a fashionista.

Jillian was also a mom. She had a one-year-old daughter named Harper Abigail Lynn Osborne – HALO for short, and she was truly Jillian's little angel. I was surprised she had come without her.

"Okay, I'll bite. What did you take up?"

"Are you ready? Okay." She folded her hands and smiled. "I've taken up the guitar."

I almost laughed out loud. Jillian had once attempted piano lessons. After only three months at it, her teacher had quit in frustration. Jillian was not a musician.

"My nanny's brother teaches the guitar," she continued. "And you know I've been looking for something new to do. So I thought, why not the guitar?"

"Jillian, remember your attempt at the piano?"

She rolled her eyes. "Don't remind me. But that was different. That was the piano, stretching your fingers all over the keyboard, left hand playing one thing, right hand playing another. How anybody can play the piano is a mystery to me."

"It's the same with the guitar," I told her.

"The guitar is *nothing* like the piano, Abs. Nothing. It's about finger placement." She wiggled the fingers of her left hand to show me how agile they were. "Trust me, I will excel at the guitar. And I've already taught myself a song."

Jillian had the zipper halfway down the case when Rosa walked in with her cup of tea. She spotted the guitar case and turned to stare at Jillian. "You play?"

"Not yet," Jillian replied, removing the guitar. "My first lesson is in fifteen minutes."

Rosa looked over the instrument, shaking her head in awe. "It's a beautiful guitar. Would you mind if I tried it?"

"Of course not." Jillian held out the instrument and Rosa took it. She cradled it under her arm, adjusted her left hand over the frets and finger-plucked the strings gently, playing a song I didn't recognize. She glanced up and saw us watching and immediately stopped.

"I'm so sorry. I get carried away."

"Wow," Jillian said. "Amazing."

"Rosa," I said, "that was beautiful. I didn't know you played."

"I haven't played for a long time. I no longer have a guitar." She held it out.

Jillian took it, laid it in the guitar case, and closed the top.

"I thought you were going to play something," I said to her.

Jillian flushed with embarrassment as she zipped up the case. "Never mind that. I have to get to my lesson."

"Thank you for letting me play," Rosa called as Jillian parted the curtain.

Jillian mumbled a hurried "You're welcome," and slipped out.

Rosa sighed sadly. "I think I made her feel bad."

"You did nothing wrong," I said. "Jillian will be fine."

Rosa set down her cup and pulled an order from the spindle. "Abby, did you notice that the big cooler has been making strange noises?"

"I heard something earlier," I answered. "Maybe the motor needs oiling. I'd better call a technician to check on it."

I hoped it was nothing major. Bloomers' finances couldn't handle much more.

CHAPTER FIVE

That evening, I pulled a pan of meatloaf and roasted potatoes out of the oven just as Marco walked into the house. I had the table already set for dinner, with two glasses of wine waiting for us.

"Something smells good," he said, bending down to give Seedy a scratch behind his ears. "Meatloaf?"

"You've got it."

"Yum." He washed his hands in the sink as I took the dish of food over to the table.

Marco brought over the sauteed broccoli, and we sat down opposite each other. He picked up his wine glass and waited for me to do the same. "What shall we toast to?"

"Finding a way to save Down the Hatch."

"I'll drink to that."

I touched my glass to his and took a sip. "Good wine."

"It's a new red blend. Joe at the wine shop thought we'd enjoy it."

Since we'd bought the house, Marco had taken an interest in wines and was in the process of starting a collection.

I took another sip and set the glass aside. "I heard some interesting news from Jillian today. It seems that Arthur McMahon had been preventing his daughter from getting married."

"Preventing how?"

"By refusing to pay for the wedding," I said. "Apparently, he was very wealthy."

"I guessed as much. I know he owns several buildings in town and some properties on the outskirts."

I toyed with my napkin. "Jillian joked that his daughter might have been the one who killed him."

"And your radar went up immediately."

"You have to admit she would've had a motive."

"As I said, many people had motives." Marco put down his glass. "How about dishing out a slice of that meatloaf?"

As I put the meat on his plate, Marco changed the subject. "I talked to my mom today, and we have something of a situation."

"Oh no. What's wrong?"

"Nothing's wrong. Not exactly."

Marco wasn't a man to mince words, so when he didn't answer right away, I knew to embrace for impact. "What's wrong, Marco?"

"She's hosting Thanksgiving dinner at her house this year. She's invited all our relatives."

I dished a large helping of meatloaf onto my plate and sat down. "Then what do we do about my family?"

"We had dinner with the Knights last year, remember? It wouldn't be too unreasonable to skip this year."

"I can't just bail on my mom. Thanksgiving is in nine days. She's expecting us."

"I haven't seen my aunts and uncles in several years, Abby. They're getting older. I don't know how long until I'll get to see them all again."

"I understand." I chewed a generous mouthful, giving me time to think of a solution, but as I swallowed and reached for my wine, no thoughts came. "My mom would be devastated. Our Thanksgiving dinner is an important tradition."

"Then I don't know what to do, Sunshine. I don't want to ignore my family and we do see your family every week."

"You're right." I sighed morosely. "We're supposed to have dinner with my family at the country club this Friday, in fact. I'm sure my mom will want to talk about Thanksgiving plans."

Marco ate a bite of broccoli and chewed thoughtfully for a moment. "We'll figure something out."

Wednesday, November 16th

When I came out into the kitchen for breakfast Wednesday morning, Marco was sitting at the counter reading the local newspaper on his laptop. "Look at this," he said and turned the computer for me to see. He scrolled back up to the top.

In all caps, the banner headline read: REALTOR FOUND MURDERED.

I read the article aloud. *"Local realtor and businessman Arthur McMahon was found in his office Tuesday morning dead from a knife wound to the back of his neck. The police are investigating but as of yet have no suspects. McMahon's business partner, realtor Grant Starling, commented that he couldn't imagine anyone wanting the well-liked realtor dead.*

"Arthur was a fine human being," Starling said. "He had just gotten engaged and had a whole new life ahead of him. This is a tragic loss to his family and our community."

A family spokesman announced that the funeral would be held this Thursday at the Happy Dreams Funeral Home at 4 p.m., with a viewing on Wednesday from 6-8 p.m."

I stopped reading and turned the computer back toward Marco. "I think we should go to the viewing this evening."

"You didn't even know Arthur McMahon." He studied me for a moment. "What's your real reason?"

I put a slice of bread in the toaster and pushed down the lever. "I want to meet his daughter."

Marco studied me for a long moment. "Why do you want to meet his daughter?"

"I'm just . . . curious."

"Curious, huh? This wouldn't be about us getting involved in the investigation, would it?"

"Of course not. I'm just a curious person."

"Yeah right."

"We can go after dinner."

Marco sighed. "Fine. I wanted to pay my respects anyway."

Seedy sat down at my feet and gazed up at me, bushy tail wagging excitedly. "Yes," I said, "we'll walk you first."

❦ ❦

There was a small stack of orders for Arthur McMahon's viewing when I got to Bloomers that morning. I checked the computer in the workroom as I removed my navy pea coat and green scarf, but only a few more orders were waiting. Not the busy day I had imagined. Then my imagination kicked back in as I envisioned a steady stream of arrangements leaving Dora's Discount Flower and Garden Center, delivered by a small army of brightly painted delivery vehicles. I shook the thought away as I heard the ding of another order come in online. Maybe today would be busy after all.

As Grace, Lottie, Rosa, and I sat in the coffee parlor enjoying Grace's gourmet blend, I filled them in on the latest news on McMahon and his daughter Crystal.

"But remember," Rosa said, "this was just Jillian's gossip, you know, from the grapevine?"

I finished my coffee and set the cup on the saucer. "Jillian's grapevine has roots all over town," I said, "so I tend to believe her."

"If Crystal does get married," Lottie said, "let's hope she comes here for her flowers."

"Fingers crossed," I said.

Rosa and I spent the rest of the morning and half of the afternoon putting together funeral arrangements for Arthur McMahon's viewing and funeral, which Lottie then delivered to the Happy Dreams Funeral Home. We used the rest of the day to sweep the floor and clean off the table and counters, leaving the workroom spotless. We were ready to close up for the day when the phone rang, and I heard Lottie answer it up front. Moments later, she stuck her head through the curtain.

"Sweetie, a man by the name of Grant Starling is on the phone. He needs an arrangement for Arthur McMahon's viewing this evening. I told him we were closing, and he asked for you personally. What do you want to do?"

"I'll talk to him." I sat down at my desk and picked up the handset. "This is Abby. How can I help you?"

"Abby, thanks for taking my call. I'm on the road heading back from Chicago and I just heard that Arthur McMahon's viewing is tonight. I know this is asking a lot but is there any way you can put together a funeral arrangement for Arthur and deliver it before the viewing? I'll be happy to pay you double for your trouble."

I glanced at my watch. "Sure. I can do it."

"Perfect. Thank you so much!"

"What would you like the card to say?"

"'Deepest condolences. Arthur will be greatly missed.' And sign it with my name. I'll come down to your shop first thing in the morning and pay you. Thank you, again."

"No problem. Happy to be of help." I hung up the phone and found Lottie and Rosa watching me.

"Okay, both of you can go home," I said. "I'll stay to make the arrangement and I'll deliver it on my way home."

"Are you sure?" Lottie asked.

"It's no trouble. I don't have kids waiting at home. Go!"

"Thanks, sweetie," Lottie called, and slipped through the curtain, followed by Rosa.

Grace came into the workroom to retrieve her coat. "While I haven't any kids at home, I'm sure Charity will be happy to see me."

I smiled. Charity was the name of a fluffy calico cat who was adopted by Grace after I thought I'd run her over.

Grace called good night from the shop, and I heard the bell over the door chime as they all left. I walked to the front and locked up behind them, then returned to the workroom and pulled my stems.

Fifteen minutes later, I wrapped the arrangement and tagged it, then picked up my purse and left through the alley door, heading for my car in the public parking lot. I drove to Happy Dreams Funeral Home, parked on the side street, and walked toward the rear entrance. As I approached, I noticed a colorful van pull away from the curb. DORA'S DISCOUNT FLOWER AND GARDEN CENTER was written on the side. A knot of anxiety formed in my stomach.

The Happy Dreams Funeral Home was a huge, Victorian, cream-colored clapboard house with dark green and light green trim and accents of mauve - a style commonly known as a Painted Lady. It had a reception area in front and two parlors, A and B, on each side that ran from the front to the back, where a small, common kitchen joined them. A curving staircase at the right rear of the foyer lead upstairs to the family's living area, which I'd heard was quite spacious.

As I approached the cement patio behind the Victorian house, I saw two people standing near the rear entrance, dressed in black, talking and laughing together as though they were attending a party. I recognized Rowell immediately. With his large potbelly and curly mop of hair, he was hard to miss. The young woman standing next to him was the Laurel to his Hardy. Thin, curvy, and tall in her stiletto heels, the woman cackled wickedly at something Rowell had said. I paused behind a trellis to listen.

"Figures Birch wouldn't show up," the woman said. She had big blonde hair, fake eyelashes that were so thick I was surprised she could keep her eyes open, and an enormous diamond ring on her left hand. She wore what appeared to be an expensive black dress with silver accents that hugged her abundant curves and black patent leather shoe boots.

Rowell was smoking a cigarette and flicking the ashes into the air. "Crystal, I wouldn't be surprised if Birch doesn't show up for the funeral either. Now that he has dad's car, we'll never see him again."

So, the blonde woman in the black dress was Crystal.

"I wouldn't be surprised if that drunken grease monkey wasn't the one who finally did us the favor," Crystal added.

"And this whole time I thought it was you," Rowell told her.

There was a brief pause before each of them broke into laughter.

My cell phone chirped with an incoming text, causing both Crystal and Rowell to turn and spot me. With a jolt, I started toward them.

Crystal eyed the arrangement in my hands. "Are you a florist?"

"Yes," I paused to say. "I'm Abby. I own Bloomers Flower Shop."

"Hi, Abby!" Crystal said brightly. "I'm Crystal McMahon and this is my brother Rowell."

Rowell dropped the lit cigarette and snuffed it with the heel of his scuffed leather shoe. "We've been introduced."

"Nice to meet you," I replied to Crystal, ignoring her brother's sneer, "and I'm so sorry about your father."

A smile flickered across her face. "Yeah, us, too. Hey, listen, I'd like to talk to you about wedding flowers, maybe get some prices from you."

"Sure," I said. "Let me know what date works for you."

"How about tomorrow?" she replied. "Say around noon?"

"Isn't your father's funeral tomorrow afternoon?"

"Oh, that's right. Okay. How about at ten?"

"I'll put it in my calendar."

Crystal's wedding was bound to be a big one. Snagging that job would be fantastic. Plus, I'd have an opportunity to question her about her father's death. But to meet on the day of his funeral seemed pretty heartless to me.

I entered the back of the funeral home. There I met Delilah Dove in the kitchen, one of the owners, who took the arrangement from me.

"So good to see you, Abby," Delilah said with a smile.

"Good to see you, too. I had a late order, so I thought I'd drop it by myself." I nodded toward the back door. "Arthur's kids sure don't seem to be in mourning."

Delilah leaned closer to whisper, "You'd never know their father just passed away – and by murder! I've seen a lot over my years of being in the business, but this takes the cake."

I stowed that away to tell Marco later. "I just saw the Dora's Discount Flower van pull away."

Delilah gave me a sad smile. "They're taking business from you, aren't they?"

"They are. I'm just not sure how much."

"They brought in sixteen arrangements."

"Sixteen?"

She put her hand on my shoulder. "I'm so sorry. But hey, you've got a sterling reputation in town. You'll be fine."

I hoped so. We'd done only ten arrangements.

"I should get home," I told her. "I've got to fix dinner so Marco and I can be back for the viewing."

"Then I'll see you later." With a smile, she left with the arrangement.

When I walked out the back door, Crystal and her brother were looking at her cell phone, laughing. When they noticed me, they grew silent.

"See you tomorrow," Crystal called as I passed by.

"I'm looking forward to it," I said.

❧ ❦

Over dinner that evening, I told Marco about my floral competitor and then related my experience with the McMahons. "You'd never have guessed they'd just lost their father."

"Maybe they weren't close to him," Marco said.

"Still," I said, "the man was murdered. You'd think they'd be a little more – I don't know - solemn. It makes me wonder."

"Wonder about what?"

"About which one of them killed their father."

"Ah, so the truth comes out." He gave me a playful smile. "I knew there was a reason you wanted to attend the viewing."

"Just you wait, Marco. Watch how they act this evening. See if you don't agree with me."

After walking Seedy, we drove downtown and cruised along Indiana Avenue looking for an open parking space. Marco pointed out a shiny red Lamborghini parked in front of the funeral home. "That's Arthur McMahon's car. One of his family must've driven it here."

"I overheard Rowell and Crystal talking about their brother Birch inheriting a car."

"That's quite a vehicle. He's one lucky guy."

"Marco, do you have car envy?"

"Come on, Sunshine. Who wouldn't love a Lamborghini?"

"It sure does make a statement."

After locating a parking spot halfway down the block, we walked to Happy Dreams and saw a sign indicating that the McMahon viewing was in Parlor A.

We stepped through the wide doorway and were surprised to find the room nearly empty. There were only a handful of people waiting in line to offer condolences to the family up front. Crystal and Rowell stood in front of the casket, while a young man with straggly hair who I guessed was Birch stood off to one side, scrolling through his cell phone. Standing apart from them was Arthur's fiancée, Honey Chen.

We signed our names in the visitor log and walked toward the front of the room where the open casket lay. I was pleased to see how nice the arrangements we'd made looked. I studied the four figures dressed in black, watching how they solemnly greeted the people who came through the line.

"Abby," Crystal said with a smile. "How nice of you to come." She batted her eyes as she looked over my shoulder. "And this must be your husband."

"Marco Salvare," he said. "We're sorry for your loss."

She blushed at the touch of his hand.

"Salvare," Rowell said curtly. To his sister, he said, "This is the man who owns Down the Hatch."

"How very nice to meet you," Crystal said in a deeper tone.

"We're going to need to talk soon," Rowell said to Marco.

"Just let me know when," Marco replied.

"Abby," Crystal said, turning toward the woman on her right, "this is Honey Chen. She was my father's *fiancée*." Crystal rolled her eyes. "Honey, this is Abby." Crystal spoke slowly to her, as though she were a child. "Abby owns Bloomers Flower Shop. And this is her husband, Marco."

"Abby and I have already met," Honey said, ignoring Crystal's rudeness. Her eyes were red and swollen. Her lip quivered as she tried to hold back tears. Compared to McMahon's children, his young fiancé seemed to be the only one truly affected by his death.

"We're so sorry for your loss," I told her. I became aware of more people coming up behind us and, with a consoling smile, moved on.

We walked to the back of the room and turned to watch the family interact with more people.

"That's the youngest son, Birch, at the end of the casket," I told Marco. "It looks like he's checked out. But watch how Crystal and Rowell are acting. Not a shred of emotion from either one. And Birch isn't even greeting anyone. Do you get the feeling that they're not sorry their dad is gone?"

"Maybe they're not," Marco said. "I told you Arthur wasn't a good guy."

"Maybe it goes deeper than not liking him," I said. "Maybe they actively hated him."

Marco poked me lightly in the shoulder. "Are we playing detective?"

"Can you blame me? Just watch them."

Grant Starling walked into the parlor, saw us, and came over. "Hi, Marco," he said in a hushed, sad voice. "Abby. Listen, thanks again for making the arrangement. Can you point it out for me?"

"It's to the left of the casket, a spray of red and white roses and carnations."

"Thanks." He looked toward the casket. "It's beautiful."

"Terrible about Arthur, isn't it?" I asked. "It must have been a shock finding him like that."

"Arthur was a fine human being." Grant glanced around and said almost as an afterthought, "This is a tragic loss to his family and our community." He reached inside his suit coat and pulled out a business card, which he handed to Marco. "I know of several properties that you might be interested in for your bar. Let me know if you want my help."

And then he walked away, heading toward an older couple who had just walked in. I watched as he smiled and held out his card.

"He's trolling for business," I said to Marco.

"It looks that way."

"And he's just repeating what he said to the press about Arthur's death."

Marco leaned over to whisper, "Are we ready to go?"

"Not yet. I want to check out Dora's arrangements."

⌀3 8⌀

Later that evening, Marco was working out with weights in the basement, and I was about to take a shower when my mother called.

"Just wanted to remind you about the family dinner at the club Friday," she said.

"Thanks, Mom. I remember."

"We're looking forward to seeing you. And while I've got you on the phone, I'm working on Thanksgiving plans. Do you want to bring something? Maybe the green bean casserole?"

"Actually, I wanted to talk to you about Thanksgiving. Marco's mom will be hosting a dinner this year and is having her family from Ohio join her."

"How is Francesca? I haven't seen her in ages."

"She's fine. The thing is, she wants us to come for dinner, too"

"You're going to have a busy Thanksgiving going from one house to the other."

"Well, I think maybe we should just go there since we see you and Dad almost every week."

"Oh, Abigail, Thanksgiving is our last remaining family tradition."

The hurt in her voice stabbed my heart. "I get it, Mom. I'll see what I can do."

There had to be a fair solution.

Thursday, November 17th

When I got to Bloomers Thursday morning, I was dismayed to see that only a few orders had come in overnight, and they were for Arthur McMahon's funeral.

"The cooler is making those noises again," Rosa said, as we had our morning coffee in the parlor.

"I've got an electrician coming this afternoon," I told her. "We should be good to go by closing time."

"I've been trying to come up with a way to increase business," Lottie said. "What if we offer a fifteen percent discount? We can print out flyers and leave them at businesses on the square."

"I can post a notice on our Facebook and Instagram pages," Grace said.

"Let's do it," I said. "We need to drum up more business."

"Speaking of business." Lottie glanced at her watch. "It's time to open. Let's get moving, girls."

I unlocked the yellow door, tied on my bright yellow apron, and within minutes, customers streamed in and headed for the parlor, eager for their daily dose of Grace's fresh coffee and pumpkin-spiced scones. Rosa and I headed for the workroom, where we began to put together arrangements for Arthur McMahon's funeral.

At ten o'clock, Lottie stuck her head through the curtain to let me know that Crystal McMahon was there for her appointment. I set aside my floral knife and the blooms I had pulled and gathered up two big wedding planners and my notebook. I walked out to find Crystal examining the crystal figurines in the display case.

"Crystal," I said, walking up to her, "how are you?"

She was wearing a two-piece white outfit that had designer written all over it, with a Louis Vuitton purse in white and matching shoes. Big diamonds hung from her ears that sparkled brilliantly in the sunlight. "As well as can be expected," she said with a shrug. She held out her hand for a limp greeting. The diamond in her engagement ring was even larger up close.

She walked over to the table in the middle of the room and picked up one of my mother's plaques. She glanced at me over her shoulder. "This is a flower shop, isn't it?"

"The best in town."

Make that – the only one in town.

"It's kind of small. And I don't see many flower arrangements."

"It's small, but we do big business. Trust me. Let's move into the coffee parlor. You can try my assistant's delicious scones."

The parlor was fairly empty when we walked in. We sat at a table in the corner near the window, where I readied my pen and notebook. Overhead, one of the fluorescent lights flickered ominously.

Grace approached the table. "What will you lovely ladies have?"

"I'll have a cappuccino," Crystal said, "with oat milk and one pump of caramel."

Grace smiled politely. "I'm afraid we don't have a cappuccino machine."

"Oh. Coffee is fine, then."

"I'll have a coffee, too, Grace. Crystal, you have to try a pumpkin scone. Our compliments."

"No, thank you. I don't like pumpkin."

"Then a blueberry scone. Grace, two blueberry scones, please."

Grace's smile faded. "I'm afraid we're all out of blueberry."

Well, that was embarrassing.

"So," I said to Crystal, "describe for me your perfect wedding."

I took notes as she explained what she'd pictured in her mind, trying all the while to ignore the annoying flickering light overhead. When she had finished, I opened one of the floral wedding planners and let her flip through the pages, taking note of the arrangements she liked. Inside, however, I was buzzing with questions.

When I couldn't ignore the buzz any longer, I said, "I don't mean to interrupt, but is there any news from the police on your dad's death?"

"Nothing," she said, still looking through the pages. "Whoever killed him was very careful not to leave any evidence behind."

"What about the security camera footage?"

Her head snapped up and her eyes narrowed. "Security camera footage?"

"I was just wondering whether the detective had seen anything helpful on it."

"I wasn't aware that they had any footage. I'll have to check with Detective Corbison about it."

Just as she finished looking at the first album, the light overhead flickered once again. She glanced up at the ceiling then down to the long list I'd made and gazed at me in concern. "That's a lot of flowers," she said. "Are you sure you'll be able to handle a wedding this size?"

"No problem," I said. "I've done it before."

"Do you have the staff?"

"We have a wonderful staff. Why don't you take a look at this planner? The arrangements are completely different than the first book."

While Crystal flipped through the pages, I noticed Lottie standing in the doorway to the coffee parlor, motioning for me to join her. I excused myself and met with Lottie in the flower shop, stepping out of Crystal's view.

"The big cooler is making a horrible noise," Lottie said quietly. "What time did you say the electrician is coming?"

"Around three," I whispered.

"That's what I thought. I'm going to see if he can come sooner."

I suppressed a sigh. Fixing our cooler was bound to cost a lot of money.

Lottie went into the workroom, and I turned back toward the coffee parlor to find Crystal standing in the arched doorway. "Is something wrong?" she asked.

"Nope," I said immediately. "Nothing at all. Have you seen anything you'd like?"

I walked her back to the table where she pointed out several enormous arrangements. "These would be fantastic."

And expensive. Yay!

"This one could be at the top of the aisle," she said pointing to one of the arrangements. "This one could be on the wedding gift table, and this one could be the centerpiece for the head table." She looked up at me. "What do you think?"

That maybe my luck was changing.

Just then, a loud, mechanical screeching noise came from the workroom, startling Crystal. "What was that?"

I glanced around and saw Lottie dash through the purple curtain in a panic. She looked over at me with urgent concern.

"What's going on back there?" Crystal asked. "Do I smell smoke?"

"No, of course not," I said. "We're having a small problem with one of our coolers. Nothing to be worried about. Everything is just fine."

I watched as Rosa left the back room next, and smoke billowed out from behind the curtain. Over my head, the fluorescent light flickered a final time and went dark.

Crystal glanced up at the broken light, then another light started flickering near the bay window. "You know what?" she said, closing the album, "I think I'll check around." She rose and put her Louis Vuitton bag over her shoulder. "Thanks for meeting with me."

I walked with her to the door. "Let me know if you want prices."

"Sure." With a *flicker* of a smile, she turned and left.

The bell chimed above me as I closed the door. I turned to find my staff standing there, regarding me sadly.

"That could've gone better," I said. "What's going on back there? Why is there smoke?"

Lottie wrung her hands. "The motor busted. The cooler is officially dead."

"Well . . ." I breathed in deeply and let it out slowly. "Let's hope that's the worst thing that happens today."

As the words left my lips, the bell over the door dropped on my head and hit the ground with a loud jingle.

The ladies gathered around to see if I was okay, but it wasn't my head that hurt, it was my pride. Bloomers was falling apart around me and all I could do was wonder what else was going to go wrong.

"Did you reach the electrician?" I asked Lottie, picking up the bell.

"He can't come any earlier. We'll have to buy some bags of ice and hope they keep the flowers cool."

"I'm leaving to get some bags now," Rosa said.

I followed Lottie into the workroom where she paused to say, "This happened to me before you took over Bloomers. We'll just have to keep the cooler closed as much as possible."

Rosa came in to get her purse and coat. "Luckily, we don't have many orders right now."

Was that luck or more bad news?

At noon, I headed to Down the Hatch to meet Marco for lunch. When I got there, Gert told me he was meeting with Grant Starling in his office, so I sat in the last booth and ordered a glass of iced tea.

Five minutes later, Grant and Marco came out and headed for the booth. "Abby," Grant said, "it completely slipped my mind to come down this morning to pay for the arrangement. I'm going down to Bloomers right now."

"Thanks," I said.

Marco shook hands with him, then slid into the seat opposite me. "I'll have a Coke," he told Gert, then settled against the back. "Bad news," he said. "Grant just informed me that Rowell inherited some of his father's properties downtown, including Five Franklin Street. He said Rowell still plans on going through with the evictions."

"He's going to put in a boutique hotel?"

"No. There's no money in a boutique hotel. Rowell wants to gut the building and turn it into luxury condos. The tenants will have to be out by the first of January, including Grant."

"Rowell said he wanted to talk to you, Marco. Maybe you can reason with him."

"Baby, Rowell and I have never seen eye to eye on anything."

"Let's take him to court."

Marco laughed. "And ask the court to do what? Order Rowell to change his mind about the evictions?"

"I guess that wouldn't happen." I rested my chin in my palm. "We're just going to have to find Down the Hatch a new home."

"Or say goodbye to it."

❧ ❦

I was feeling very low when I returned to Bloomers, and even lower after the electrician came.

"You're going to need a new refrigeration unit," he told me.

"A new refrigeration unit," I repeated. "How much is that going to cost?"

His answer made my jaw drop. "How soon can you get it here?"

"I can try to have it overnighted," he told me, "but that's going to add to the cost."

I had no choice. "Let's do it," I told him.

After he left, I got on the computer to see whether any new orders had come in, but my inbox was empty. Our orders were down, our expenses were up, and Marco was about to lose his bar. What else was going to happen?

The purple curtain parted, and Jillian's guitar case poked through before my cousin herself appeared. "Hello, ladies," she said. "Hi, Abs."

Upon seeing her, an idea popped into my head. "I'm very happy to see you, Jillian."

"You are?"

"Let's go sit in the parlor and talk."

CHAPTER SIX

Jillian waited until Grace had brought over our coffees to say, "The reason I came in was to show you my progress on the guitar. I've been practicing all day. But now I'm curious. Why are you so happy to see me?"

"I'm having some financial problems here at Bloomers," I explained. "My main cooler needs a new refrigeration unit, expenses are up, and so are my maintenance costs."

Jillian leaned forward and said in all seriousness, "How much do you need?"

"No, Jillian. What I need is information. Crystal McMahon approached me about doing her wedding flowers and then backed out. The thing is, I really need her business to help keep the shop profitable."

"How can I help?"

"You're close with Crystal, right?"

"I mean, we're friends but I wouldn't say *close* friends."

"Close enough to find out where Crystal is going for her wedding flowers?"

"Oh, that's no problem."

"And I also need to find out how much she's going to be charged."

"Okay, that might be a little harder. Why do you need to know that?"

"Because I want to make sure Crystal comes back to Bloomers by giving her a competitive bid."

She pursed her lips, thinking, then turned her head to look over at her guitar in the corner. Her eyes flicked back to me, and she smiled slyly. "Okay. I'll get you that information on one condition. You get Marco to let me play a song at Down the Hatch."

My mouth fell open "You want to do *what?*"

Her smile expanded. "Let me play my guitar at Down the Hatch."

"You don't even know how to play."

"Not like tomorrow or anything, but when I'm *proffected*, I want to display my skills at the bar."

Jillian had always had trouble with big words. "You mean proficient."

"That too."

"Jillian, I –"

"Look, Abby, you need my help, and I've agreed to help you. All I ask in return is this one little favor."

"I'll ask Marco, but I can't give you any guarantees."

"Then I can ask Crystal, but samesies. No guarantees."

"Fine. Just get me the info and I'll make it happen. Deal?"

"One more thing. I want to play for you the song I've been practicing."

I glanced at the clock and Jillian saw me. "Don't you dare say you're busy. This will only take two minutes."

My shoulders sagged. I looked around the coffee parlor, for the first time feeling relieved that we had no customers.

Jillian unzipped her bag and set her guitar in her lap. She eased one arm around the neck then moved her fingers awkwardly over the fret until she found the correct position. Her other hand raised and came down heavily across the strings, and then she began to warble in a high-pitched voice:

Abby Knight is a florist magnifique.
But solving crimes is what really makes her tick.
With her husband Marco at her side,
She handles the toughest crimes with pride,
She's a florist whose puzzle-solving is her schtick.

Jillian gave the guitar a final strum and gazed at me hopefully.

It was the longest two minutes of my life. And I'd once been trapped inside a burning shed. "That was — *great*, Jillian."

"Wasn't it? I've got lots more ideas for songs, too. The patrons of Marco's bar are going to love me."

I had a feeling Marco wasn't going to agree.

❧ ☙

"It's okay, Sunshine. We'll manage. That's what savings are for."

I had just told Marco what the cost would be for a new refrigeration unit, and he'd barely blinked an eye. Instead, he'd torn into his leftover meatloaf, obviously famished. I, on the other hand, had little appetite. I pushed the food around my plate. "What if we need those savings? What if our roof leaks or the furnace goes out?"

"What if the world ends tomorrow?" Marco retorted.

"I know you're joking, but that would solve a lot of problems."

"Listen, Abby, get the cooler fixed, replace the part, whatever it takes to keep Bloomers going. We can't both lose our businesses."

At that, I paused. Marco was right. This was just a small setback in the grand scheme of things. But I hated to hear him talk like that, like his bar's closing was a foregone conclusion. It just wasn't like him. "You can still talk to Rowell, Marco, explain what a gem Down the Hatch is, give him its history. What's the worst that could happen?"

"All he cares about is money, Abby." Marco finished chewing. "Here's an idea. Why don't we go on a date tomorrow? Just you and me and a great Italian meal at Adagios."

"There's a slight problem," I said. "Tomorrow is Friday. That means dinner at the country club."

As Marco let out an irritated groan, my cell phone rang. I went to the kitchen counter to take the call and saw Sean Reilly's name on my screen. Before I could answer it, there was a knock on the front door.

As Marco got up from the table to get the door, I answered my phone. "Hey, Sean. What's up?"

"Detective Corbison is on his way over. He doesn't like to announce his arrival, so I wanted to give you a heads-up."

I walked into the living room and saw Corbison step into the house. "He just walked in, Sean."

Detective Al Corbison walked into the living room and glanced around, as though taking stock of the situation. He saw me in the kitchen talking on the phone as Reilly continued. "Okay, but I wanted to let you know not to answer any questions."

"Why not?"

"Just don't," Reilly commanded. "I'll explain later."

"Have a seat," Marco said to Corbison as they entered the living room. "Can I get you a glass of wine? Water? Beer?"

"No, thanks," the detective said, sitting in one of the two easy chairs opposite the sofa. He waited until

Marco and I had taken seats next to each other on the sofa to say, "We talked about sharing information, so I thought maybe we could have a chat."

There was something about the way he said it that raised my suspicions. Add to that Reilly's warning and I was on high alert.

"Sorry to interrupt your phone call," Corbison said. "I hope it wasn't important."

"It was . . . my mother."

"Was it now?" Corbison replied wryly.

I didn't like his tone. "No problem. I can call her back. What would you like to chat about?"

"We have an eyewitness who claims to have seen Devona Esmond leave the McMahon Realty Office late on the evening Mr. Mahon was killed," Corbison explained. "I was wondering if you saw anything. That's just one building down from your bar."

"I wasn't paying attention," Marco said. "There was a lot of activity that night. There was a big game on tv, so we had a full house, people coming and going. Wish I could be of more help. What about security cameras on some of the businesses?"

"We're in the process of contacting business owners. I just thought you might have some information."

I wasn't buying it. Corbison was after something.

"Also," the detective continued, "Kenton Lang claims he was at the bar from the time your meeting ended until eleven o'clock. Can you back up his claim?"

Marco hesitated. "After the tenants' meeting, Kenton came in and sat at the bar. He usually stays until close, but I had to cut him off early. Sometime around ten."

"And why did you cut him off?"

Marco hesitated again. "He was – a little angry – about being evicted."

I decided to throw a question back at Corbison. "What about Arthur's children? Have you spoken with them? Are you looking at them as persons of interest?"

Corbison raised his shoulders casually. "We're looking into his kids, but as of right now there are no witnesses or evidence pointing us in that direction."

"Well, I was at the viewing, detective, and I overheard Rowell and his sister Crystal talking, *laughing* about their brother, Birch, killing their father. Rowell then said that he'd thought Crystal did it. That seems like a pretty good direction, don't you think?"

Instead of writing the information down, Corbison leaned back in the chair. "Why didn't you come to me with this information sooner?"

"Because it was just gossip."

"Yet you thought it was important enough to mention to me now."

We glared at each other.

Marco raised his palms. "Let's take a beat. Abby, would you mind getting me some water?"

I snatched the glass from his hands and went to the kitchen, Reilly's warning etched in my mind. I quickly rejoined my husband who had successfully quelled the confrontation and had Corbison back on track. I stood behind the sofa, my nerves jangling.

"You said your meeting with McMahon was at nine-thirty, is that right?" Corbison asked.

Before Marco could answer, I retorted, "Is that what you have in your notes?"

Corbison shot me a perturbed glance.

"It was eight-thirty," Marco corrected.

"Oh, that's right. I have you and the others attending the meeting at *eight*-thirty. How long did the meeting last?"

"Half an hour."

"And you said previously that the mood there was angry, correct?"

"That would be a fair assessment," Marco answered.

Corbison wrote it down. "Did you go straight back to the bar after the meeting? Walk around the square to clear your head? Go see your wife at Bloomers?"

"Bloomers closes at five," I interjected.

Corbison ignored me, his gaze on Marco.

Marco rubbed his chin, hopefully getting the same feeling that I was that Corbison was trying to trip him up. "I went back to the bar. As I said, it was busy that night –"

Stop talking, Marco.

"— but I decided to try again –"

Stop talking.

"— because I thought –"

My reflexes kicked in. I sloshed the glass of water so that the liquid swirled over the edge and down the back of Marco's head. Marco stood immediately, pulling his wet collar away from his neck. He twisted to look at me with eyebrows raised in confusion.

"Marco, I'm so sorry. Let me get a towel."

But I wasn't sorry. I was relieved that my husband had stopped talking, and I was surprised that he would go along so willingly with Detective Corbison's questioning. Obviously, the detective was trying to trip him up. But why?

When I handed Marco the dish towel, he still had a look of bewilderment on his face.

"You were saying?" Corbison asked.

"I think we'll stop the interview right there," I told him.

Corbison tapped his notebook with his pen a few times and put them both into his inside jacket pocket. Giving me a hard look, he said, "Interesting timing."

He put on his overcoat, his eyes watching mine, then turned and walked to the door, where he stopped. "We'll talk again," he said to Marco.

"With our lawyer present," I shot back.

Corbison turned to me with a sly grin. "Tell your *mother* I said hello."

Marco closed the door and turned to study me. "Did you really spill water down my neck?"

"I was trying to keep you from talking. That was Reilly on the phone warning us about Corbison. He told me not to answer any questions. And I'm pretty sure Corbison knew it was Reilly on the phone. Something is going on, Marco. We need to call him back."

Marco picked up his phone and punched in a number. "Sean? Corbison just left and Abby's here with me. You're on speakerphone. What's up?"

"The camera at McMahon's office was damaged, Marco. There's no evidence you or anyone else were ever there that evening. All Corbison has is your admission that you went back to meet with McMahon alone. That's why he came to see you, to question you further about that. I wanted you to know that before Corbison interviewed you."

"Thanks for the heads up, Sean. I'll keep that in mind."

"One more thing, Marco. They found the murder weapon. A steak knife."

"Why is that concerning?" I asked Reilly.

"It looks like it could belong to a restaurant," Reilly answered. "Or a bar and grill."

"Corbison thinks the murder weapon is from Down the Hatch?" Marco asked.

"Look," Reilly said, "I know you didn't do it, but with your admission about your private meeting, the murder weapon, and the fingerprints he found at the scene, it wouldn't be hard for Corbison to link it to you or Kenton, because both of you were at the bar before the murder."

"What fingerprints?" Marco asked.

"Both Kenton's and yours were found on the door handle to the building."

That spelled trouble for Marco.

"Can you get me a picture of the murder weapon, Sean?" Marco asked. "I need to know if it's one of my steak knives."

"I'll do what I can," he told Marco. "Just be careful when you speak to Corbison from now on."

"Thank you, Sean."

"Thanks, Reilly," I called.

Marco hit END and slid the phone into his pocket. "Now I need to go change my shirt."

"Didn't you notice," I asked, trailing after him, "that Corbison was trying to trip you up?"

"Yes," he answered. "My mistake was in trusting him." Marco pulled a clean T-shirt over his head. "I think it's time we got involved."

❧ ❧

We settled back in the living room with glasses of wine, Marco in the easy chair, me on the sofa, Smoke curled up beside me, and Seedy at Marco's feet.

"Where do we start?" I asked.

"Let's list what we know," he answered.

"Okay. We know Arthur was killed with a steak knife. We know that he'd just had dinner with his kids - who don't seem to care about him. We know that the realty office's security camera wasn't working. We know that you, Kenton, and Devona had just met with Arthur. We know that your fingerprints and Kenton's were on the building's door handle. And we know that Corbison knows you went back to see Arthur later that evening."

"Which makes me a viable suspect," Marco said.

"True. So, where *do* we start?" I asked.

"I suggest we start with Kenton. He was very angry after the meeting, and I'd like to know what he did after he left the bar that night. The problem will be getting him to talk to us. He's very suspicious of everyone. But he seems to trust me, so I'll try to get him to meet with us."

"We need a way to get to McMahon's kids, too. I was very close to getting information from Crystal, but it didn't work out. However, I've convinced Jillian to help me."

"Jillian?" Marco asked.

"She knows Crystal, although she did have one condition."

"That sounds ominous."

"She wants to play her guitar at Down the Hatch."

He stopped sipping his wine to stare at me over the rim.

"And I promised her it would happen," I added.

"Jillian plays the guitar?"

"Well, not exactly."

"Then I'm confused."

"She's *learning* the guitar."

"And she wants to practice at my *bar?* Have you heard her play?"

I was afraid to tell him about the song she'd played for me, so I just said, "She's still learning, so let's not worry about that just yet. And who knows? Maybe the bar will close, and we won't have to worry."

"Funny."

"Anyway, you have an in with Grant Starling. I'm sure he has lots of information about McMahon's kids. Plus, you know Rowell. You might be able to get him to talk to us."

"There's no way Rowell is going to talk to me about anything other than my moving out."

"Marco, if we're going to investigate McMahon's murder, we're going to have to find a way. And there's also the youngest son, Birch. We'll have to find out more about him. In the meantime, once I get info from Jillian, I'll figure out a way to speak with Crystal."

"Okay, here's the plan," Marco said. "We'll start with the two most obvious, Kenton Lang and Devona Esmond. Also, Corbison seemed very interested in the security cam footage from around the square, so I'm going to contact the shop owners nearby, see if they'll let me look at their archives."

"I'll grab a new notebook so we can keep track of our information."

Marco held up his palm for a high five. "Let's do it, partner."

"Team Salvare is back in action." I hit his palm with mine and sat back against the sofa. "Don't forget we have dinner at the country club with my family tomorrow."

"I can't wait," Marco said under his breath and took a big drink of wine.

CHAPTER SEVEN

Friday, November 18th

I was on my way to work the next morning when a shiny red Lamborghini came tearing up the street behind me, swerved around me, and headed into the New Chapel Savings Bank's ATM driveway.

"Well, look who we have here," I said to no one in particular. "New Chapel's wealthiest grease monkey. No sense wasting an opportunity."

I stopped in front of the driveway exit, got out of the 'Vette, and put up the hood. Then I waited. A few minutes later, Birch McMahon tried to exit the ATM drive and found himself blocked. He honked the horn and I shrugged. "It stalled," I shouted.

Birch got out of the car and came toward me. He looked like he'd just gotten out of bed. His long-sleeved white T-shirt with a beer logo on the front was wrinkled, his jeans were frayed at the bottom, and his toes hung over his brown leather sandals, the toenails badly in need of cutting. It was autumn. Wasn't he cold?

"What's the problem?" he asked.

"I don't know," I said. "She just stalled."

"Why don't you try to start it so I can see what's going on."

"Thank you." I got back into the driver's seat, thinking quickly. I lightly twisted the keys in the ignition a few times before starting up the engine.

Birch lowered the hood gently and swaggered up to my window. "Seems to be working fine now. What is this, a sixty-two? It looks brand new."

"Nineteen sixty. She was in bad shape when I first got her," I patted the steering wheel, "but a good paint job and a seat reupholstery made her beautiful again." I glanced down the street. "Listen, I'd love to hear about your Lamborghini. Do you have time to grab a cup of coffee? I know a great little coffee and tea shop just around the corner."

Ten minutes later, Birch and I entered Bloomers, where I stepped behind him to signal to Lottie with a quick wave not to say anything. We entered the coffee and tea parlor where I did the same to Grace, who had her mouth open, ready to speak.

"Table for two, please," I said.

"Yes, of course," Grace replied. "Right this way." She led the way to a table in front of the big bay window. As soon as we were seated, she said, "Our scone of the day is pumpkin spice. Now, what may I bring you to drink?"

"I've heard so much about your special blend of coffee," I said. "I'll try that."

"Same for me," Birch said.

"I'm so glad my car is okay," I told him. "I bought it with my own money. My dad couldn't help me. But you probably don't have that problem."

"Are you kidding? I've had my share of clunkers. They were all I could afford. My dad liked to keep a tight fist on his money."

"Liked?"

"He passed recently. You might have read about his death in the papers – Arthur McMahon. His office is right up the block here."

"I heard about that. Was he a realtor or something?"

"That's him."

"Oh, wow. I heard he was stabbed. Do the police know who did it?"

"Nope." He stopped as Grace brought our coffees.

I said nothing, thinking hard as I laced mine with cream from the little pitcher on the table. How did I get him to talk about the murder?

"The coffee is on me," Birch announced as he put a spoonful of sugar into his cup. "And lunch, too, if they have it."

"We don't serve" -I caught myself and said, "*They* don't serve lunch here."

"Care for a scone then?" he asked.

"No, thanks. Coffee is enough." I took a drink and set my cup in the saucer. "So," I said, "any suspects in your dad's death?"

Birch's expression tensed. "We're not here to talk about my dad, are we? Tell me more about you."

"Aren't you just a little concerned about the cause of his death?"

He looked out the window, a sly smile playing about the corners of his mouth. "No, I'm not." He took a drink of his coffee and leaned back. "Tell me more about your Corvette."

I gave him the specifics, then asked, "When did you get your Lamborghini?"

Birch took time to sip his coffee before finally answering, "Yesterday, actually."

"No kidding!"

"Yep. You wouldn't believe the engine in that beauty. It's got a V twelve, sixty degree, MPI fuel supply system."

I had no idea what he was talking about. I pretended to study him for a moment. "You must have saved up quite a lot of money to afford that car."

"To be honest, I inherited it."

"Ah," I said. "Then it was your dad's."

"Yep. And now it's mine." He finished his coffee quickly and held up his hand for another cup.

"That was very generous of your father."

Birch laughed sharply. "Generous isn't the word I'd use. At least when it came to me." He shook his head. "He thought I was a disappointment. I couldn't do anything right in his eyes."

"That's awful."

"I know. He just had a dinner to announce his wedding plans and I wasn't even invited. I learned about it from my sister – and I sort of crashed their little party." He paused as Grace poured him more coffee.

"I'm so sorry," I said.

"I thought for sure I was cut out of the will, but I inherited a bundle. And actually, I wasn't the true disappointment. That honor goes to my brother Rowell, although he would never admit it."

I leaned in. "What do you mean?"

Birch studied me for a moment. "I don't know why I'm telling you all this."

"Maybe because I'm a good listener." I smiled. "You were saying about Rowell?"

"Just that he did everything my dad told him. He followed every path my dad laid out. He didn't have to make any decisions for himself or work for what he got. And now he just sits on his fat butt and waits for his paycheck. He's the disappointment. Not me."

"Did Rowell inherit the business?"

"No. I don't think he wanted the responsibility, just the money." Birch took a sip of coffee, studying me. "You're awfully curious about our inheritances."

"I'm just awfully curious. Period. Blame my father, who was a cop. So," – I paused cautiously – "you were saying Rowell was the true disappointment?"

"If you really want to see a trainwreck, you should meet my sister, Crystal . . . But I'm sorry. What kind of date am I, taking up all your time talking about my family? What do you say we go out for dinner and have a real conversation?"

"I'd love to talk more but I'm married." I held up my left hand to show him my ring. "Unfortunately, dinner is out of the question."

"Married? But I thought . . . You asked me . . ."

"To talk about cars."

Birch's eyebrows drew together in confusion. He set down the cup with a hard clink. "Then why did we end up talking about my father's death the whole time?"

"I just wanted to talk –"

"Wait a minute. Who are you?"

"Birch, calm down. I can explain."

"Are you a cop, too? Was this just a trick to get me to talk?"

"Look, the truth is I'm a private investigator, but I really was interested in your car. As you must have noticed, I love sports cars."

"You're a private investigator? Are you investigating my father's murder?"

"Well, actually –"

"Actually?" He shoved back his chair and stood up. "You tricked me."

"I didn't mean to." *The lie just slipped out.*

He leaned toward me, pointing his finger at me. "This conversation had better not get back to Rowell or Crystal, do you understand? Just leave me the hell alone."

And with that, he stormed out.

I swiveled around and saw Lottie and Grace standing at the coffee counter in the back of the room, arms folded, waiting for an explanation. I sighed and stood up.

"Well, that didn't go well," I said and began to tell them why.

&3 8&

At lunchtime, I slid into the back booth opposite Marco. "Hey, babe."

His attention was focused intently on his phone screen. He mumbled a quick greeting.

"What are you working on?"

"Grant sent me some properties to look at."

"Anything good?"

"Eh."

"Are you hungry?"

"Uh-huh."

"Anything sound good?" I waited a few seconds for Marco to answer then I snapped my fingers, but even that didn't get his attention. "Marco, what do you want for lunch?"

"Um . . ."

I picked up the menu and held it in front of my face. "I went on a date this morning."

My comment registered several seconds later. I heard him set the phone down, then he reached across to lower the menu. "Care to explain that?"

"Welcome back," I said with a grin. I set the menu down and leaned in to answer quietly, "It was a coffee date, and it was with Birch McMahon, whom I tricked into accompanying me to Bloomers."

Gert stopped at our table to ask for our orders in her gravelly voice. "What sounds good today, lovebirds?"

"I'll have the Hatch Burger," Marco said, "with a Coke."

"Hi, Gert. I'll have the ham and cheese on whole wheat," I told her. "And an iced tea."

Marco leaned against the back of the bench and crossed his arms. "You want to tell me how you tricked Birch into a coffee date?"

"It wasn't *actually* a date. But Birch kind of thought it was . . . until I started questioning him about his family. It didn't end well – he stormed out – but I did get some interesting information."

I gave Marco a run-down on my conversation, stopping just as Gert brought our drinks to the table.

"So, Birch got the car he wanted," Marco summed up.

"It also sounded like he and his siblings inherited a good amount of money," I added, "making my case for the kids' motives all the more realistic."

"And your case for their motive is?"

"It's all about money, Marco. I think one of the kids killed him for the inheritance."

"If I may suggest an alternate opinion –"

"Which you usually do."

"— Arthur had just announced his plans to turn the building into a hotel, displacing the tenants."

"You still think one of the tenants killed him?"

"I think we should start with them."

"Okay, fine," I said, "we'll start with the tenants."

"I'm glad you agree."

"And once we rule them out, we can focus on the real investigation."

Marco flashed a good-humored smile. "What makes you so sure the kids are guilty?"

"Besides the obvious motive," I enumerated on my fingers. "Birch hated his father, Rowell wanted money, and Crystal wanted her dream wedding. On top of that, none of them have shown any remorse about losing their dad. So, here's what I was thinking. They had dinner at Adagio's with their father the night of his murder, which means that all of them were on the square that night. We should try to track their movements from the restaurant."

"Another reason I need to go around to the other businesses nearby to see if I can get a look at their security footage."

"Exactly what I was thinking."

"I'll make it a point to do that today."

And with that our food arrived, so we put business aside and had a nice lunch together.

Back at Bloomers, Grace gave me the bad news that the electrician had called to say the part for the cooler wouldn't be in until Tuesday.

My stomach knotted. *Four days?*

"Looks like we'd better take out stock in ice," Lottie said.

"And the lights in the coffee parlor are flickering again," Grace informed me. "We'll have to get someone up on a tall ladder to change the fluorescent bulbs. Shall I have the electrician do it when he comes back?"

"I don't have a tall ladder and neither does Marco, so I guess we'll have to." Which would mean putting up with a flickering light for four more days.

Feeling very blue, I headed back to the workroom, stepping through the purple curtain at the back of the shop into the room that was my paradise - and I immediately felt better. The room smelled of roses, lavender, eucalyptus, and moist, tropical air, and even with no window, it felt like a garden. Wreaths and swags hung from pegs on one ivory latticed wall, and rows of shelves above a Formica counter and deep sink on another wall held all manner of vases and containers of dried flowers.

A long, slate-covered worktable sat in the middle of the room, with drawers underneath for the floral knives and sheers, diagonals, awls, pruners, and other tools we used on a daily basis. A shelf at the bottom held foam, wire mesh, and *papier mache* containers.

99

Against the side wall sat a stainless-steel walk-in cooler where we stored fresh greenery and flowers. Beside it sat a smaller cooler where we kept finished arrangements.

Rosa had three order slips laid out on the table. "Abby, I need your help. We have to pull the flowers for all three orders, so we don't open the cooler more than we have to."

"Okay, let's make a list of what we need."

I went to the desk against the opposite wall and got a pen and pad of paper, which I used to write down the names of the flowers. With the list in hand, Rosa and I stepped into the big cooler only to find it was not very cool at all.

"We need more ice," I told her, as we began to pull the stems. Behind us, the heavy door shut and latched.

Rosa gasped. "We are locked inside!"

"No worries," I said, flipping the latch. "These new doors are made to open from the inside."

She made the sign of the cross. "*Gracias a Dios.*"

I placed the flowers on the table, went to the desk drawer, and opened the petty cash box. It was empty.

"We used it up," Lottie told me when I went up front to inquire. She was dusting the nearly empty shelves, her brassy curls pulled back with a pink polka dot hair scrunchie.

I'll have to charge the ice," I said, even though I knew our credit card was nearly maxed out.

A customer came up to the counter carrying two of my mother's inspirational plaques. "I can't decide," the woman told us. "Which one do you like?"

"This one," I said, pointing to the plaque in her right hand that said, *Opportunities don't just happen; you make them.*

"That one," Lottie said, pointing to the other plaque. It read: *There is nothing impossible to those who will try.*

The woman studied one and then the other, then shrugged. "What the heck? I'll take both."

When she'd gone, Lottie said, "Well, 'least now we can buy the ice."

"I'll go get some. I'll have to remember to tell my mom that her plaques are selling well."

Lottie reached beneath the cash counter and pulled out a note. "You can tell your mother tonight. She called to remind you about dinner at the country club."

Oh, *joy.*

⋐ ❧

On our way to the country club that evening, Marco told me he'd found six businesses on the square with security cameras, including Down the Hatch. "Everyone said I could look at their footage, but it's going to take quite a while to go through it all."

"I don't work on Saturday," I said. "I can start going through it then. You'll just have to show me how."

He turned into the club's parking lot and parked the Prius beneath an elm tree. He came around to my side of the car and held out his hand. "Let's do this thing."

My mother had always dreamed of being able to dine at the posh country club, but it wasn't until my brothers, both doctors, became members that her dream had come true. Now she held family dinners there once a month, bringing together our big family – my brothers and their wives, my niece Tara, my mom and dad, Jillian and Claymore, and now their baby Harper, and of course Marco and me.

New Chapel country club sat on ten acres of land on the eastern border of the city in a beautiful hilly area surrounded by trees and edged on one side by Maple

101

Creek. The golf course was highly regarded in the sporting world, or so my brothers said. The pool was Olympic-sized, surrounded by aqua-colored lounge chairs and umbrella-covered tables. The clubhouse was a tribute to what money can buy.

The long brick and concrete structure sprawled across the top of a hill, with the left wing devoted to banquets, the center span holding offices, washrooms, and a coatroom. The right wing contained the kitchen, the bar, and two adjoining dining rooms, complete with fireplaces and soaring windows that look out onto a flower and shrub garden, with the golf course beyond it. Just outside the windows was a patio for outdoor dining during the warmer months.

Marco and I entered the main dining room, a huge room of white linen-covered tables, vanilla-scented candles, hushed conversations, and air so icy in the summer that you could see your breath. At one end of this room was the bar, a polished oak beauty with brass foot rails and televisions mounted on the end walls. The table where my brothers held court sat in the corner farthest from the bar, in front of a window overlooking the gardens, nearest to the oversized fireplace.

I'd never felt comfortable at the club, and that was especially true after my then fiancé, Pryce Osborne II, jilted me a month before our wedding. He and his family were practically founding members of the club. They had been highly embarrassed when I flunked out of law school, so much so that Pryce couldn't stand the thought of being married to me. I was beyond thankful for that now. Had I married into Pryce's stuffy family, I would've never met and married the man of my dreams.

The man of my dreams now held my hand as we walked through the dining room to the family gathering, where it appeared we were the last ones to arrive.

"You don't have to get upset, Mom," I heard my brother Jordan say. "We have to be fair, is all I'm saying."

"You're saying I shouldn't set a place for you and Kathy," my mother replied. Then she felt my hand on her back and turned. "There you are, Abigail," she exclaimed. "I thought you'd gotten lost."

"Just a busy day, Mom," I said as I took a seat beside Marco at her end of the table. Beside her sat my brother Jordan, an orthopedic surgeon, and his wife Kathy, the parents of my niece Tara, who was seated across from me. Tara aimed a pained expression at me as I sat down, finishing with an exaggerated eye roll. From the conversation I'd overheard, I knew exactly how she felt.

Next to me was my oldest brother Jonathan, a heart surgeon, and his wife Portia. Portia had grown up in the lap of luxury, while my brothers and I had lived off a cop's meager salary, which was why I was always ribbing Jonathan about his acquired tastes for the finer things in life. He took it in good humor, but Portia took it as an insult.

I waved at her, but Portia had other matters on her mind. "I agree with Jordan and Kathy," she said in her soft voice. "We should take turns."

"And whose turn would it be this year?" Mom fired back. "I'm assuming it wouldn't be mine."

Portia looked at her husband for support and his cheeks flared hotly, a sign of agitation that I hadn't seen from Jonathan since we were kids. He was not one for confrontation. He raised his hands to calm the mood, his cheeks matching the color of his short, smartly parted hair. "Maybe we can work something out."

That was obviously not the answer Portia had wanted. She dotted her mouth with a napkin to mask her scowl.

To help our brother, Jordan chimed back in. "Why don't you invite all of the families over next year?"

"Well, it's a little late to tell me that now," Mom said.

Jillian and Claymore were seated at the far end of the table with baby Harper sound asleep in her carrier. Jillian raised her hand. "We could host at our house," she said. "But I don't cook, and I certainly don't know how to roast a turkey." She turned to Claymore. "Is it too late to hire a caterer?"

Claymore cleared his throat and took a drink of his wine.

"We've already ordered drinks," my dad said, as the waitress came back to our table. "What will you and Marco have?"

I opened the wine menu and ran my finger down the list of red wines, but my mind was on the Thanksgiving dilemma. It was the same argument that my family had been having since Jonathan and Jordan started dating. My mom has always been adamant about family traditions. As my brothers married and started having their own families, the traditions started changing, but Thanksgiving had always been the one holiday that held fast.

I couldn't help but agree with my brothers. It was getting harder to juggle all the families and holidays. Everyone had a different idea about what was right and what was fair. Every family had their own traditions. But what if we could start a new tradition? What if there was a way to make everyone happy?

"Have you decided?"

I glanced up at the waitress, snapping me back to reality. "I'll have a glass of Liberty School Cabernet." I closed the menu to hand it back when a flier slid out and landed in my lap.

"I'll have a beer, whatever's on tap," Marco added.

On the flier were three bold words: THANKSGIVING MADE SIMPLE. And a picture of a large, juicy, sliced turkey. My eyes opened wide. There it was - the answer I'd been hoping for. And it had just landed directly in my lap.

The waitress walked away, leaving the table painfully quiet. I glanced at my mother, who was pretending to read the dinner menu, although she always ordered the same chicken salad every single time. Portia was having a silent conversation made up completely of eye gestures with Jonathan. Jordan and Kathy were watching Tara, who was texting me beneath the table.

Tara: *Please help me. This is torture.*

I set my phone down and lifted the flier. "Look here. The country club has a turkey dinner buffet on Thanksgiving. We can invite all the families to the club and celebrate together. Thanksgiving made simple."

My mom peered over her menu. "Turkey buffet?"

Jillian made a face, as though she found the idea distasteful. Claymore kept his mouth shut.

Seizing the opportunity for a possible peaceful solution, my dad interjected. "Why not a turkey buffet? It sounds delicious. And there's more than enough room for everyone here."

"I've already purchased a turkey, and all of the sides and ingredients, Jeffrey. What will we do, let that go to waste?"

Tara looked up from her phone. "There's a shelter that hosts Thanksgiving dinners for the homeless. You could donate an entire Thanksgiving dinner."

"That's a great idea, Tara," my dad said.

"And here you can relax, Mom," I added. "Let someone serve *you* for a change."

My mom set her menu down with a stubborn sigh. "It's not tradition."

"Do you remember what you told me about our family heritage?" I asked.

The waitress came back with our drinks and asked if we were ready to order, to which everyone answered "yes" in unison. As the waitress made her way around the table, I had a chance to quietly continue the conversation with my mom.

"You said a fear of losing control runs in the family. And isn't tradition just another way to keep control?"

My mom sipped her wine, thinking.

"Wouldn't it be nice to have the extended families come together?" I asked.

"We can't assume that your brothers' in-laws will all drop their plans and meet at the club."

Jordan handed his menu to the waitress and turned to Mom. "Kathy's family is in town this year."

"We'd be happy to have my parents join us here," Kathy said.

"Awesome!" Tara exclaimed.

Portia spoke up next, a quiver of excitement in her normal fragile voice. "We can have management set up two long tables for us right here by the fireplace."

"Then it's settled," Jonathan said, his cheeks resuming their normal pale palette. "We'll start a new Thanksgiving tradition." He double-checked my mom's expression. "As long as you're okay with that, Mom."

At the end of another long sigh, she said, "If that's what everyone wants, then go ahead and make a reservation."

It wasn't the answer I'd hoped for, but it was an answer, nonetheless.

I felt Marco nudge my shoulder. "Shall I let you break the news to Francesca?"

Oh, shoot. I hadn't even thought about Marco's mom. "What do you think she'll say?"

He smiled. "I think she'll be happy she won't have to cook. Good idea, Sunshine."

My niece Tara caught my attention. "Working on any fun murder investigations?"

"Fun?" I made a face at her.

"You know you love it," she replied. "Come on. Spill."

"Are you working on the realtor's murder?" my dad asked. His wheelchair was parked at the end of the table. He'd been a cop before an armed drug dealer shot him in the right thigh. An operation to remove the bullet had caused a stroke, resulting in partial paralysis and subsequent retirement from the force.

"We're just getting started," I told him.

"I want to help!" Tara said, her eyes lighting up with excitement.

I wasn't surprised. My intrepid niece was fond of saying she wanted to be just like me, catching murderers and solving mysteries. A few weeks ago, she had come to me for help when her friend's mother went missing. We had solved the case but had nearly been burned alive after being locked in a storage shed. Clearly, that hadn't dampened her enthusiasm.

"No way," her father Jordan said. "No snooping, no spying, no getting yourself almost killed."

"Listen to your father," Kathy added. "Abby and Marco are professionals. They know what they're doing."

My brother Jonathan snorted. "Is that why Abby has almost gotten herself killed – how many times now, Ab?"

"If you ask me," my sister-in-law Portia said, "it's a good thing she has Marco."

At that, all eyes turned to Marco. He put his hand on my shoulder and gave it a squeeze. "It's a good thing we have each other."

I flashed Portia a quick glare.

"See that, Claymore?" Jillian said to her husband. "Aren't they adorable? Maybe we should go into business together."

Claymore looked at her in surprise. "Are you saying you want to become a CPA?"

"No, silly. You need to come into business with me. Although, you might need a new wardrobe."

Claymore cleared his throat and proceeded to finish his wine.

As the waitress delivered our drinks, chatter around the table continued.

"Seriously, Aunt Abby, " Tara asked quietly, "can I help with the investigation? Anything at all?"

I glanced at Marco, then said in a hushed voice, "You could help us go through security camera footage tomorrow to see if we can spot any of our suspects. Okay with you, Marco?"

"Bring your laptop with you," he told Tara.

"What time?" she asked.

"I can take a couple of hours off mid-afternoon," Marco said.

"Let's make it two o'clock," I told him. "I'll pick up Tara and meet you at the house."

"That works for me!" Tara said excitedly.

My brother cleared his throat. I looked over to see Jordan and Kathy staring at me.

"Can I go to Aunt Abby's house on Saturday?" Tara asked obediently.

Before I could receive the standard lecture about keeping my niece out of trouble, I looked past them and saw a face I recognized – Honey Chen, former fiancée of Arthur McMahon – working as a waitress?

"Marco," I said, indicating with my head, "that's Arthur McMahon's fiancée. I'm going to talk to her."

I stood up and walked over to the waitress station across the room near the kitchen. Honey was standing with her back to me, looking down at something in her hands. She was wearing a white button-down shirt with black pants and shoes, and a black apron around her waist. She was a lot shorter without her designer heels on, maybe an inch shorter than me, with dark black hair pulled up in a tight bun above her head. "Honey?"

She turned around, her eyes red-rimmed, her face blotchy, as though she'd been crying. In her hands she held a cell phone, which I could see was flooded with text messages.

I was taken aback by her expression. "Are you okay?" I asked.

She wiped a tear streaming down her cheek. "Abby?"

"Yes, from Bloomers."

Her phone vibrated in her hand. Instead of checking the message, she slipped the phone into the front pocket of her black serving apron. "What can I do for you?"

"I just wanted to say again how sorry I am for your loss. I didn't know you worked here."

"This is where Arthur and I met." She wiped another tear running down her cheek. "It's where we were going to be married."

"I'm sure this must be a difficult time."

She lifted a corner of her apron to wipe her cheeks dry. "You have no idea."

"I don't know if you're aware, but I'm also a private investigator."

"Okay."

"I'm looking into Arthur's death, and I was hoping to talk to you."

"Table fifteen needs you now," came a voice from behind me.

Honey nodded at the waitress, a tall, thin woman with auburn hair, and sucked in her breath as if she were trying to collect herself. "I'm too busy to talk to you right now," she said to me and hurried away.

The taller waitress stood at the entrance to the kitchen's swinging double doors, watching me. "Is there something I can do for you?"

"No, thanks. I was just talking to Honey."

The waitress walked toward me. "You know Honey?"

It was a simple enough question, but judging by the way she asked, it seemed loaded. This woman knew Honey, and she knew something about her situation. "Yes, I know her, and I'm worried about her."

At that, the waitress moved closer and lowered her voice. "Me too. That creep won't leave her alone. She's been fighting tears all day."

Creep? What creep? I had just assumed that Honey's tears were from the recent loss of her fiancé, but this so-called creep warranted further investigation. "I wish there was something we could do about it," I asked, thinking as quickly as I could.

"What can you do? We've all had overprotective boyfriends, but this one takes the cake."

She has a boyfriend? Now there was a twist I did *not* see coming. "I didn't know she was dating . . . again . . . so soon after the tragedy."

The waitress shook her head sadly. "I don't think she has a choice."

"What do you mean?"

She stopped talking when Honey ventured back to the station with an armload of empty plates. Honey gave me an awkward smile as she passed by, then pushed her backside through the kitchen doors and disappeared inside. Before I could finish my conversation, the other waitress waved her fingers at me and followed Honey into the kitchen.

CHAPTER EIGHT

With my curiosity now approaching one hundred fifty percent, I waited eagerly by the kitchen, dodging several harried busboys carrying heavy tubs full of dirty dishes. Finally, Honey slipped through the kitchen doors and almost slipped past me too.

I stepped in front of her. "I don't mean to bother you –"

She came to an abrupt stop and said, "Then why are you?"

"Honey," another waitress said, coming up to us. "Table eight is looking for you."

"I have to go," Honey said to me.

"Would you be able to meet with me?" I asked her. "I'd like to know more about Arthur's children. I think one of them might be involved in his death."

At the mention of Arthur's kids, her wary expression turned to one of interest. "When did you have in mind?"

"How about noon on Monday? At Down the Hatch Bar and Grill. I'll buy you lunch."

Honey thought about it for a moment. "Okay, I'll see you then."

When I got back to the table, Marco said to me quietly, "Any revelations?"

"We made arrangements to meet on Monday for lunch at the bar. I'll fill you in on the rest after dinner, including the fact that Honey has a boyfriend."

"Interesting."

"Abs," Jillian said from across the table, "don't look now but Pryce is heading this way."

My ex-fiancé? The rat who had jilted me two months before our wedding? And now he was headed my way?

"Marco," I said, "kiss me."

"What?"

I pulled him in by his shirt and gave him a deep kiss. From the corner of my eye, I saw Pryce pass by the table and continue on.

"What was that about?" Marco asked, sitting back in shock.

"Yes, Abigail," my mom said. "What was that about?"

"Pryce," Jillian said.

And everyone said, "Oh-h-h."

Saturday, November 19th

Saturday afternoon, while Tara and I waited for Marco to get home, I got on social media websites and found photos of all three of Arthur McMahon's children plus Devona Esmond. Unfortunately, Kenton Lang had no presence on the internet that I could find.

I showed each photo to Tara and gave her their names. "These are the faces we're looking for."

"Oh, yuck. Crystal looks like a Jersey housewife."

"And she's the attractive one of the bunch. Here's Rowell."

She immediately shielded her eyes. "I'm going to puke. He's so gross."

I chuckled at Tara's comedic expression and switched to the next picture.

Tara curled her lip. "Who's the homeless guy?"

"That's their younger brother, Birch."

"You told me he was rich," Tara said. "He doesn't look rich."

"His father was rich," I explained. "Now he's dead and they're all rich. That's why we're looking into them."

Tara thought for a moment. "I'm with you Aunt Abby, I think one of the kids did it."

"Marco still wants to rule out the tenants first, so keep your eyes open for this woman, too. Her name is Devona."

Tara studied the picture carefully. "She's really pretty. Look at that long hair."

"She may be wearing it in a thick braid behind her head. Keep that in mind when you're watching the tapes."

"Can you copy the photos and text them to me?"

"Sure," I replied. "If you show me how."

Ten minutes later, Tara was reclining in Marco's favorite chair listening to music on her laptop while I sat on the sofa scouring the internet for a picture of Kenton Lang. I heard the door to the garage open and Marco come inside.

"We're in the living room," I called.

"I'll be there in a minute," he replied. "I have to say hello to Seedy and Smokey boy."

He came into the room a few minutes later and took a small thumb drive out of his pocket. "I've got the files."

"Where are the tapes?" I asked.

"What tapes?"

"I just imagined you'd have video cassettes," I said.

"That's old technology, Sunshine. Everything is digital now. I've got footage from six security cameras on here. Give me your laptop and I'll download the files. Tara, you're next."

After Marco had downloaded the files, he said, "Remember, this isn't like watching a movie. We won't see clear images, just quick shots of people walking by. So, any time you see someone you recognize, pause the video and we'll inspect it.

"Abby, I've given you footage from Churchill's department store and Adagio's restaurant. That's where the McMahon family had dinner the night of Arthur's death. The camera is located inside, with a view of the front door and long windows facing the street. Hopefully, you'll be able to identify all three children leaving the restaurant and which direction they go."

"I can handle that."

"I'll go through the footage from Down the Hatch and Bingstrom's Jewelers."

"What about me?" Tara asked.

"I've given you Ascott's Shoe Store and Windows on the Square Boutique, which is just up the street from Adagio's. You should have a pretty good view of the street and sidewalk. You can work with Abby to locate the children once they leave the restaurant."

"Okay, boss."

"Some of the cameras overlap," Marco continued. "If you see one of our suspects, I can check from a different angle, and we can track their movements. Unfortunately, the only camera that would have a direct shot of the McMahon and Starling Realty office is at the courthouse and they wouldn't release their file to me."

"What about the realty office?" Tara asked. "Do they have a security camera?"

"They do," Marco said, "but it wasn't working the night Arthur was killed."

"Isn't that convenient?" Tara replied. "Maybe the killer broke the camera."

Marco and I looked at each other. Tara was on the ball.

"That's a good theory," I told her.

Tara pulled up the shoe shop's file on her laptop. "This video is eight hours long! How am I ever going to find anyone?"

"We don't have to watch the whole day," Marco replied. "We want to scroll forward to seven-thirty p.m. That's when Arthur left the restaurant and went to Down the Hatch to talk to me."

"I've got it right here." I turned my laptop screen for Tara and Marco to see. "Timestamp seven thirty-one p. m. You can see Arthur leaving the restaurant with Honey. She gives him a peck on the cheek and gets into a white car parked right out front. Then Arthur walks away from the restaurant toward the bar."

"My timestamp is in military time," Tara said.

"Then just subtract twelve," Marco told her.

"Oh my God." She rolled her eyes. "Math."

Marco set his laptop down and crouched next to the recliner. He helped Tara scroll forward to the correct time. "There. From your view, you can see Arthur walking down the sidewalk toward the realty office. Now just watch the footage and pause when you see someone. Got it?"

"Got it."

"Good." Marco took his seat next to me on the sofa and scrolled forward through his footage from Down the Hatch. "Here Arthur is entering the bar."

"What's the timestamp?" I asked.

"Seven-thirty-five," Marco said and nodded confidently. "I think this is going to work. We can track everyone around the whole town square."

"Who should I search for next?" Tara asked.

"Just let your video play and let me know if you see any of the people I showed you," I instructed.

"This is so exciting!" Tara settled back into the recliner, her eyes glued to the screen.

Marco relaxed next to me and rested his computer in his lap. I pressed play on my file and started the search. After a few minutes, I paused the video to show Marco as each of Arthur's children started to leave the restaurant. Crystal left first, so Marco checked his camera and Tara checked hers.

"She walks around the corner and disappears," Tara said.

"That means she wasn't heading toward the realty office," Marco explained. "But it doesn't mean she's in the clear. Keep your eye out for her."

Rowell left the restaurant next. Tara's footage showed Rowell getting into his black BMW parked on the street by Windows on the Square. Next up should've been Birch, but he didn't follow his siblings out of the restaurant. I scrolled through the restaurant footage until eleven p.m. when the lights in the building turned off.

"How did he get out of the restaurant without being caught on camera?" I asked.

"Maybe you scrolled too quickly," Marco said. "You'll have to rewind and start again."

I sat back with a sigh. This was not going to be as easy as I thought.

"Here I am." Marco paused the video and turned his laptop so I could see, then hit play. The footage showed him walking out of the bar. "This is when I left for the tenant's meeting. Timestamp is eight-thirty." He scrolled forward to show me when he returned from the meeting, then paused the video at nine-oh-eight. "And here is when I left to speak to Arthur alone."

I glanced at my husband. "What time did police estimate Arthur's death to be?"

"Sometime between eight and midnight," he replied.

I sighed again.

"Here I am returning at nine-eighteen," Marco said. "Ten minutes alone with Arthur before coming back to the bar. From that point, I have witnesses until after midnight."

"Ten minutes is not enough time to kill Arthur and clean up before going back to work. Don't you think?"

"I don't know, Sunshine. I guess it depends on what other evidence they can use against me. If Corbison wants to target me, he has a good place to start."

I sat up and squared myself in front of my laptop screen. "Then let's make sure he can't finish."

After twenty minutes, Tara sat up and stretched. "This is so boring."

"Hold on," Marco said, sitting forward. "Look who I see walking past the window at nine-forty-five p.m."

I squinted at the screen, where I could see several patrons sitting at the tables near the bar's front window. As Marco let the footage play, I saw a woman walking outside on the sidewalk. It was brief, but the light from the bar was just enough to make out the dark hair as she passed.

Tara squeezed onto the sofa beside me. "Who is that?"

"Looks like Devona," Marco said.

"How can you tell that's her?" I asked. "It's blurry. Can you zoom in?"

Marco tried it without luck. "The resolution just gets worse."

Tara pulled up the picture of Devona on her laptop. "She doesn't look like the woman in this photo. Her hair is different."

"But the color is the same," Marco said. "And I've seen Devona wear her hair pulled up like that."

"You know who else that might be?" I asked. "Honey Chen. The day I met with Honey, she had her hair pulled up, too."

Tara flopped back with a groan. "This is pointless. Can we order pizza?"

❧ ☙

After our pizza break, we got back to it. I started watching the footage from Churchill's Department Store while Marco started on the files from Bingstrom's Jewelers. Because of the added security, the jewelry store had outdoor cameras facing the sidewalk.

"Look, Abby," Marco said. "Here's the same woman. Nine forty-five pm."

"She's turned away from the camera," I said. "There's no way to identify her."

"Whoever she is, she stops right after Down the Hatch. That's the entryway into the apartments upstairs. I think it's Devona."

"Or," I countered, "it's Honey. You can't see which door she goes in. She could've entered the realty office. The doors are right next to each other."

Marco ran his hand through his hair and sat back against the couch. He blew out a deep breath. "Whose idea was this?"

"That's what I'm saying," Tara added.

A few minutes of frustrated silence later, Marco sat up and showed me the screen. "Doesn't this look like Kenton Lang? It's a side view but it looks like he could be standing outside the realty office. Time stamp ten-fifteen p.m."

"I can't make out his features."

"But that's the long army coat he always wears."

118

"Couldn't he also be going up to his apartment?" I asked. "Didn't you kick him out of the bar around ten?"

Marco pulled up the file from Down the Hatch and scrolled through it until ten o'clock. "Okay, here's Kenton leaving the bar at eight after ten." He switched back to the Bingstrom's file and leaned in closer to the screen. "Kenton's just standing on the sidewalk."

"Maybe he's about to go into the stairwell to his apartment," I said.

"Or maybe he's waiting for an opportunity to go back into the realty office," Marco countered.

After a few more minutes, Kenton opened a door and dashed inside, but it was unclear which doorway he entered.

"Do you think he went to McMahon's office?" I asked.

"We'll have to ask him about that."

"Hey!" Tara blurted, "isn't this the fat guy in the photo?" She swiveled her laptop for us to see the footage from Ascott's Shoe Store. And we could indeed see a heavy-set man in a dark suit walking away from the camera.

"What's the time stamp?" Marco asked her.

"Twenty-two thirty o'clock minus twelve."

"Ten thirty," Marco said dryly.

I rewound the video for another look, but the man's image flashed so quickly and was so blurry that I couldn't get a good view. But it seemed too coincidental that a heavy-set man wearing a dark suit and fitting the description of Rowell McMahon happened to be near his father's office around the time the murder occurred.

"That has to be Rowell," I said.

Marco leaned in for a closer view of the blurry image. "I think it looks more like Roger Ascott if you ask me." He pressed a few buttons simultaneously on the keyboard, which captured an image of the screen.

"But why would Roger be at his store that late?" I asked.

Marco didn't have an answer.

"I think we need to talk to Roger," I said.

Tara squeezed in between us on the couch, and we watched as she scrolled carefully through the rest of the night. Finally, around two in the morning, the footage ended.

We ran through the rest of the footage but didn't see anyone else we recognized. In the end, we had seen a woman who resembled both Devona and Honey, a heavy-set man who might have been Rowell, and Kenton Lang. It gave us a place to start.

❧ ☙

"Let's interview Kenton Lang first," I said, as Marco helped me take the empty plates back to the kitchen. "He should be at the bar this evening, right?"

"I don't know. He hasn't been back since I kicked him out."

I rinsed the plates and handed them to Marco to put in the dishwasher. "Then let's drop in on him at home."

"That won't work. He doesn't like visitors. He won't answer the door."

"Can you call him?"

"Yeah," Marco replied. "I have his number at the bar" – he glanced at his watch – "and I should be getting back there anyway."

"Why don't I take Tara home and meet you down there? Maybe we can meet with Kenton tonight."

"Sounds like a plan." He kissed me, stopped to pet Seedy, called goodbye to Tara, and headed out the door into the garage.

I finished cleaning up in the kitchen, then Tara and I left, too, heading to her parent's house several blocks away.

"Thanks for letting me help, Aunt Abby," she said, "even though I didn't help very much."

"What are you talking about? You helped quite a bit."

"But we didn't see any of Arthur's kids near the realty office, unless you count Rowell, which you can't because Marco isn't sure it was even him."

"I'm going to talk to Roger Ascott tomorrow to find out what time he left the shoe store," I said. "If it wasn't Roger in the video, then I'll bet it was Rowell."

"What happens if it *was* Rowell?" Tara asked.

"Then we'll have to dig deeper, find more evidence against him."

After I pulled into her driveway, Tara gave me a quick hug and popped open the passenger door. "If you need any more help just let me know."

I waited until she was safely inside the house and then headed toward Down the Hatch, parking in the public lot a block away. When I got to the bar, the place was packed, and Rafe - Marco's brother – plus Chris and Marco were behind the shiny wooden bar. Marco, who was pouring beer from the tap, glanced up, saw me, and winked.

I walked up to the bar and ordered a glass of Cabernet. "Did you call Kenton?" I asked him.

"I had to twist his arm, but he said he'd come down at eight o'clock." Marco glanced at his watch. "Half an hour from now."

I looked around, saw that the booths were all occupied, and took a seat on a stool. Marco was busy, so I took out my phone and scrolled through the news.

"Hey, Red," I heard, and glanced to my right to see a blond-haired man around my age smiling at me. "You look familiar."

"Ever do business at Bloomers Flower Shop?" I asked.

"Can't say that I have. Why?"

"I'm the owner."

He set his elbow on the bar and leaned toward me with a flirtatious grin. "What else can you tell me about yourself?"

"She can tell you she's married," Marco said, standing behind the bar with his arms folded.

The blond glanced back at me and smiled smugly. "A ring don't mean a thing to me."

As the man leaned in closer, Marco placed his hand on the bar between us, his wedding band smacking the polished wood loudly. "Married to me."

The man took a step back and then pulled out his wallet. "I was just about to go anyway." He paid his tab quietly and slunk out of the bar.

"You're welcome," Marco said. He looked so pleased with himself that I didn't have the heart to tell him I could've handled the guy myself.

At eight o'clock on the nose, Kenton Lang opened the door and stepped into the bar, his head on a swivel as he scoped out the people around us. He had on his beat-up green army jacket and a pair of dark blue jeans with worn black sneakers. He saw Marco and headed for the bar.

Marco leaned over and said to his brother, "I need to leave for about ten minutes. I'll be in the back."

"Kenton," Marco said, "let's go talk in my office."

Kenton's eyes widened in alarm. "Why in your office?"

"It's quieter," Marco replied. "And we won't be disturbed." He nodded at me, so I got up and headed past the long bar and up the hallway.

I was already there when the two walked in. "Hi, Kenton," I said softly.

He turned toward Marco. "Why is she here? She's not wearing a wire, is she? Or you? Is this a setup?"

"Nothing of the sort," Marco told him and tugged down the neck of his black T-shirt to show him. "Have a seat and we'll explain everything." He indicated one of the black leather slingback chairs facing the desk.

Kenton sat down and I sat in the chair beside him, while Marco took a seat behind the desk. "Abby and I are looking into Arthur McMahon's death," he said to Kenton, "because we know the police are going to be looking at you and me as suspects."

"That's what I'm afraid of," Kenton replied. "That's why I kept my answers short and vague. You know?"

"What have you told them so far?" I asked, pulling out my notebook and pen.

"What are you writing?" he replied instantly, half rising from his chair.

"I'm taking notes. It helps me remember our conversation."

"We do this with everyone we talk to," Marco assured him. "No reason to be worried."

Kenton slowly lowered himself into the chair. He took a deep breath and then said, "I told the cops I went straight home after you tossed me out of the bar that night."

"You know why I had to cut you off," Marco said.

"I know, man. You did what you had to do. And it's a good thing you did. Wait a minute. Are you going to tell the cops what I tell you? You know they'll come after me if they find out I lied."

Marco scratched his chin, a sure sign that he was now carefully crafting his answer.

"What did you lie about?" I asked.

Kenton looked at me, twitching in his seat. "Don't write this down. I don't want any evidence in writing."

I did as Kenton asked and put my notebook and pen on Marco's desk.

Kenton seemed to relax. "I didn't go straight home after Marco kicked me out. I wanted to talk to Arthur, you know? Set him straight. But I saw someone in his office. I could see them through the blinds. I didn't tell the cops because I didn't want them to know I was there." He looked back across the desk at Marco. "You can't tell the cops what I tell you."

"I won't tell Detective Corbison that we spoke, but if you have any information that will help me find Arthur's killer, I'll have to share it."

"Just keep my name out of it and I'll tell you what I saw."

Marco nodded. "I can do that."

"On second thought –" Kenton sprang from his chair, "— I'll show you what I saw."

Marco and I gave each other a puzzled look as Kenton headed for the doorway.

"Come on."

We followed him out of the office, through the bar, and outside, where he walked over to the realty office's plate glass window. He cupped his hands against the glass and peered inside.

"You can just make out the people through the wooden blinds," he told us. "Especially after dark with the lights on inside."

"What did you see?" I asked.

"The blinds were partly opened. I could see the outline of a woman. It looked just like Devona, but her hair was pulled up."

"Devona?" I asked. "Are you sure?"

"Yeah. You heard me right. Devona was inside Arthur's office. They were fighting."

"Did you hear what was being said?" Marco asked as I did my best to memorize Kenton's words.

"I heard shouting. I heard the woman call Arthur a liar. I don't know what he was lying about, but she said it over and over again. I thought maybe he needed some help, so I tried the door, but it was locked."

Which would put Kenton's fingerprints on the doorknob.

"I also saw Devona throw something at Arthur. I don't know what it was, but it clinked against the blinds right near me."

I made a mental note: *What could Devona have thrown at Arthur?*

"How long did you listen to the argument?" Marco asked.

"A couple minutes maybe. Then I see this car coming down the street with one headlamp out," he continued. "It was creeping along real slow and then it pulled up next to a car parked at the curb, so I ducked into the entrance to my apartment and hoofed it upstairs. The car was still there when I got to my window, and then it pulled away."

"Did you get a look at the make and model of the car?" Marco asked.

"It was dark colored, maybe black, or dark gray. That's all I know."

"Did anyone get out of the car?" Marco asked.

"Not while I was watching."

"Did you see anyone else out here that evening?" Marco asked.

"No one I recognized. And like I said, I didn't tell the cops I was there. I just hope you remember our little deal. If you talk to the cops, keep my name out of it." Kenton walked over to the door that separated the two halves of the building and disappeared inside.

"That was interesting," I said as we walked back to the bar. "Kenton thinks he saw Devona in the office, but it could've been Honey. It sure looked like Honey in that security footage I saw."

"You know what I found interesting? Kenton said he tried the building's door, but it was locked. Does that mean Devona locked it after she went inside so no one else could come in? Or was Kenton lying?"

"His story matches up with what we saw on the security cam footage. What would be his reason for lying?"

"To prove that he couldn't have gone inside himself."

"Which would take him off the suspect list," I concluded.

"Exactly. Look how adamant he was about us not giving him up to the police. He's frightened." Marco opened the door for me. "Here's another thing that interests me. The car with the headlight out. We need to find out if that matches any of our suspects' cars."

"How are we going to find that out?"

He smiled and put his arm around my shoulders. "It's called an investigation, remember?"

"Very funny." I retrieved my purse and called it a night. "I'm going home to write down all of my mental notes before they escape my brain."

"I have to close the bar tonight," he replied, "so don't wait up."

I gave him a kiss and left.

Sunday, November 20th

Early Sunday morning, Marco's cell phone rang. I was in the kitchen making breakfast and my handsome hubby was in the basement working out. I heard him answer the phone and knew immediately that Francesca was on the other end. I could tell because Marco's tone changes when he speaks with his mother. It becomes gentler. After the call, he trotted up the basement stairs with a wide grin.

"You seem happy."

"Just talked to my mom."

"Oh yeah?"

"She's all in for Thanksgiving dinner at the country club."

"That's great! And the rest of your family is okay with it?"

"Yep." He gave me a big, sweaty hug. "You may have just saved Thanksgiving for all of us."

"Not all of us," I replied, squirming out of his grasp. "My mom didn't seem very happy about starting a new tradition."

"You can't make everyone happy. You have to do what's right for you."

I wasn't worried about making everyone happy. I was worried about ruining Thanksgiving for the one person who cared most about family traditions. Marco could tell I wasn't satisfied with his affirmation and leaned in for another hug. "I'm sure she will be fine once we're all together."

I blocked him playfully with my hands. "No more hugs until you shower. Hurry up. Breakfast is almost ready."

After a big helping of hot apple cinnamon oatmeal and some extra creamy coffee, we bundled up and took Seedy for a walk in the park a few blocks from our house. On our walk, we began to discuss the murder investigation.

"I still see a strong motive for Arthur's children," I said. "Money. But I see only weak motives for Kenton and Devona – being kicked out of their apartments."

"Maybe they had issues with Arthur that we don't know about," Marco countered. "For instance, what was Kenton doing spying through Arthur's window? Could he have been waiting for Arthur to be alone? And what was Devona yelling about? If it was Devona. I suggest we interview her next. We just need to make it seem like we don't suspect her."

I pondered that for a few moments. "Has she been interviewed by Corbison?"

Marco turned Seedy around and we headed back toward home. "I don't know."

"If she's been interviewed, she may already be worried about being considered a suspect."

"And be more willing to let us help." Marco smiled at me. "Good idea, babe. I'll try to get an interview tomorrow."

"Okay. But remember, I'll be at Down the Hatch talking to Honey tomorrow at noon."

When we got back to the house, Marco placed a call to Sean Reilly, who it turned out was off duty. Marco explained what we had learned from Kenton and then let Reilly talk.

"We'll do that, Sean," Marco said. "Thanks for the information. You know we always appreciate the help."

He hung up and walked into the kitchen, opened the refrigerator, and took out a beer. "Sean thinks we should go see Corbison, fill him in on what we learned from Kenton."

"Without giving up Kenton as our source?"

"Yes. He also gave me a new piece of information. An eighteen-carat gold bracelet was found at the scene of the crime that Corbison believes belongs to Honey Chen."

"Eighteen carat, wow!" I said. "Is that why he thinks it's Honey's?"

"Yes, plus it has an inscription of a heart and an eternity sign inside."

"Then maybe it *was* Honey I saw on that security camera. And maybe it was Honey whom Kenton saw yelling at Arthur." I stooped to pet Smoke, who had come to see what we were doing. "And maybe I can find all that out when we have lunch tomorrow."

CHAPTER NINE

Monday, November 21ˢᵗ

Monday mornings at Bloomers usually started with a hearty breakfast of *Huevos Rancheros* made by Rosa. We'd had to skip the previous Monday because of all that was going on, but today we were back in the swing of things, which made all of us happy.

That was until Rosa and I opened the big cooler to find that the flowers were wilting, their stems were going limp, and the ice had melted. We hadn't ordered more flowers because we weren't sure what time the cooler was going to be fixed, but I had no choice now. We needed fresh blossoms.

"I'm going to Dora's Discount Flowers," I said.

"No, Abby," Rosa demanded. "You cannot go there. You'd be putting money into the hands of our competitor."

"I have to go there if I want money coming into *our* hands." I glanced at the clock on the wall. "I won't have enough time to go now. I have to meet someone for lunch. It'll have to be afterward."

❧ ❧

Shortly before noon, I walked up Franklin Street and crossed Lincoln to get to Ascott's Shoe Store. The brightly lit store had shelves along the walls filled with shoes and smelled of fresh leather and shoe polish. Specializing in the sale and repair of dress shoes, Ascott's business had been around since his grandfather started it in the early sixties.

"Well, if it isn't Abby Knight!" Roger Ascott called as he came out of a doorway in the back. He was a portly man of medium height, with wispy, light brown hair, a wide smile, and a bulbous nose. Always dressed to impress, Roger wore a tan blazer with an argyle tie. His dark leather watch matched the color of his wingtip oxford dress shoes. He gazed at my tan leather loafers for a moment. "Size six-and-a-half, medium width, right?"

"Right on the money," I said. "But I didn't come in for shoes today."

"Ah, so the detectives are back at it. Does this have anything to do with the security footage Marco asked me for?"

"You guessed it. In fact, Marco and I were studying the camera footage and saw someone walking down Franklin Street. We can't identify the man, so we'd like to verify that it wasn't you. Did you stay late on Monday night?"

"I'm not a suspect, am I?"

"Oh, no! Not at all. But someone who resembles you may be. What we need to know is whether you left your store around ten-thirty."

He scratched his head. "Well, I can tell you I stayed late Monday, Tuesday, and Wednesday evenings to work on inventory."

Just then, Roger's wife came out of the back room with several shoe boxes stacked in her arms. Mrs. Ascott was a short, squatty woman with an oval face and thick, curly, golden hair. She set the boxes down at the counter and joined her husband. "Hello, Abby. How good to see you."

"Hello, Mrs. Ascott."

"Oh, no. That won't do. You just call me Elma. All of our customers call me Elma."

"Well, actually, I'm not here to buy shoes."

Elma's smile quickly dissipated. "Not here to buy shoes? Then why are you here, my dear?"

"I was just asking Roger a few questions about last Monday night."

Her jaded smile faded further as she turned to focus on Roger. "What about Monday night?"

Roger began fidgeting with his tie as he fumbled over his words. "Monday night I was, uh, I was staying late, working on inventory, like I said."

"Do you leave out the front door when you stay late?" I asked.

He rubbed his nose and looked away with a shrug.

"Answer the woman, Roger."

"No," Roger answered. "I'm sure I left out the back door."

I showed him the picture we'd captured from the security video outside his store. "We're trying to verify who this man is."

"It's not me. I swear."

Elma asked for the picture and studied it closely. "This looks exactly like you, Roger. Why did you leave out the front door? The only time you leave out the front door is when you go to Down the Hatch after work. Did you go to the bar that night, Roger?"

He wiped a thick band of sweat from his forehead. "No, of course not."

Elma folded her arms slowly across her wide bosom. "Roger is not allowed to go to the bar during the weeknights. Are you, Roger?" Her eyes grew narrow as she glowered at her husband. "He promised only to go to the bar on the weekends. Didn't you, Roger?"

"I – I swear to you. It's not me."

The poor man gulped down a lump in his throat and shifted his eyes nervously between me and his wife. Before I got him into any more trouble, I said, "Good. I didn't think it was you, but I had to check."

"What are you saying?" Elma asked.

"There's a man who looks just like Roger. He's our suspect. Don't worry, Mrs. Ascott. We have security video from Marco's bar. Roger wasn't there Monday night."

Roger smiled in relief.

His wife uncrossed her arms. "Call me Elma, dear."

"Okay. Thank you for your time. I'll be going now."

Roger waved and said, "Tell Marco I'll see him on Saturday."

Elma recrossed her arms.

I left the shoe store quickly. I only had a few minutes until I was supposed to meet with Honey Chen at Down the Hatch.

As I approached the bar, I saw a dark gray sedan pass me and double park near the entrance. Honey opened the passenger door but didn't exit. She seemed to be arguing with the driver, a male with a shaved head except for a thick patch of dark hair on top. Was that her boyfriend?

I hurried into Down the Hatch and took a seat in an open booth. A few minutes later, Honey walked in the door, glanced around, and spotted me.

"Thanks for meeting me," I told her as she slid onto the orange seat across from mine.

"I haven't been here since college," she said, looking around. "Looks like nothing has changed."

Gert, the waitress, stopped by the table to drop off menus and take our drink orders. "I'll have an iced tea," I told her.

"Diet cola," Honey said. "Any kind." She picked up the menu and looked it over. "What's good here?"

"They have excellent sandwiches. My favorite is the ham and Swiss."

"Then that's what I'll have."

"Same for me," I told Gert.

Honey put the menu aside and looked me dead in the eyes. "Why are you investigating Arthur's murder?"

She wasn't wasting any time. I didn't want her to know Marco was a potential suspect, so I said, "Arthur was Marco's landlord. My husband just wants to see justice done, and unfortunately, sometimes the police are slow to make that happen."

"I see." She unrolled her napkin and laid it in her lap. "And what did you want to know about Arthur's kids?"

I slid my notebook and pen out of my purse. "Do you mind if I take notes?"

"I guess not."

"Thanks," I said and opened the notebook. "A gold bracelet was found in Arthur's office after his death. Did the police ask you about it?"

"Oh, yes. They asked. And I told them it wasn't mine." She glanced around and then leaned toward me to say quietly, "If you want to know about the bracelet, ask Devona Esmond."

"What do you mean?"

"I saw her at the country club wearing the exact same bracelet that Arthur had given me. If the detectives found a gold bracelet in Arthur's office, it's Devona's."

I stopped writing. "Devona was at the country club?"

"Yes, for some sort of charity event."

"Why would Arthur give Devona a gold bracelet?"

Honey gave me a look of disbelief. "Seriously? Why do you think?"

"Arthur was seeing Devona, too?"

She gave an angry nod. "I couldn't believe it at first, but I got over it."

I pondered that for a moment. A fiancé cheating on his intended wife? That had to make Honey very angry. "Did you know Arthur was seeing Devona when you agreed to marry him?"

"He told me that his relationship with Devona was over."

"Was it over?" I asked.

Honey looked down at her wrist. "I had my doubts."

"Then why did you accept his proposal?"

She pinned me with another direct gaze. "I'm not going to lie to you, Abby. I live paycheck to paycheck, with student debt up to my ears. Arthur asked me to marry him. He said he would make my dreams come true. How could I turn that down?"

"What was your dream?"

She smiled and looked off distantly. "I've always wanted to run a boutique hotel."

"Did Arthur know that you were marrying him for his money?"

"He wasn't stupid." Honey reached into her purse to retrieve her cell phone. I hadn't heard the phone ring, but the screen was bright with an incoming call. She ended the call and set the phone face down on the table.

"Did you have any feelings for Arthur at all?" I asked.

"Of course. He was always good to me. He wanted companionship and I wanted a secure future. It would've worked for both of us. Now I'm back where I started, with nothing."

"Did Arthur make any provisions for you in his will?"

"No. He was going to wait until after we were married."

"Did his kids know that?"

Honey shook her head and furrowed her brows. "No way. He didn't trust his kids."

I wrote it down and then waited as Gert delivered our meals. If Devona's bracelet was the one found in Arthur's office, then Devona had some serious explaining to do. That was, if Honey was telling the truth. "I notice you're not wearing your bracelet."

She rubbed the inside of her wrist. "I had to pawn it."

"You did? Why?"

She picked up her sandwich. "The catch was too big. It dug into my skin."

"Couldn't a jeweler have fixed that?"

She took a bite of her sandwich and chewed thoughtfully. "I suppose," she said. "But when I saw Devona wearing the same bracelet, I didn't want it anymore."

"You didn't want an eighteen-carat gold bracelet your fiancé had given you?"

Her phone vibrated against the table. She put down the sandwich to silence it once again. "Okay, the truth is, I have bills to pay. I'm a waitress, Abby."

And Arthur's money would've been the answer to her prayers. "Is that what happened to your engagement ring?"

She looked down at her empty left hand. "Yes." She sighed sadly. "It was the most beautiful ring, too."

"I'm sorry."

Her gaze lingered on her left hand. "Me, too."

I jotted it down. I found Honey convincing for the most part. Pawning her jewelry for money was believable, considering her circumstances, but maybe just

136

a bit too coincidental seeing that the police found the same bracelet at the scene of the crime.

"Which pawn shop did you go to?"

"I don't know. Why?"

"You don't know where you sold your jewelry?"

"Why do you need to know that?"

"So I can verify your story."

"I didn't kill Arthur, Abby."

"I didn't say you did. It'll help us rule you out if we can verify that you pawned your jewelry."

"I don't remember where."

"Well, there's a pawn shop here in town, and there's one in Maraville."

She shrugged. "In town."

I made a note of it. We ate in silence for a few minutes and then I asked, "How did Arthur's children take the news of your engagement?"

"How did they take it?" Honey laughed dryly. "You should've seen my car. Crystal smashed the passenger side windshield of my brand-new white Porsche."

"Wow. You have a Porsche?"

She blushed. "I did. It was a gift from Arthur, but I had to sell that, too."

I noted the sale of the Porsche and continued. "When did Crystal smash the windshield?"

"On the night of Arthur's death. Right after he announced our engagement at dinner. Crystal must've followed me home because as soon as I parked and went inside the mansion, I heard something smash. I ran out and saw Crystal running back to her car. And that's when I saw the windshield."

"Wait. You live in a mansion?"

"*Lived.* I moved in with Arthur after we got engaged."

"Did you report the smashed windshield to the police?"

"No, I wanted to talk to Arthur first."

"Did you see him that night?"

She looked down, toying with her napkin as though she didn't want to meet my gaze. "No, I called him, but he didn't answer."

"Did you drive downtown?"

"What I meant to say was that he didn't answer *right away*."

"So you *didn't* drive downtown that night?"

"No. Not at all." She still wasn't looking at me. I made a note of it.

"Have you had any contact with Arthur's kids since his death?"

"No. They avoided me at the funeral."

Honey's phone vibrated against the table. She turned it over to look at it then immediately dropped it into her purse. She signaled to Gert, who came right over. "Can I have a to-go container for this?"

"I'll box it up for you," Gert said, picking up her plate.

"Is something wrong?" I asked.

"No. I just need to go."

"Is someone bothering you?"

"No."

"I'm sorry, but I've noticed quite a few missed calls and messages on your phone. Are you sure everything is okay?"

"Yes, Abby. Everything is fine."

"I saw you arguing with someone in a dark gray sedan outside the bar. Was that your boyfriend?"

She stared at me in surprise. "Excuse me?"

"You have a boyfriend, right?"

She glared at me. "That is *none* of your business." She finished her soft drink and gathered her purse. "I need to go."

"You had to sell your car. Is that why he's driving you around?"

"We're done here, Abby."

"If something is going on," I told her, "or if you need help, you can let me know."

"I don't need your help."

"Honey, I'm truly sorry for everything you've been through."

"I'm sure you are." She gave me a fake smile. "Guess I'll see you around." She accepted the box from Gert and walked out of the bar.

I jumped up and went to the window, where I saw her getting into the same dark gray sedan.

Marco had been watching from behind the bar and came over, sliding onto the bench across from me as I regained my seat. "How did it go?"

"I think I just saw Honey's boyfriend. He dropped her off here and picked her up. And the interesting thing is that he was driving a dark gray sedan. Remember Kenton telling us he saw a dark-colored car with a headlight out outside the realty office that night?"

"There are a lot of dark-colored cars out there, Sunshine."

"Yes, but Honey was very evasive when I questioned her about her coming back to see Arthur that night. It just seems a bit too coincidental that her boyfriend is driving a car similar to the one Kenton saw creeping down the street."

"Then we need to get a look at that car at night when the headlights are on."

"That means we need to find out where her boyfriend lives." I thought for a moment. "I wonder whether the waitress I talked to at the country club could help. I'll have to stop by there and have a chat."

Marco pointed to my plate. "You've barely touched your food."

I picked up the sandwich and took a bite. "And I'm starving. I got so wrapped up in Honey's interview that I forgot to eat."

"Tell me what you learned."

I chewed a mouthful then gave him a rundown on Honey's responses to my questions about the bracelet and ring, and about her mad dash to escape when I mentioned her boyfriend.

"So, Honey knew about Arthur seeing Devona," Marco said. "I wonder if Devona knew about Honey."

I swallowed a bite and wiped my mouth. "I don't think it mattered. I honestly don't believe these women really cared for Arthur. It was all about the money."

"Jealousy is a powerful motive for murder, Sunshine, especially in the heat of the moment. Remember what Kenton said?"

I had already taken another bite, so I shook my head instead of answering.

"He said that he heard Devona – at least he suspected it was Devona – calling Arthur a liar. He said she repeated the phrase several times. Doesn't that sound like jealousy to you?"

I finished a quick drink of iced tea. "Could be. Or she could've been talking about her eviction."

"It would've been very easy for Devona to go up to her apartment and grab a steak knife before visiting Arthur again that night." Marco shook his head sadly. "Things are not looking good for Devona."

"I agree," I said. "But I still got the feeling that Honey was hiding something. Maybe it was her boyfriend. Or maybe it was the fact that she couldn't remember where she pawned her jewelry." I sat for a moment, thinking. "Honey works at a restaurant. She has access to steak knives. What if Honey and her boyfriend came back downtown with plans of their own?"

"What we need to know is exactly whose bracelet the police found," Marco said. He looked over at the bar and saw that it was nearly empty. "Let's take a quick trip over to the pawn shop."

CHAPTER TEN

"Before we go to the pawn shop, let me run down to Bloomers first to let Lottie know."

I slipped on my navy pea coat, wrapped my Kelly-green scarf around my neck, put my purse over my shoulder, and took a quick walk down to the flower shop which, unfortunately, was empty. I found Lottie, Rosa, and Grace sitting in the parlor drinking tea and looking bored.

After letting them know where I was going, I walked out the front door ready to hop into Marco's silver Prius. Except there was no Prius, just Marco, wearing his black down jacket with his faded blue jeans and his scuffed brown leather boots.

"We're walking?"

"It's only two blocks."

"Did you just move here? It's five."

"Okay, five short small-town blocks. You're dressed for it. The sun is out. It's a warm thirty degrees. I think you can make it."

Thirty degrees was not warm, especially with a sharp breeze, and it wasn't a question of me making it. It was a question of me showing up with bright red cheeks and frozen fingers. I stuffed my hands in my coat pockets and plodded along beside him. "Next time warn me."

"Is someone in a bad mood?"

"No. I'm just worried that Bloomers' business is drying up."

"Things will get better, Sunshine. Think positively."

I held his hand firmly in mine. "Thanks, I'll try."

We continued to make small talk until we reached the pawn shop, owned by the same man who owned Bingstrom's Jewelers.

Marco held open the door so I could enter. "After you."

We walked up to a glass counter containing at least a dozen watches, where a middle-aged woman smiled at us. "Can I help you?"

"Is Steve Bingstrom here?" Marco asked.

"He's in the back. Would you like me to get him?"

"If you would," Marco said with a smile.

She blushed, a typical female reaction to my handsome hubby. "I'll go get him."

In a few moments, a tall, trim man with light brown hair parted on one side and combed back came striding toward us. "Marco!" he exclaimed, holding out his hand for a handshake. He had on tan pants, a brown button-down shirt, and a tan and brown plaid sports coat, looking every inch the successful businessman he was. "Any luck with the security footage I gave you?"

"I think so, but we have a question," Marco replied. "You remember my wife, Abby."

"Good to see you again, Abby," he said, shaking my hand. "How can I help?"

"Well," I started, "we were told by a woman named Honey Chen that she pawned an eighteen-carat gold bracelet and an engagement ring. The bracelet has a heart and an eternity sign engraved inside. We wondered if she brought them here."

"I can verify that those pieces were pawned," Steve replied. "Beautiful pieces, too, and quite valuable. But it wasn't a woman who sold them to me. It was a man."

"Can you describe the man?" I asked.

Steve thought for a moment. "I'd say he was in his mid-thirties, dark hair on top with shaved sides, and tattoos covering his neck and arms."

"That sounds like the guy I saw with Honey," I told Marco.

"Is there a problem with the items?" Steve asked. "Should I alert the police?"

"No," I replied. "I think it was a legitimate sale."

"Let us do a little more investigating first," Marco told him.

Marco and Steve chatted for a few more minutes, then we thanked him for his help and left.

I wrapped my green scarf tightly around my throat and braced myself for the chilly wind. "That explains why Honey didn't know where her jewelry was pawned. She let her boyfriend pawn them."

"It appears that Honey was telling the truth about pawning the jewelry," Marco said as we headed back to Bloomers. "And that makes Devona Esmond the stronger person of interest."

❧ ☙

When I got back to Bloomers, Lottie and Rosa were still on their lunch break, so my trip to Dora's Discount Flower and Garden Center was put on hold. As I rang up another sale of one of my mother's inspirational plaques, Jillian came in lugging her guitar case.

"Just finished another lesson," she said, setting the case on the floor.

I put the plaque in a bag and handed it to the customer. "Thank you. Have a nice day." I waited until the door was closed – listening for the familiar jingle of the bell – only to remember that the bell had fallen on my head. We still had to get that fixed.

"What's up, Jill?"

"I got you the information you wanted. Crystal is going to use Dora's Discount Flower and Garden Center for her wedding. Can you believe it? I mean, if anyone can afford an over-the-top wedding, it's Crystal. What does she need a discount for? A bushel of apples? A crate of cucumbers?"

"What are you talking about?"

"Dora's doesn't just sell flowers, Abs. She sells fruits and vegetables, too. It's a big place. Oh, and they also sell the most delicious dark chocolates from France."

"Wait one second. You've been there?"

Jillian's eyes widened. Her mouth opened as though she were about to speak and stayed that way while she tried to think of an answer. It was a telltale sign that she was about to lie. "No," she said with a rising inflection. "I've heard about it is all. From a friend. A good friend of mine."

"What's her name?"

Again, Jillian's mouth opened as she tried to come up with a reply. "Okay. Okay. I went to Dora's *one time*. But just for the chocolates."

"It's okay, Jill. I'm not angry about it."

"Hey! Here's a thought. Let's go there. You're not busy." She glanced around at the empty shop. "You are *really* not busy. What do you say?"

"I say we go," Rosa said, coming out of the workroom.

"What?" I asked in disbelief. "You told me earlier that you didn't want to go."

She placed her hands on her tiger-stripe-printed leggings and raised an eyebrow. "I have to see this place that is stealing our business."

Lottie was right behind her. "Go ahead, sweetie," she said to me. "Check out the competition. Grace and I will handle everything here."

Like there was something to handle. Thank goodness for the coffee and tea parlor. I grabbed my coat from the rack and my purse from under the counter. "Let's go then."

"Yay!" Jillian said happily. "I'll drive."

❧ ❧

We took Highway 30 to Maraville and pulled off the side of the road at a large, gray warehouse with a big sign on the front that read: DORA'S DISCOUNT FLOWER AND GARDEN CENTER. Jillian parked her Volvo SUV in the gravel lot in front of the building and we walked through the big center doors. Inside, to our left, was the garden center, where we could see rows of plants of all kinds. Beyond that was an outdoor area where larger plants and shrubs were sold.

Directly in front of us was a fountain surrounded by small ice cream tables, with a counter in the back outfitted with coffee makers and tea servers and a glass case filled with an assortment of sweets. I glanced at Rosa. "Grace is not going to like this."

To our right was a big area filled with bins of fruits and vegetables. And just beyond that was the floral department, where dozens of arrangements sat on shelves, and flowers of all sorts stood in large containers, with a stack of baskets nearby for people to use to select their flowers. At the back of this area was a counter staffed by two women. A sign over the counter read:

DORA'S FLORAL SHOP – with a sign beneath that said: NEW CUSTOMERS RECEIVE AN EXTRA 15% OFF.

There went Lottie's sales promotion.

I picked up a red rose and looked at it. "It's not as fresh as it should be," I said and put it back. I checked out a container of daisies and had the same comment.

"Look how close the flowers are to the fruits," Rosa said. "There's the problem."

"What problem?" Jillian asked, plucking a lily from its container.

"The problem with flowers near ripe fruit," I said, "is that harmful ethylene is produced which causes the flowers to wilt faster."

"You'd think they'd know that," Jillian said, eyeing the women behind the counter. "Maybe we should tell them."

"Is there a problem?" I heard and turned to see Patrice Englund standing behind me, arms folded across her red dress. Patrice was the forty-something owner of Englund's Finest Gift Shop on the town square. Now, with her dyed-blond hair, overly tanned skin, and plastic face, she gave me a haughty smile.

"Yes, there's a problem," Jillian said, stepping up. "Why? Do you work here?"

"I own Dora's," Patrice said, then turned back to me. "My little shop on the town square has done so well that I decided to open up a flower and garden center. I named it after my dear mother." She put her hand to her heart as though she was humbled by her own goodwill. "Goodness, I hope our operation isn't hurting your little flower shop. But there's nothing wrong with a little healthy competition, is there?"

I didn't respond to her snarky comment. Patrice Englund was Lottie's nemesis. Lottie had trained her at Bloomers, hoping for a reliable assistant, but Patrice quickly proved herself to be not only unreliable but also unbearable. After Lottie sold the flower shop to me, Patrice left and opened up a gift shop in direct competition with Bloomers' small gift department. Now it appeared she was trying to steal the rest of our business.

"You said there was a problem?" Patrice asked Jillian.

"No problem," I answered for her, then aimed my gaze at my cousin. "No problem at all."

Jillian understood to keep quiet.

"We should be going," I said. "Lots of orders waiting. Let's go, Jill. Nice to see you, Patrice."

"You, too," she said with a pasted-on smile. "Come back any time."

I looked around for Rosa but didn't see her. "Where's Rosa?"

"She might be waiting outside," Jillian replied. "She said something about it being stuffy in here."

We walked out to the SUV, but Rosa wasn't there. I pulled out my cell phone and called her, but she didn't pick up.

"Maybe she went back for some coffee," Jillian said. "I'll go look."

She headed back inside while I waited. Five minutes later Jillian walked out with a to-go coffee cup in one hand and a piece of chocolate in the other. She was followed by Rosa, who was loaded with paper bags. Sticking out of the bags were bunches of flowers.

"You said we needed flowers," she said with a smile. "I waited until that *espantoso* woman was gone and I bought them."

"Rosa, you're amazing. I don't know what *espantoso* means, but I'll agree with you."

"I think the word is *horrible*," she said and raised the bags. "This will be a good test because I'll bet these flowers won't last three days."

"We only need them to last one day," I replied.

I was quiet on the ride home, wondering how I could meet with Crystal and talk her into using Bloomers instead of Dora's.

When we got back to the flower shop, I filled Lottie and Grace in on Dora's as Rosa and I unpacked the flowers in the workroom. "It's a big operation," I told them. "It could really hurt our business, not to mention that our fifteen percent discount is still no match for their prices."

Grace cleared her throat and assumed her lecture pose. "There will always be those who'll go for the bargains and those who'll prefer higher quality," she said. "Let us not forget that."

"Oh!" Jillian said. She had scooted onto one of the stools at the worktable. "They have a very nice coffee and tea shop, too."

Grace pressed her lips together. She didn't have a quote for that.

"Hi ho," I heard. The purple curtain parted, and my mom walked in carrying a tote bag. "I brought more plaques. I noticed that most of my first batch have sold."

"They've done very well, Maureen," Lottie replied.

Mom began to unpack them. I picked one up and read: *You are the artist of your life. Don't hand the paintbrush to anyone else.* The next one read: *If you want the rainbow, you have to put up with the rain.*"

Lottie looked them over. "These are wonderful, Maureen. I'm sure we can sell them quickly."

Jillian picked up a plaque and read it aloud. "When you can't find the sunshine, be the sunshine." She pursed her lips and then smiled. "I'll bet I can write a song about finding the sunshine."

After that trip to Dora's, I was hoping for a little sunshine myself.

"In fact," Jillian continued, "maybe that will be the first song I sing at Down the Hatch!"

Oh no. She remembered our deal.

The gang shot Jillian a puzzled look as she lifted her guitar case from the floor and clunked it onto the worktable.

"What do you mean?" my mom asked.

"Marco is going to let me showcase my new talent at his bar."

"I didn't know you had a new talent," Mom said.

She opened her mouth in shock. "Abby hasn't told you? I play the guitar now. I've even written a few songs. I can play one for you right now."

My cell phone rang, and Marco's name appeared on the screen. "Busy?" he asked.

"You caught me at the perfect time." I walked into the kitchen as Jillian unzipped her guitar case. "What's up?"

"Two things. One. I found out that Corbison has interviewed Devona. And two, I asked Devona to meet me at seven o'clock at the bar this evening to talk about Corbison's investigation."

"Was she suspicious?"

"Not at all. Why don't you go home and have dinner, walk Seedy, and meet me here at the bar?"

"As long as you have a glass of wine waiting for me."

"Deal."

❧ ❧

When I walked into Down the Hatch that evening, I saw Devona sitting across from Marco at the last booth sipping a beer. She had on a light blue sweatshirt with a white sports logo on the front, and she'd left her long, curly black hair loose on her shoulders instead of pulled back. She saw me and smiled, displaying bright pink lipstick.

149

"Here she is," Marco said, standing up to let me into the booth. "I told Devona you'd be joining us. What'll you have to drink?"

"A merlot," I answered.

He lifted one eyebrow. "Not your usual cabernet?"

I winked at him. "I'm branching out."

As Marco walked up to the bar to get my wine, I said to Devona, "I hear that Detective Corbison questioned you."

"He did." She shuddered and rubbed her arms. "The way he studied me made me nervous, like I was some sort of lab specimen."

"I was also a suspect in a murder investigation, so I know what you mean."

Her eyes widened. "You were a suspect?"

"I was the main suspect. Fortunately, Marco and I found the real murderer and cleared my name. That's what we want to do for you now."

Marco set my glass of merlot in front of me and slid in beside me.

"I was just telling Devona about the time I was accused of murder," I said. "We agree that Corbison can be very intense."

"What kinds of questions was he asking you?" Marco asked Devona.

"Well, he knew about our tenants' meeting, so basically, he wanted to know what I did after the meeting. I told him I walked to the drug store and then went up to my apartment because I had to get up early for work the next day."

I pulled out my small notebook and a pen. "Where do you work?"

"You're going to take notes?" she asked.

"We talk to a lot of people," I said. "I have a hard time keeping all the information straight."

"Okay," she said slowly, then proceeded to watch as I wrote down her answer. "I work in the lab at the hospital."

"After you left the tenants' meeting," Marco said, "did you see anyone hanging around outside the realty office?"

"Not that I can remember."

"Do you know of anyone who would've wanted to harm Arthur?"

Devona took a sip of beer, contemplating the question. "I honestly don't know. People say he's a cutthroat, but he didn't seem that way to me. He was a good person who made a lot of mistakes."

"Like what?"

"I don't know. Going back on his word. Breaking deals. Kicking us out of our apartments with no warning." She looked at Marco. "We both know that didn't resonate well with Kenton."

"What kind of deals did Arthur break?" Marco asked.

She stuttered. "I – I don't know. I was just . . ."

"Did he break a deal with you?"

Devona looked down at her glass, not wanting to meet our gazes as she answered, "Not personally. I just meant that he kicked us out of our apartments."

I shifted the notebook so Devona couldn't see my notes. Her answers were vague but indicative of something more specific. I wrote down that Devona seemed to have had a stronger relationship with Arthur than we'd realized.

Marco must've been thinking along the same lines. "How well did you know Arthur?"

She shrugged casually, but the tone of her voice was more restricted. "How well could I know him? He was my landlord."

"You can be honest with us," Marco told her. "If there was a relationship, it would help to know about it."

151

"I am being honest." Her tone shifted further, sounding more defensive and hostile. "I did not have a relationship with him."

Marco waited a beat, giving time for Devona to calm down, but it seemed to be too late. She checked her watch and started drinking her beer in longer gulps. I tilted the notebook for Marco to see, indicating with my pen the next question he should ask. I figured we might as well try to get some honest answers while we could.

"Did Arthur ever give you any jewelry?" he asked.

"No," she answered quickly. She sipped her beer again and set the glass down. I noticed bright pink marks on the rim from her lipstick. Then I noticed her hand reach for her wrist below the table. It was brief, almost as if it were subconscious, but to me it was a clear signal that she was lying. She quickly reached for the beer again, saying, "Why would you ask that?"

Before Marco could respond, I jumped in. "I notice you have a mark on the inside of your wrist. Is that from a bracelet?"

She rubbed the inside of her arm. "No. I scratched myself there."

"Devona," Marco said, "I'm just going to be blunt about this. We have a source who says that Arthur McMahon gave you an eighteen-carat gold bracelet. We also know that such a bracelet was found at the murder scene."

"It wasn't mine," she said instantly.

"We know it was yours."

"Then why are you asking?" she shot back. "Why are you trying to catch me in a lie?"

"I didn't expect you to lie," Marco said.

"Okay, fine. He gave me a bracelet. What does that prove?"

"Why did Arthur give you a bracelet?" I asked.

She blushed hard, tracing a drip of condensation that had run down the outside of her beer mug with her finger. "It was a gift for something I'd helped him with."

That had been one *expensive* gift.

Marco locked eyes with her keenly. "Did you leave your bracelet in Arthur's office the night of the murder?"

She returned the look. "You were there. Did you see me leave my bracelet behind?"

"Devona," Marco said, "did you go back to Arthur's office after our meeting? I'm not accusing you of anything. I just need to know whether you were there or not."

She gripped her glass with both hands. "I didn't go back."

"If Detective Corbison were to get a search warrant for your apartment," Marco quizzed, "would he find your bracelet there?"

Devona set the glass down hard on the table, sloshing the liquid up and around the sides. "Just whose side are you on?"

"Your side," Marco said at once. "But we need to have the full story. Did you return to Arthur's office later that night?"

"I told you. No." She sat back with a stony look on her face.

"We have security footage of someone matching your description walking near the office building at nine forty-five."

"It wasn't me."

"We also have an eyewitness who saw you in Arthur's office around ten o'clock."

She looked away.

"The eyewitness heard you call Arthur a liar," Marco continued. "What did he lie about?"

She slammed her hand against the tabletop. "I thought you were on my side!"

Marco sat back. I could tell he was getting frustrated, so I waited a moment before trying a different tactic.

"Please believe us," I said. "We need the truth so we can stay ahead of Corbison's investigation."

"What do you mean by stay ahead?"

"He's a good detective," I answered. "If we know that you lied about being in Arthur's office that night, then Corbison does too. It won't be long until he brings you in for more questioning."

She turned her head away, thinking, and finally said, "Then what do I do?"

"You can start by telling us the truth," I replied.

She pressed her lips together, staring at the top of the table. Finally, she looked up at me. "Okay. I went back to talk to him, to try to get him to let me stay in my apartment. But he was alive when I left."

I wrote down her answers while Marco proceeded with the interview. "We need to know what was said and what happened when you left. Did Arthur leave at the same time? Did he make a phone call? Did someone else come to see him?"

She shook her head, clearly flustered. "No one came to see him. The phone kept ringing, but he didn't answer. That's all I remember."

"What did he say when you asked him if you could stay in your apartment?" Marco asked.

Devona heaved a big sigh. "He said the same thing he'd told us earlier, that he'd promised his fiancée that she could have a hotel. He said he'd help me find a new apartment."

"Did you throw your bracelet at him?" I asked.

"I don't remember," she answered.

"We have a witness who saw you throw something."

"Who could've seen that?" she asked angrily. Her eyes grew wide. "Did Grant Starling tell you that?"

"Would he have been right?" I asked.

"Then he must've been in his office next door."

"Did you throw your bracelet?" I repeated.

"Okay, yes, I threw the bracelet. Arthur gave it to me as a promise, and when he broke that promise, I didn't want the bracelet anymore. But I swear Arthur was alive when I left."

I wrote it down. "What was the promise?"

"He said he would marry me," she answered spitefully. "He said I'd never have to worry about money again."

I stopped writing. "He promised to *marry* you?"

"Yes. Months ago. And then Honey Chen sank her greedy little hooks into him. When he started talking about her again that night – I just lost it. That's why I threw my bracelet." She sat back with a huff. "Now what do I do about Corbison?"

"You'll have to explain yourself," Marco said.

"I can't do that. He'll come after me."

"Do you have an alibi?" I asked. "Any proof that Arthur was alive when you left?"

"If Grant was in his office, he'd know. He'd be able to provide an alibi." Her eyes narrowed. "But if Grant *was* in his office, then *he* was the last person to see Arthur alive."

Good observation. I wrote down her answer and underlined it.

Devona finished her beer and scooted to the end of the bench. "I hope you meant it when you said you wanted to clear my name. I didn't kill Arthur. I hope you can find the person who did."

She got up, made her way through the crowded bar, and left.

I looked over my notes. "Do you believe her?"

Marco sat next to me, thinking. He leaned back against the booth with a sigh. "I want to."

"But?"

"Arthur broke his promise to marry her. That had to hurt a lot – enough to make her throw away an expensive bracelet."

"But did it hurt enough to make her stab him in the neck?" I asked.

"I wouldn't think so, but I've been wrong before. We need to know what kind of steak knife it was and where it came from. I think I'll call Corbison and see if he'll share that info."

"In the meantime," I said, "we should take a look at Grant Starling."

"We didn't see Grant on any of the cameras," Marco reminded me.

"The murder occurred in his office building. Devona mentioned that she thought Grant could've been in the office that night. He might have stayed late. Or maybe he left for the night but came back through the alley door."

Marco scratched his chin. "I haven't considered the alley door. Usually, the back exits are for emergencies."

"We use ours at Bloomers all the time for deliveries," I told him. And as I talked, I began formulating a new theory about Arthur's death. "We drive right up the alley and load the van from the back door. Marco, anyone could've parked in that alley and never been caught on camera."

He put his arm around me and pulled me close for a kiss on the cheek. "For a florist, you're a pretty smart detective."

I smiled and turned my head to accept a second kiss. "I think we should include Grant in our list of suspects and find out who else has a key to the back door."

"What would be Grant's motive?" Marco asked.

"I guess it depends on what Grant stood to lose when Arthur married Honey, or what he stood to gain by Arthur's death, like the realty business."

Marco's cell phone rang. He looked at the screen and said, "Speak of the devil."

CHAPTER ELEVEN

"Grant, hello," Marco said. He listened for a minute and then replied, "Sure. I can make it tomorrow morning. I'll watch for your text. See you then."

I picked up my wine glass and took a sip. "What was that about?"

"Grant found a building for me to look at. It's near the college and it's been empty for several months."

I put down the glass. "I'm coming with you."

Marco's brows lowered in puzzlement. "Why? You'll be working."

"Marco, he's a suspect. What if he knows you're investigating? What if he's the killer and is luring you to an abandoned building?"

"What if your imagination is running wild?"

I scowled at him. "Are you willing to take the risk?"

"Devona was only assuming Grant was in the building," Marco explained. "Kenton was the one who saw her throw the bracelet. Not Grant."

"He's still a suspect."

"But here's the thing. You know that inner sonar you have?"

"Radar."

"Yes. Well, my inner radar is telling me that Grant isn't the killer."

"You just said you've been wrong before." I reached for his hand and covered it with mine. "Just humor me. Let me come along to see the building. What can it hurt?"

He studied me for a long moment and finally nodded. "Okay. Grant's going to text me the address. I'll forward it to you. We're meeting at one o'clock."

"I'll be there." I gathered my purse and slid out of the booth. "I'll see you at home later."

He stood up, gave me a quick kiss, and strode off. I stood for a moment to watch my handsome husband go. I wasn't about to let him meet a potential murderer in an empty building alone. Plus, it might give me an opening to ask Grant a few questions of my own.

Tuesday, November 22nd

"Look at this lily!" Rosa exclaimed, holding up the offending blossom. "It's already starting to droop."

"Sweetie, we can't use these flowers." Lottie stood at the open door of the broken cooler, gazing at the flowers inside. "It would ruin our reputation."

"I agree," I told her.

Rosa dropped the lily onto the work counter. "Dora's flowers are worse than I thought. It won't be long until that place goes down."

Lottie turned to face us. "Until then, we have to figure out how to fill these orders."

"The refrigeration unit is going to be installed this afternoon," I reminded her, "and my flower order is set to arrive then, too. We'll have to buy some fresh flowers at the discount center to make it through the day." I glanced at the spindle. There were only a handful of order slips on it. "Who wants to go?"

Lottie threw her hands in the air as she left the workroom. "Lordy, I don't think I could handle seeing that woman again."

Rosa sighed and reached for her coat and purse under the desk. "I will go."

About fifteen minutes later, Lottie came through the curtain holding an order slip. "There's a woman up front who'd like four centerpieces for a big dinner party she's throwing at Adagio's in their banquet room. She needs them by four o'clock today."

"Tell her yes!" I said instantly. "We should have our floral delivery by two."

"Will we have enough time?" Lottie asked.

"It's going to be close," I said.

"The electrician will be working in the cooler," Lottie reminded me. "Where will we put the four centerpieces?"

I thought for a moment. "It's November. We'll set them in the back of our delivery van until it's time to drop them off."

"Good thinking, sweetie. I'll go tell our customer she'll be good to go at four."

Finally! Back in business.

❧ ❦

At one o'clock I pulled into a parking space across the street from the address Marco had given me and got out of the car. Marco's Prius was parked out front. I sized up the big square building before crossing the street. It was brown brick. Good. It had several windows across the front. Good. It had a nice center door. Good. And there was a public parking lot half a block away. Not bad.

I opened the door and walked inside. The all-gray interior was lit only by sunlight coming through the western-facing windows, showing lots of dust mots in the air. The gray linoleum floor was covered with a heavy layer of dust, and a musty odor prevailed.

"Here you are," Marco said, coming through a doorway in the back. He walked up to me as I took off my gloves. "What's your first impression?"

"It's a decent-sized space but it needs a thorough cleaning. Did you see the kitchen?"

"It's okay, nothing to brag about." He looked around. "The space lacks coziness."

"The walls can be painted a warm color and we can hang artwork."

"The ceiling is too high."

"We can put in a drop ceiling."

He looked around again. "I just don't like it. It's too far from the downtown area."

"But it's close to the college."

The door opened and Grant Starling stepped inside. The sunlight streaming through the windows highlighted his brown hair starting to gray at the temples. He was smartly dressed in a black wool jacket, light blue button-down shirt, and black pants with black dress shoes.

"Sorry I'm late," he said, walking up to us. "I had a last-minute business call." He put his hands on his hips and glanced around with a smile. "So, what do you think?"

"It needs a lot of work," Marco said.

"Just about any property I show you will need work to turn it into a bar," Grant replied.

"And it's too far from downtown," Marco added.

"I can't do anything about that, unfortunately."

"I think we need to keep looking," Marco said.

"No problem. It may not be today, however. I've had to take over Arthur's clients and some of them are in the middle of buying homes."

And there was my opening.

"Did Arthur have a lot of clients?" I asked.

"A healthy number," Grant replied.

"Was he having problems with any of them? Any friction? Any unhappy clients?"

"Not that I'm aware of. Why?" Grant glanced at Marco. "Did someone hire you to investigate?"

Why did he look at Marco for verification?

"It's an independent investigation," Marco told him.

"Sorry," I said. "I should have led off with that."

Grant folded his arms over his coat. "You're investigating, too?"

"We work as a team," I answered.

"I see. Is there anything else I can tell you?"

"Did anything strange happen in the days before Arthur's death?" I asked. "Anything that struck you as out of the ordinary?"

"Not that I can think of."

"What kind of relationship did Arthur have with his tenants, if you know?" I asked.

Grant looked at my husband with a smile. "Actually, I think Marco can answer that better than I can."

Well, that wasn't helpful. "What about individually? Like his relationship with Devona, for instance?"

Grant studied me for a moment. "His relationship with *Devona?*"

"We know she and Arthur were close before Arthur became engaged to Honey Chen," Marco said.

"Then you know more than I do," Grant said.

"Did you ever hear Arthur and Devona arguing?" I asked.

"How would I have heard that?"

"You have an office right next to Arthur's, correct?"

"I do, but I can't say that I ever heard him arguing with her."

I decided to try a more direct approach. "Were you at your office the night Arthur died?"

"I see." Grant rubbed his chin. "You have to view me as a person of interest, but I can assure you that I had nothing to do with his death. I'll help you in any way I can, but I'd hate for you to waste your time on me."

"You can help by answering the question," I told him. "Where were you the night Arthur died?"

He took a moment, as if thinking, then said, "I had a business dinner after work, and then I watched TV the rest of the evening with my wife. She will attest to that."

Of course his spouse would verify his alibi. That didn't put my mind at ease, so I decided to do a little fishing. "Who owns the realty business now?"

Grant gave me a searching look, as though trying to figure out where I was going with my question. "I own the business now. It was in our partnership agreement that if something happened to one of us, the other would get the business."

"Did you also get the Five Franklin Street building in your agreement?" I asked.

"No. That would be Rowell."

At that, Marco asked, "Does Rowell have a key to the building?"

"He does."

"What about a key to the alley door?"

"Both locks use the same key," Grant replied.

I stored that piece of information for later. Anyone who had a key to the realty office would've been able to enter through the back-alley door.

"Do you know when Rowell usually comes to the building?" Marco continued. "We'd like to talk to him."

"Rowell isn't on a schedule that I know of," Grant replied. "Sometimes he's there in the mornings when I arrive. Sometimes he stops by at the end of the day. He also has an office at one of the properties he manages. You might have better luck there. I can text you the address."

"That would be helpful," Marco said. "Thank you."

Grant glanced at his watch. "Is there anything else I can help you with? I have another showing in twenty minutes."

"Just a few more questions," I told him. "Were you the one who found Arthur's body?"

"I was."

"When you came in that morning, which door did you use?"

"The front. We hardly ever use the alley door."

"Did you call the police?"

"I did, yes."

"What about the press?"

"No, of course not."

"Did you notify anyone else?"

"I called Rowell to let him know, and I called Arthur's fiancée, too."

"What about the security system?" Marco asked. "We know the camera facing the front door was broken. Is there a camera facing the alley door?"

"No. I'm afraid not," Grant answered.

"What about an alarm system on the alley door?"

"No, but that reminds me. I've been wanting to put one in. Maybe you could assist me with that, Marco."

"I'd be happy to," Marco said.

"Any other questions, then? Because I really need to shoot out of here."

I wracked my brain for more questions, but before I could speak, Marco let him off the hook.

"That should do it," he said.

Grant started toward the door. "Great. I'll keep looking for a space for you."

"Something downtown," Marco reminded him.

"Unfortunately, there's nothing available right now," Grant answered. "But I'll keep my eyes open."

Grant walked us out and locked up. After he drove away, I stood with Marco by his car.

"Well, Miss Detective," Marco said, "what's your feeling about Grant now?"

"Remember when we talked to Grant at the funeral?" I asked. "He gave us the same answer he gave to the newspaper as if he'd rehearsed it. That's how he seemed to be answering us just now."

"I thought he was being pretty straightforward about his willingness to help."

"I'd sure like to verify his story about being at home that evening," I said. "But I'm certain his wife will back him up no matter what."

"Feel free to check out his alibis," Marco said casually.

My phone buzzed and I saw the name on the screen flash *New Chapel Electric*.

"There's my electrician," I told Marco. "Right on time." I gave him a kiss. "See you at supper."

❧ ☙

By three o'clock, my main cooler was up and running. Rosa and I put all of the flowers that had been delivered inside and continued working on the four table arrangements. At four o'clock, they were all ready, so we loaded them into the van for Lottie to deliver. Three more orders had come in while we were working. We pulled the orders and started to work, Rosa humming

165

happily for a change. And to top it off, the electrician had replaced all of our fluorescent lights in the parlor and attached the bell back above the front door. I felt hopeful for the first time in days.

On my way home from work, I swung by the country club to see if I could find the waitress I had talked to the Friday before. I walked through the club's lobby and stopped at the restaurant's doorway, where the hostess asked me if I had a reservation.

"Actually, I'm just here to talk to someone." I glanced behind her and caught a glimpse of the red-headed waitress at a far table. "I see her now," I told the hostess.

I waited until the waitress had finished with her table and headed back to the kitchen. As soon as she turned in her order, I stopped her.

"Hi," I said cheerfully. "Do you remember me? I spoke with you Friday night about Honey."

She glanced around the room, clearly distracted. "What can I do for you?"

"Can you tell me anything more about Honey's boyfriend? The one who was harassing her with texts?"

The waitress looked me over. "You came back to the club just to ask me about Honey's boyfriend?"

"I'm concerned about her. Harassment is a serious offense."

"Okay. And?"

"And I'd like to talk to her boyfriend. Do you know his name? Where he lives?"

"Why don't you just ask Honey?"

"I tried to talk to her about him, but she got defensive. I want to help her, but I'm having trouble making her understand that. Any information you can give me would be very helpful."

She glanced around again, checking her tables. "I don't know much. I know he goes by the name Razor, and he works at that tattoo parlor down by the railroad tracks." She saw someone signal to her and said, "I gotta go. That's all I know."

"Thanks. You've been very helpful."

I left the country club and drove home to make dinner and feed the pets. When Marco got home, I had spaghetti Bolognese and a nice red wine waiting for him. Over dinner, I told him about my conversation with the waitress.

"What are you thinking?" he asked when I'd finished.

"That we need to take a trip to that tattoo parlor." I twisted a spool of noodles around my fork. "I'm also thinking we have too many suspects."

"I agree. Let's list them."

Marco held up his fingers as I began to list our suspects. "First, there's Kenton and Devona, whom we've already talked to. Then we have the kids - Rowell, Crystal, and Birch. Finally, we have Honey and her boyfriend."

"That's seven," Marco said.

"And don't forget Grant," I reminded. "Eight suspects."

"I guess we could add him too."

"See what I mean? Too many."

"Let's make some sense out of this." He finished a sip of wine. "Where's your notebook?"

I got up from the table and dashed up the hallway to the spare bedroom, which we'd turned into an office. Seedy had lifted herself from her normal spot beneath my seat and followed behind, her tail wagging happily. I gave her a pet and promised she would get her rawhide treat after dinner. When I sat back down, I flipped to an open page as Seedy resumed her position beneath me.

"Make a numbered list, one through eight," Marco advised.

"Way ahead of you."

Marco waited as I wrote down eight names, then asked, "Is there anyone we can cross off the list?"

"Nope. Not yet."

"Is there anyone you think is the least likely suspect?"

"At this point, I don't know," I told him. "Maybe Kenton?"

Marco shook his head. "Kenton has too many strikes against him. He was angry at Arthur when he left the bar, he was caught on camera outside the realty office, and his fingerprints were on the door handle."

"Devona?"

"We can't rule her out until we are positive Arthur was alive when she left the office."

"Then who do *you* think is the least likely?"

"Of the three we've talked to, just Grant," Marco replied. "We have no evidence that he was in the office that night, and we don't have a clear motive."

I checked the list. "That leaves Arthur's kids and Honey and her boyfriend."

"Then let's start digging deeper into Arthur's kids."

I rubbed my hands together. "Finally."

"Grant is supposed to text me the address to Rowell's office. Why don't we head there tomorrow at noon? I'll bring ham and cheese sandwiches."

"Sounds perfect and delicious."

CHAPTER TWELVE

Wednesday, November 23rd

My hopes for a surge in business did not pan out. Only four orders were waiting when I got to work that day. Mid-morning, I was putting together an order for a birthday party when the purple curtain parted, and a stroller appeared with baby Harper inside.

"Good morning," Jillian sang as she pushed the stroller into the room.

"You're in a good mood," I told her.

She unfastened the harness and picked up Harper. "It's a beautiful day outside," she replied, "and tomorrow's Thanksgiving. I'm so happy that you came up with the idea of having our family gathering at the country club. It'll be so much fun!"

"I'm glad you think so. I'm not so sure my mother feels the same."

"Aunt Mo?" Jillian waved away the thought with her free hand. "She'll come around. Don't worry. Oh, and guess what? I've been invited to Crystal McMahon's bachelorette party. Isn't *that* fun?"

My ears perked up. "When is her party?"

"This Saturday evening. Private dining room at the Marriott Hotel." After a few moments, Jillian snapped her fingers in front of my face. "You've got that far-off look in your eyes. What are you thinking?"

"I'm wondering why the party is so soon after her father's death."

"Well, duh. Now she's free to get married as soon as she'd like. She's been waiting a long time for this."

"Why did she need her father's approval to get married?"

"She didn't need his approval. She needed his money."

"Why? If she wanted to be married, she could've gone to the courthouse."

Along with a haughty scoff, my cousin rolled her eyes to the ceiling and back. "Abby, it's not about the license. Crystal is more interested in the event, the pageantry, the excessive, outlandish spectacle of it all. That's what she's been waiting for."

"Then I may have to crash that party. I need her business."

"Are you serious?" Jillian switched baby Harper to her other shoulder and looked at me askew. "Just how do you intend to do that?"

"I'll take her a floral arrangement and hope she invites me to stay."

"And then what? Are you going to make a sales pitch for her wedding in the middle of her party?"

"That's exactly what I'm going to do."

"It won't work."

"Why not?"

Jillian laughed. "Do you understand who you're talking about? This is Crystal *McMahon*, the most elite, most posh, most conceited, and self-entitled spoiled brat you've ever met in your life. And this is her bachelorette party you're planning to crash. She's going to expect to be treated like a queen all night. She's not going to care what you have to say."

Jillian had a good point. I had to come up with another way. "What can I do?"

"There's nothing you can do, Abs. All Crystal wants is for people to bathe her with compliments, spoil her with gifts, and serve her the finest champagne all evening."

"So, she'll be drinking champagne all evening?" I asked.

"She'll be drinking something. Whatever the most expensive drinks they have to offer, I'm sure."

"Then I'll wait until the end of her party to talk to her."

"Abs, that party may last until two in the morning! Are you really that desperate for business?"

"Yes, among other things."

"What do you mean?"

"Never mind. All you need to know is that I have to talk to Crystal. And I may need your help crashing the party.

Jillian shifted Harper once again and said in a conspiratorial whisper, "Is Crystal a suspect?"

"If I tell you, I'll have to kill you."

"Oh my God, she is!"

"Jillian, I'm serious. You can't tell anyone."

She made a zip motion across her lips. "I won't tell a soul."

"Won't tell a soul what?" Lottie asked as she came through the curtain.

I looked at Jillian.

"I can't tell you, Lottie," Jillian replied. "I made a promise."

Lottie stopped to admire the baby. "Hello, you little cutie pie. And Jillian? Good for you for sticking to your promise."

"I didn't hurt your feelings?" Jillian asked in amazement.

Lottie shook her head. "No, sweetheart. Abby will tell me later."

❧ ❦

At noon, I stepped out the door and found Marco waiting for me in his silver Prius. I hopped in and fastened my seatbelt. "Hi, handsome. Where are we going?"

Marco handed me his phone, showing a text message from Grant Starling. "That's the address for Rowell's office. Will you be my navigator?"

I typed the address into my phone's map. "Okay, head south on Franklin and turn right onto Indiana Avenue."

"You've got it."

I unwrapped the ham sandwich Marco brought for me and took a bite. "Does Rowell know we're coming?"

"No. He'd just have some excuse for why we couldn't see him."

"Smart."

We spent most of the ride in silence as I devoured my sandwich. Marco crossed the old two-lane highway and headed toward the outskirts of the county.

"Guess what?" I asked as I finished the last bite. "I'm going to Crystal McMahon's bachelorette party Saturday evening."

"She invited you?"

"No, she invited Jillian. I'm going to make a surprise entrance with a floral arrangement."

"I hope you're not being overly optimistic that you can interview her there."

"Don't worry. I think I have a plan. Turn left at the next light."

"I'm not sure crashing a party is the best way to gain her trust."

"But an expensive gift might work," I hinted.

Marco glanced my way. "How expensive?"

"I'll explain later."

Marco turned onto a county road and headed toward the railroad crossing. The car bumped and bounced over the uneven railroad tracks. "Are you sure we're going the right way?"

"I'm just following the GPS," I told him.

We traveled east for a few minutes, passing by several old businesses that looked abandoned, a power station, and a few rundown auto body shops. I wasn't very familiar with this part of town, even though I'd been born and raised in New Chapel. Closer to the road were older homes with unkempt front yards, and far beyond the tree line were newer homes behind gates and lavish front lawns.

"Take a right at the next stop sign. It should be the first building on the left."

Marco did as told and turned left into the parking lot of an old, two-story, beige brick building that looked to be an old shopping center. I finished my drink, wiped my mouth, and got out of the car. Just inside the main glass doors, we found a directory on the wall. In the list of businesses we saw, *McMahon Enterprises, Suite 7.*

We walked down the hallway and entered suite 7. It was a large, unfinished space with high open ceilings that revealed dusty pipes and electrical wiring hanging far above our heads. At the back of the suite was a beautiful, large oak desk and a dark red leather high-back chair. Behind the desk, in complete contrast to the uncovered cement walls, were towering wooden bookshelves with intricately carved trim housing all sorts of books, manuals, and three-ring binders.

The lavish, obviously expensive office furniture looked ridiculously out of place in the dusty industrial space. In one corner of the room sat stacks of cardboard boxes. Another corner housed a metal ladder and construction equipment. The cement floor was dirty. The windows were painted shut. And Rowell McMahon was nowhere to be seen.

Marco and I approached the desk. The computer monitor was off, and piles of paper were scattered across the top revealing one clean space for the keyboard and mouse. As I looked at the mess, I caught a glimpse of something that looked very intriguing. Under an empty take-out container and a used, maroon, cloth napkin sat a long, legal document with blue backing.

I carefully moved the mess to the side. "Marco, look," I whispered, although we appeared to be alone. I swiveled the document so he could see it.

"Abby, be careful. Rowell could come in at any minute."

I set the will aside. "Maybe he's not even here. Grant said he doesn't keep to a schedule."

"No, he's here somewhere. I saw his black BMW out front."

"Why don't you call him? We could be here all day waiting for him to show up."

Marco reached into his pocket for his phone while I made my way around the desk and perused the bookshelves. *How to Make a Fortune in Five Days, Real Estate Law for Dummies,* and *Beat the Odds at Online Poker,* were just a few of the titles I saw.

"What do you want?" I heard a deep voice grumble from the speaker on Marco's phone.

"You said we needed to talk," Marco replied. "I'm at your office. Ready to talk."

"I'm not at the realty office today," Rowell replied.

"Neither am I."

There was silence on the other end while I assumed Rowell was processing the information. "You're here right now?"

"Yes."

"I'm busy, Salvare. Now get the hell out of my office or I'll call the police."

The phone went dead, and Marco sighed in frustration. "I knew he wouldn't talk to us."

"It's okay," I said. "We'll find a way." As I rounded the desk, something caught my eye. I brushed aside a few documents and the cloth napkin on Rowell's desk to reveal a large day planner, opened to the current month. I pulled out my cell phone and snapped a few pictures. "Marco, take a look at this."

"Don't touch anything," Marco said. "He's not bluffing about calling the police."

"I'm not touching anything," I promised. "Just taking pictures. But look. He has hardly anything written down on his calendar. The only thing he has regularly scheduled is a bowling league on Monday nights."

Marco glanced at me. "Every Monday night?"

"That's what it says here. Every night this month."

"Arthur was killed on a Monday night."

"Then we need to talk to someone at the bowling alley, see if we can confirm Rowell's whereabouts."

"And if Rowell won't schedule a meeting, we might just have to surprise him."

"Looks like we're going bowling!" I said.

Just then we heard a toilet flush somewhere in the distance, the sound echoing throughout the large space.

"Let's get out of here," I whispered.

Thursday, November 24th

175

Thanksgiving Day

The parking lot was almost full by the time we arrived at the country club. Along with the chill in the air came a buzz of excitement as Marco and I exited his Prius amidst a throng of families coming and going, greeting each other with smiles and hugs, and bidding fond farewells with full stomachs. Grandparents walked hand in hand with grandchildren. Proud parents took family photos by the front entrance. I squeezed Marco's hand as we entered the building,

The smell of sweet, buttered rolls and salty gravy filled the main dining room, causing my insides to rumble with anticipation. But there was also a creeping unease as I looked around the large room. Would everyone be here? Would they be happy? The turkey buffet had been my idea. Was it going to be a success or a bust?

At the back of the room, just as Portia had promised, two long tables had been set up near the fireplace. I saw Jillian place baby Harper in a highchair at the first table. As we approached, she held out her arms and crushed me in a hug. "I'm so glad you're here. Now we can eat! My little angel is hungry."

Claymore stood and shook Marco's hand as the rest of the family shared their greetings around the table. Francesca stood and waved us over to the second table, which was filled with Marco's extended family. Next to Marco's mom was his brother, Rafe, sister Gina and her family, and other members of the Salvare clan. Everyone looked happy. And everyone looked ready to eat.

We took our seats near my brother Jonathan and his wife, Portia. Across from Marco and me were two open spaces for my mom and dad. I was dismayed to see them still empty. Jordan and Kathy came in next and found an open seat near Jillian at the head of the table.

Tara followed behind, looking cute in a short, tan and cream-colored print dress that set off her flaming hair. She came up behind me and pulled out the chair next to me. "Is this seat taken? Never mind. It is now."

When Jordan sat down, I leaned in so that both he and Jonathan could hear me. "Have you heard from Mom?"

Jordan shrugged and Jonathan shook his head. "Dad?"

Same response.

The waitress came around taking drink orders, informing us of the self-service buffet, and after she had made the rounds, some of the extended family stood and headed toward the middle of the dining hall where a wide buffet stretched the length of the room. There was a line of people at one end and several turkey carvers at the other. In between, a plethora of side dishes, gravies, jellies, and rolls awaited our consumption.

Tara practically dragged me from my seat. "Come on, Aunt Abby. I'm famished!"

"We can't start without your grandparents," I said. "They should be here any minute."

Francesca and Marco's family left their table next, leaving most of the Knight clan sitting in tummy-rumbling silence. After I'd checked my watch for the third time, Marco put his arm around me. "They'll be here. Stop worrying."

"Abby," Jonathan said. "We're all hungry. We might as well eat."

Jillian excused herself politely from her seat and bent down next to me so I could hear her whisper, "How much longer are we going to wait? I'm literally getting hangry."

My cousin had a bad habit of making up words. "First of all, Jill, hangry is not a word. And second…"

"Not so fast. Hangry is *too* a word. It was added to the Oxford English Dictionary in twenty-eighteen."

I looked over my shoulder at her, *literally* caught off-guard. "How do you know that?"

Jillian huffed. "I know things, Abs."

Just then, my phone rang in my purse. I pulled it out and saw my mom's name on the screen. With fingers *figuratively* crossed, I answered, "Hi, Mom."

"Abigail," she said, "will you and Marco come out to the car? I'm having trouble with your father's wheelchair."

I let out an audible sigh of relief. "We'll be right there." I hung up and looked over the expectant faces. "They're here. You call all eat now."

Before I'd even finished my sentence, the table was empty.

Outside in the parking lot, as Marco helped my dad into the wheelchair, my mom gave me a big hug. "Thank you, sweetheart."

"I was so worried you weren't going to come," I said, holding onto the hug a little longer than normal.

She smiled as she held me at arm's length and looked me in the eyes. "I wouldn't do that to you."

"You're not angry?"

"Well," she said, "it's not our tradition, but I'm glad we can all be together."

"Me too, Mom."

We walked and talked as Marco wheeled Dad through the parking lot. Just as we were making our way up the ramp in front of the building, I noticed a car with only one headlight idling by the curb.

At that moment, the passenger door opened, and Honey Chen stepped out. She was wearing a black apron and had her hair pulled back into a tight braid. The car, a dark gray sedan, pulled away, but not before passing closer, revealing the driver, a man with hair that was shaved on the sides and long on top.

"Marco, look."

"I see it," he responded as the man sped away.

"Did you see that the headlight was out?"

"I did. Just like the car Kenton described he saw the night of the murder."

"Then maybe Honey *did* come down to the realty office that night, but she wasn't the one driving."

"We need to take a closer look at that security video."

"Is this about your murder investigation?" my dad asked.

Before I could answer, my mom looped her arm through mine. "You can talk about your case all you want after dinner. Right now, it's time to give thanks."

❧ ☙

Thanksgiving dinner was amazing. The food was delicious and plentiful. Everyone was in a good mood – even baby Harper had settled down – and I was beyond happy to have pulled off the event. As we ate, we discussed the many things for which we were most thankful. Tara was the first to start on dessert, and I followed quickly behind her, gaping at the selection of pies, cakes, pastries, and gourmet coffees. With a full belly, I sat back and watched as the extended families chatted and mingled. I saw my mom sitting with Marco's mom, both talking and laughing.

I sat with my dad for a while after sneaking him a second piece of pumpkin pie.

"You know," he said softly, "your mom will never admit this, but I think she's having a good time."

"I think so, too."

"You're a good daughter. I've always been thankful for that, my little Abracadabra."

I gave him a big hug. "I'm thankful for you, too, Dad."

❧ ☙

179

Later that night, I was laying on the couch working on my laptop. Seedy was sprawled out on the floor below me, and Smoke was curled up on my husband's lap. Marco lay fully reclined in his favorite chair with his eyes sinking lower every time I checked on him. He'd wanted to watch football, and I'd wanted to watch an old movie, so we'd compromised by watching an old movie about football.

After searching through the security videos for nearly an hour, I sat up suddenly, startling poor Seedy. "I found it!"

Marco jolted and wiped a bit of drool from his mouth. "What's wrong?"

"Are you sleeping? It's only eight-thirty."

"It's Thanksgiving. Give me a break."

I kneeled next to Marco to show him the footage. "Kenton was right," I told him. "The car has one headlight out. It creeps along the street and stops in front of the realty office. It's partly blocked by the cars parked along the curb, but it looks just like the one we saw Honey exit today. I think it's very possible Honey and her boyfriend were working together."

Marco thought for a minute, petting the sleepy cat in his lap. "What's the timestamp?"

"Ten-fifteen."

"Grab your notes," he said. "Go to the Honey interview."

I searched the notebook. "Got it."

"You asked her if she called Arthur, right?"

"Yes, and her answer is underlined, which means that I thought she was lying."

"What did she say?"

"She said she called Arthur, but he didn't answer. When I pressed her on it, she said he didn't answer *right away*. Then I asked her if she'd driven downtown that night and she said, no, not at all."

"Okay, here's a theory," Marco began. "Crystal smashes Honey's windshield. Honey calls Arthur to let him know but he doesn't answer. Honey calls her boyfriend to drive her downtown so she can talk to Arthur in person. Then Kenton sees her car and runs upstairs."

"The question is, then, what does Honey do? I can't tell if she gets out of the car or not."

"I have no idea," he said, "Does she confront Devona in the office? Does she leave then, or does she stay to have it out with Arthur?"

"And what about the boyfriend?" I asked. "Why would he agree to drive her downtown?"

"I honestly don't know."

"This is making me crazy, Marco."

"Then maybe it's time for some new information. Why don't we go talk to Honey's boyfriend tomorrow?"

Black Friday, November 25th

Friday was a busy day on the town square, with lots of people taking advantage of all the pre-Christmas sales. I put a sandwich board out on the sidewalk advertising a twenty percent discount on all orders, and that attracted a lot of attention. Some customers wanted an arrangement to brighten their homes, but many came to pre-order their holiday flowers. The coffee parlor, too, was busy from the time we opened until we closed at five.

"The sandwich board was a good idea," Lottie said as we prepared to go home that afternoon. "I think we should do it again next week to draw in more customers."

"Let's do that," I said. "We need to keep the name Bloomers in people's minds so we're the first florist they think of when they need flowers."

Rosa was checking something on her phone. "Look," she said, showing us the screen. It was a media ad for Dora's Discount Flower and Garden Center. Prominently on the top was displayed: *Take 20% off everything!*

Curses.

CHAPTER THIRTEEN

Friday evening after eating supper and taking Seedy for a walk, Marco and I headed out to see the man called Razor. We drove to the south side of town and turned into a parking lot in front of a small, blue, wood-sided building with a sign on the front that said *Cutting Edge Tattoos*. And beneath it: *No Appointment Necessary*.

We walked into a dimly lit reception area and went up to the counter that ran along a back wall. On the wall were pictures of hundreds of tattoos. A young woman who appeared to be about eighteen years old stood behind the counter looking at her phone. She had long, dyed black hair, heavy purple eye makeup, and nude lipstick. She was wearing a glittery white top with black jeans.

"Hello," I said to get her attention.

She looked up from her phone with disinterest. "What do you want?"

What did we *want?* Before I could stop myself, I said, "Excuse me? Is that how you treat your customers?"

The young woman lifted a slender metal device to her lips and pressed a button. She inhaled deeply and exhaled casually, enveloping her head in a cloud of sweet-smelling vapor. In a mocking voice, she said, "Let me guess. You want a butterfly on your ankle."

That did it. "Is a butterfly more embarrassing than a purple snake crawling up your arm?"

The woman looked down at her arm. Marco reached his hand around me and gently caressed my shoulder, trying to calm me down.

He took over then, smiling at her with his intense gaze. "We're here to see Razor. Is he here?"

She went back to scrolling through her phone. "Do you have an appointment?"

"The sign says no appointment necessary," I told her.

She glanced up at me with a smirk. "Yeah, well, there is now."

"What is that supposed to mean?" I shot back.

"He's with a customer, that's what it means."

I balled my fists at my side, my Irish temper flaring hotly. Before I could burst into flames, Marco guided me away from the reception desk and said, "We'll just wait over here."

As the girl went back to her phone, Marco ushered me to a far corner of the room where I waited for my internal temperature to cool down from a rolling boil. My understanding husband rubbed my back gently. He knew all too well how to handle the Knight temper.

As I calmed down, I began to look at the tattoo pictures decorating the walls. "Look, Marco," I said, pointing, "there's a cat tattoo that looks like Smoke."

"Cute." Marco's gaze traveled across the wall. "Maybe they have a three-legged dog as well."

"You could get that heart tattoo and put my name inside it."

"No way," he said. "Tattoos are forever."

"And our marriage isn't?"

He raised an eyebrow.

"Marco!"

He grinned. "I'm just teasing. How could I ever replace my Sunshine?"

"You couldn't. So don't even tease about it." I scanned the wall and picked out another. "Look at that four-leafed clover. Maybe I should have it tattooed on my wrist for good luck."

"Have you ever had any needling done?" Marco asked. "Because I don't think you'd like the pain."

"You're right. I can hardly stand to pluck my eyebrows."

The black curtain in the side wall parted and an older man walked through followed by the guy I'd seen in the gray sedan. The sides of his dark hair were shaved. The top was long and brushed back like a limp mohawk. He had a black nose ring and colorful tattoos covering his neck and arms.

As the older man stood at the counter taking out his wallet, the girl said, "Hey, Razor. Got a couple here who want to talk to you."

Razor was dressed mostly in black. He looked us over as he walked up to us and spoke with a slight, almost imperceptible lisp. "You wanted to see me?"

There was something incredibly familiar about the man, but there was no way I would've forgotten someone who stood out as Razor did. Not only did he have a nose ring, but his eyebrow was pierced, and both of his ears were lined with metal loops.

Marco showed him his P. I. license. "We'd like to talk to you about a case we're working on. Do you have five minutes?"

Razor stuck his hands in his pockets. "You'll have to be more specific."

There was the lisp again. I noticed that Razor wouldn't look me in the eyes. As I studied him further, looking past the ink and metal, a light bulb went on, and I had to stop myself from laughing out loud. "Todd? Is that you?"

He looked down at his shoes and then nodded shyly. "Hi, Abby."

The smile on my face must have grown three inches. I looked up at Marco, who was watching me in utter confusion. "This is Todd Burns," I explained. "We went to high school together." I looked back at Todd, whose cheeks were flushed in embarrassment. "We were lab partners in science class. Remember? You were the smartest kid in class, and I was terrible at lab, so I always asked you to be my partner."

"I remember," he said shyly.

"You certainly have . . . changed. I almost didn't recognize you."

"That's kinda the point," he said. "And no one calls me Todd anymore. I go by Razor now."

"Wait a minute," I said, trying not to laugh. "You go by the name Razor Burns?"

"No," he answered quickly. "Just Razor. Call me Razor."

From what I remembered, Todd Burns had been a good kid. He'd been a bit nerdy, with a serious lisp, but he was always kind to me. It struck me odd now that this was the man we had come to interview. This was the murder suspect we'd been talking about.

Breaking up my stroll down memory lane, Marco said, "Is there somewhere we can talk in private?"

He shrugged. "Sure. Follow me."

We walked through the black curtain and up a short, narrow hallway into a treatment room, an area the size of a large closet, with what looked like a dentist's chair inside. A counter filled with tools and lotions hung on the back wall, and a rolling stool sat underneath.

Razor folded his arms across his chest. "What case are you working on?"

Marco took the lead. "The Arthur McMahon murder."

A muscle in Razor's jaw ticked. "What does that have to do with me?"

"It's our understanding that you're seeing Honey Chen."

"I don't know any Honey Chen," he replied.

"Are you sure?" I asked.

He nodded.

"Because her name is tattooed on the side of your neck," I pointed out.

He ran his fingers over the tattoo. "Yeah, okay, I know Honey. So what?"

"Do you own a dark gray sedan?" Marco asked.

"I might."

"Did you give Honey a ride downtown last Monday evening?" Marco asked.

"How should I remember that?"

"It was the evening Arthur McMahon died," I told him. "A car like yours was seen pulling up in front of Arthur's realty office."

"I don't remember that at all," he replied. "I think you've got the wrong car."

"We don't have the wrong car," Marco told him. "Not only do we have an eyewitness, but we also have your car on security cam footage. That puts you at the scene of the crime. Maybe a visit from the New Chapel police would help jog your memory."

Normally, my husband could be very persuasive, but Todd was clever. "I know how this goes," he said. "All I have to do is give you one piece of information, and you'll use that to target us. Besides, if there was any evidence against me, the detective would've already questioned me."

Fortunately, Marco was pretty clever, too. "Private detectives work a lot faster than the police. I'm sure when we share our information with Detective Corbison, he'll be more than happy to pay you a visit."

Todd pushed his hands further into his pockets. "Here comes the intimidation."

I stepped forward. "Todd –"

"It's *Razor*."

"Okay, Razor. Listen. I understand why you don't trust us, or the detectives, but we're not trying to target you."

"Then you're trying to target Honey."

"We're trying to find the truth," I reasoned. "If she's innocent, then maybe your cooperation can help prove that. Did you let Honey drive your car that night?"

"No. Why would you think that?"

"Because her windshield was smashed," I replied. "She wouldn't have been able to drive downtown."

He scratched the back of his neck. "She can't drive my car. It's a manual transmission."

"Did you drive Honey downtown?"

"She didn't kill anyone," he insisted.

"How can you be sure?"

"Because she was with me all night."

Finally, we were getting somewhere. I could tell Razor was getting anxious, so I didn't bother pulling out my notebook. I figured it would spook him even more. I gave him a second to calm down, then continued my questions. "Did you drive Honey downtown?"

He pressed his lips together – I knew he was about to deny it – so I looked him in the eye and said, "Todd. *Razor*. Come on. Be honest."

"Okay," he finally said. "Yes."

"Did you drop her off at the realty office?"

"No. I absolutely did not drop her off anywhere."

"Then tell us what happened."

"She wanted to talk to Arthur," Todd finally explained, shifting from one foot to the other. "But when I pulled up at the office, she didn't get out of the car."

"Why not?"

"I don't know why. She wouldn't say. But then we saw a woman exit the realty office, and Honey seemed really upset by that. At that point, she told me to take her home."

"Where did you go next?"

"Back to my apartment." Todd looked incredibly hesitant, staring at the ground while answering, but at least he was talking.

Before I could ask my next question, Marco put his hand out to stop me. "Where is your apartment?"

Again, Todd shifted. He took his hands out of his pockets and fidgeted with his smartwatch. "Student housing on Campus Boulevard."

"At New Chapel University?" I asked.

"Yes."

"Are you going to school there?"

He nodded but didn't give any more information, so I continued, "Why did Honey come back to your apartment?"

"Because that's where she felt safe. That was her home. Not in some mansion like Arthur wanted."

"Are you saying Honey *lived* with you?" I asked in surprise. "While she was engaged to Arthur?"

"No, not after she got engaged. She moved into his mansion then. But my apartment was her true home."

"Why didn't Honey feel safe at the mansion?"

"Because of that rich psychopath who busted her windshield."

I could understand why he would think of Crystal McMahon as a rich psychopath, but I still felt as if Todd was holding something back. "Were you still dating Honey while she was engaged to Arthur?"

"No." His voice took on a hard edge and his lisp became more prominent. "She moved out when she got engaged, okay? We didn't see each other after that . . . well, until, you know."

"Her engagement must've hurt," I said.

"Yeah, well, I survived. She did what she had to do. Now I think you should leave."

Before I could ask another question, Marco put his hand on my back and said to Todd, "Thanks for talking to us." He guided me out into the hallway and toward the black curtain.

"Why did you stop me?" I asked as we stepped into the reception area.

"He was getting agitated, and we got everything we need."

I started across the parking lot, headed for Marco's Prius, then realized Marco wasn't beside me. I turned around just as he disappeared around the corner of the tattoo shop. I hurried after him, my shoes crunching the gravel beneath my feet. "Marco, what are you doing?"

He stopped in front of Razor's dark gray sedan parked behind the building and pointed to a plastic card hanging on the rearview mirror. "Check it out. He was telling the truth about being a student. There's a parking pass for New Chapel University." He leaned over the hood to look through the windshield. "Building N." He straightened with a smile. "Razor just gave us an alibi without even knowing it."

"What alibi?"

We walked back to the car while Marco explained. "Student housing will have a record of every student entering and exiting the building. We can find out if he was telling the truth about heading right home after driving Honey downtown. I'll give the university a call Monday."

"What if they don't have a record?"

"Then they'll have security cameras. Either way, we can verify Razor's story."

"That's good because I don't think Razor or Honey had anything to do with Arthur's death."

Marco waited until we were inside his Prius to ask, "Why do you say that?"

I buckled my seat belt and thought about my response. I needed a better answer than that it was just a gut feeling. "I don't think Honey wanted Arthur dead. I think she was fully prepared to marry him for his money."

"And leave Razor behind?"

"Maybe not. Honey could've married Arthur, divorced him a few months later, and hooked up with Razor again as a wealthy divorcee. Her killing Arthur doesn't make sense."

Marco started the engine. "If you say so."

I put my hand on his. "Just think about it."

CHAPTER FOURTEEN

Saturday, November 26th

Our day off started with an early morning rainstorm, which was unusual for late November in Northwest Indiana. Marco and I used the excuse to take the day off and spend some quality time with our furry family. Marco used a laser light to rile up Smoke until he was running back and forth through the hallways, chasing the red dot up the walls and down the stairs into the basement. After a few minutes of mayhem, Seedy was worked up as well, chasing the cat around the house, skidding to a short stop in front of the basement stairwell.

We ordered Thai food for lunch and ended up lounging in the living room with two pooped pets, watching a new streaming murder mystery series on TV. I explained my plan to infiltrate Crystal McMahon's bachelorette party that night, and Marco actually thought it was a good idea.

"Except, how expensive is this champagne going to be?" he asked.

"It doesn't have to cost much," I clarified. "It only has to appear so."

"You think Crystal will fall for it?"

"I hope so. I can't think of any other way to get her attention. Hopefully, with Jillian's help, I can pull this off."

"Well, it looks like the rain has stopped for now. Let's head over to the wine shop and talk to Joe."

The shop was small, squeezed into a strip mall just off Highway 30, but the walls were lined with shelves from floor to ceiling, with bottles of all shapes, sizes, and colors taking up every inch of shelf space. The higher-end bottles were showcased in a glass cabinet behind the register. Marco talked with Joe while I inspected the assortment of wine labels, looking for anything that caught my attention.

"What about something like this?" I asked.

Joe was an older Greek gentleman of average height. He had a full head of white hair combed back from his tanned, wrinkled forehead. Always wearing gold jewelry and an unbuttoned linen polo and crisply ironed slacks, Joe reminded me of an old-fashioned movie star.

He approached and lifted the bottle from the shelf. "This is a good year – full-bodied, not too sweet – but anyone who's anyone knows this label. It's very distinguishable. From what Marco's told me, you're looking for something unique."

"With a fancy label," I added and pointed to a bottle behind the counter. "Like that one."

Joe rounded the counter and lifted a key chain from his pocket. He unlocked the glass case to retrieve the bottle. "Nineteen ninety-two Chateau Neuf-du-Pape."

He told us the price and Marco's jaw dropped.

"We're looking for something similar, but less expensive," I explained. "Something rare. Something with an incredibly ornate label that would trick someone into thinking it was expensive."

"Ah," Joe exclaimed, "a challenge. Let me take a look in the back room and see what I can find."

While we waited, Marco picked out a bottle of merlot to add to our collection.

I checked the price and nudged him playfully. "I thought we were looking for inexpensive wine today."

He smiled and held the bottle up. "This will be our reward for solving the case."

"And if we don't solve it?"

"Let's just say I trust that we will."

"You just want the wine."

"That, too."

Joe came out a few minutes later with a bottle in each hand and one under his arm. He set the three bottles on the counter near the register, pushing one forward. "This Rose´ is very rare, but a bit pricey."

I checked the label. "A little too pricey."

He moved on to the next one. "This Malbec is almost twenty years old – aged to perfection – but again, a little on the expensive side."

"Next," Marco said.

"Well, there's the sparkling wine." He spun the bottle so we could see. "This winery went out of business a few years ago. It's nothing special but it has a real fancy golden label."

"That's the one," I told him. "How much?"

He pushed the bottle across the glass countertop. "On the house."

"No," I said. "We can't take it."

"Sure you can. I didn't even know we had it. And between you and me, there was a reason the winery went out of business – some of the worst sour grapes I've ever tasted." He wrinkled his nose and gave a wink. "It's all yours."

I thanked him and accepted the bottle.

Marco gave me a concerned look. "Are you sure?"

I studied the label. The lettering was intricate, the design was ornate, and there were plenty of decorative golden accents. "It's perfect. As long as she doesn't drink it."

❧ ❧

We avoided talking about the investigation the rest of the evening to give ourselves a break, but as the time grew near for me to head to the hotel for Crystal's bachelorette party, we began to discuss what to ask her.

"We didn't spot Crystal on any of the videos," Marco reminded me, "but we do know she followed Honey back to her father's mansion. It would be helpful to find out where she went after she attacked Honey's car."

"I also want to see what kind of relationship Crystal had with her father," I said.

"You can ask her about her brother's relationships, too."

I glanced at my watch. "That'll have to do. I've got to get dressed and scoot down to Bloomers to pick up her arrangement."

I donned a black skirt and light blue pullover, slid into black flats, and changed to a black purse. I put blush on my cheeks, a light pink lipstick, ran a brush through my red hair, and I was ready to go. "I don't know when I'll be home," I told Marco. "That'll depend on Crystal."

"Just don't get drunk yourself, Sunshine."

"Marco, when have you ever known me to drink to excess?"

"Have you forgotten the dinner when you were introduced to my mother? As I recall, she kept refilling your wine glass until I had to practically carry you home."

"Okay, once." I kissed him. "I'll be good, I promise."

After picking up the floral arrangement, I drove the 'Vette south to Highway 30, where the Marriott was

195

located. I pulled into the parking lot and spotted Jillian's Volvo parked in the first row. Inside the lobby, I asked a woman at the reception counter where the Crystal McMahon party was and was directed down a hallway toward the back of the building.

I could hear music coming from within one of the rooms and stepped inside. The banquet room looked as though it had been professionally decorated for a sweet sixteen party. Purple and pink streamers were twisted around each other and strung across the room. Big bunches of shimmering helium-filled balloons were swaying above each table. And a wide banner ran the length of the back wall that read CONGRATULATIONS, CRYSTAL in pink glitter.

Long tables full of appetizers ran along one side of the room where men in fancy suits stood, ready to serve. In one corner of the room was a man standing behind a booth wearing headphones and staring at a laptop monitor. In front of him was a small area for dancing with multi-colored lights flashing and swooping across the floor. The opposite corner housed a full bar stocked with top-shelf liquor.

Standing at the back of the room was Crystal surrounded by women in skimpy dresses, watching her unwrap gifts. She was dressed in a skintight lavender evening gown accentuating her unnaturally large curves, a silver and crystal tiara on her head, with a silver sash over her shoulder that read BRIDE-TO-BE.

I spotted my cousin and made my way to her, careful to not let Crystal spot me. I kept the bouquet of flowers at my side, with the sour wine in my purse. Jillian was wearing a knee-length royal blue silk dress with silver heels and a slender silver purse over one shoulder. A silver and diamond pendant hung around her neck. She had pulled her long copper locks up into a loose bun on the back of her head, displaying matching silver earrings. She looked stunning.

"Abby," she exclaimed. "You actually came!"

I shushed her, even though we were standing away from the group of women and the music covered her enthusiastic greeting. "I don't want to interrupt," I told her.

She turned for me and asked, "Do you like my dress?"

"Jillian, you look gorgeous."

She smiled and said, "So do you."

There was a lull in the music while Crystal unwrapped her next gift. She shredded the beautiful wrapping and tossed it aside, then held up the box for everyone to see. "A blender," she said as if she couldn't possibly hide her disappointment.

A short-haired woman at the front of the crowd responded, "It crushes ice. We can make margaritas!"

Crystal set the box down. "I have a blender, but thanks, Tiff."

The next gift garnered an almost identical response. Jillian and I watched as Crystal continued to open gifts, each one more expensive than the next, with the bride-to-be barely cracking a smile. Finally, Jillian held my hand as Crystal reached for the last gift.

"This one's mine," Jill said. "I'm nervous."

Crystal shook the box, an action which caused Jillian to wince and crush my hand in hers. Crystal opened the gift and pulled the cloth wrapping from a gorgeous crystal vase. She looked the vase over, then glanced up to find Jillian in the crowd.

"It's a Waterford," Jillian told her.

"A flower vase," Crystal said. "Thanks."

"And what would a flower vase be without the flowers to go with it?" I asked as I walked through the group of women, with Jillian following closely behind me.

Crystal watched with interest as I pulled the flowers from the bouquet and arranged them quickly inside the vase. "Abby Knight. The florist," she said slowly. "Excuse me, but, I don't remember inviting you."

I turned the vase for her to see. "It's Abby Knight Salvare, and I know I wasn't invited, but Jillian said you'd be celebrating –"

"Well, aren't you thoughtful," she replied sarcastically. "This doesn't have anything to do with my wedding plans, does it? Because I've chosen Dora's to do my flowers."

"Let's just say this arrangement is to make your party brighter," I countered.

Another lull in the music left me standing in complete silence. I felt as though I were standing before a judge, awaiting a verdict. That's when I remembered my true plan. "But that's not all I brought you." I pulled the fancy bottle from my purse and presented it, the lights from the DJ booth reflecting brilliantly off the golden label. "It's one of a kind."

At that, Jillian huffed.

Crystal accepted the bottle of sparkling wine and inspected it carefully. Then she held it up for all to see and said, "Now *this* is what I'm talking about!"

"I remember this winery, Abs. It's not even –"

I cut Jillian off immediately. "Not even making this wine anymore."

"Yeah," Jillian laughed, "because the wine was so –"

"Rare," I interrupted again. I shot her the look that meant to keep quiet. "Luckily, I happened to have one bottle left. I couldn't think of anyone more deserving."

The music started up again and Crystal instructed her court to move to the dance floor. Everyone obeyed dutifully, leaving me, Crystal, and Jillian huddled near a pile of ruggedly ripped wrapping paper.

"Thank you," Crystal said, as my plan fell into place. "I'll get us a couple of champagne flutes and we can enjoy this bubbly together."

"No," I spouted before she could turn to leave.

Crystal looked confused. "Why not?"

"Because this . . . um . . . this is a special bottle."

"So you've said."

"*Very* special. In fact, I think you should save it for your wedding night." I gave her a sultry wink, or at least as sultry as I could muster. "Share it with the groom."

Crystal smiled and nodded as though we were sharing a secret. "I like where your head's at. Jillian, put this with the other gifts, put some water in that vase of yours, and then the two of you are joining me on the dance floor. Come on!"

Three long hours later, after Jillian had introduced me to every single person there, and I'd painfully realized the true meaning of small talk, I finally found Crystal standing at the bar alone – or rather, wobbling – as she chatted up the bartender.

"Abby," she said in a slurred voice, "the little florist from Bloomers. How are ya, babe?"

Her gaze was unfocused as she smiled at me. "Are you still drinking wine? You need something stronger! How about a chocolate martini? Bartender, one chocolate martini for my little friend here." She pushed her empty glass forward. "And one for me, too."

"How are your wedding plans coming along?" I asked. "Do you have your gown?"

"Want to know a secret?" She put one finger to her lips. "It's an off-the-rack gown. Don't tell anyone."

"I won't tell a soul."

"I needed it right away."

"Why's that?"

"Because I've been waiting two years now. Can you believe it? Enough is enough! Know what I mean?"

"I do know what you mean."

The bartender delivered our martinis and Crystal immediately took a drink of hers. "Dee-lish-*ous*!" she proclaimed.

I picked up the glass and forced myself to take a sip. The last time I'd had a chocolate martini had been at Jillian's bridal shower, where I'd ended up pouring mine in a nearby plant. I hadn't ever liked alcohol because I could never get used to the burning sensation.

"You like it?" Crystal asked.

"It's . . . um . . ."

She frowned. "You don't like it?"

I took another sip and smiled as the alcohol slid down my throat like molten rock. "Yum," I said cheerfully.

"Let's go sit down. Me and you. Have a little chat."

I followed her to one of the tables in the center of the room. Most of the ladies had left for the evening. Those who'd stayed, I gathered, were considered to be part of Crystal's inner circle, consisting mostly of single bridesmaids and young divorcees. That circle had quickly started to look a little square as they continued to drink and dance late into the night. Fortunately for Jillian, she had to leave early to help put Harper to bed, which left me right where I wanted to be. "So, Crystal, why did you decide on Dora's to do your flowers?"

She set her glass down carefully and turned to face me. "Don't get angry, but Dora's is a big place. And I'm having a big wedding. I just didn't feel right being in your little shop."

"Do you know Sara Sanford? I think she's a member at the country club."

"I know Sara!" Crystal gushed. "Nice girl. *Beautiful* girl."

"I did her wedding. And it was a big one. Tons of floral arrangements."

She closed one eye and tried to focus on me. "Seriously?"

"Seriously." I waited until she'd taken another drink then said, "Tell me what your cost is going to be at Dora's, and I'll beat it."

"I don't know, Abby."

"I'm right in town. You won't need to drive out to Maraville for meetings. And I'll be at your wedding venue myself, no sending the hired help like Dora's does." Which I didn't know but it sounded good.

She turned to face the bar, sipping her martini. I waited patiently, my foot bouncing under the table in anticipation.

She finally turned to me and closed one eye. "That was a very nice gift you got me, so nice of you. You're a good person." She smiled crookedly and threw her arm around my shoulders again. "You got the job, babe. I can come see you on Tuesday."

I did it! But I couldn't act too excited. I had to keep my cool and finish the mission. On to part two. I paused and pivoted. "How are things going for you? It must be rough now with your dad gone."

She took a big gulp of her drink, then said in a whisper, "Can I tell you another secret?"

I leaned in closer.

"I didn't like my dad very much. He's the reason I haven't been able to get married."

"Still," I said, "he was your father. He must've had *some* good qualities."

"He was good at making money." She leaned toward me. "He wasn't so good at making friends."

"Are you saying he had enemies?"

She held a finger to her lips again. "Right under his own nose."

"Who would that be?"

She shrugged.

"Someone close to him? Someone he works with?"

She scrunched her face. "Huh?"

"Nevermind."

"You haven't even touched your drink!"

I forced myself to take another sip. The only flavor besides vodka was a disgustingly sweet syrup that must've passed for chocolate. I set the glass down. "I'm sure your dad was very generous to you in the end."

"Ha!" she said. "We came close to losing it all because of *Honey*." She sneered at the name then added, "The black widow."

"What do you mean?"

"What do I mean? I'll tell you what I mean. Dad would've given everything to that spider once they were married. He was going to change his will!"

"Did he tell you that?"

"Dad wouldn't tell us anything. What were we talking about?"

"Your dad's will."

"Oh yeah. I mean, it's bad enough that she got his life insurance."

Life insurance? I took a moment to mull over the information, but still had to ask, "Honey was his beneficiary?"

Crystal tried to put her elbow on the bar, and it slipped off, nearly toppling her. "Yep. Honey gets a million dollars."

Well, that put a different spin on things.

Crystal held up her index finger. "*However,* she doesn't get a dime until the murder case is closed." She leaned toward me and put her hand to the side of her face to whisper, "I phoned the insurance company. They were very helpful."

And I was very surprised. "How were you able to get all this information?"

Her head teetered between her shoulders as she smiled. "I have my ways."

"Do the police know about the insurance policy?"

She giggled and hiccupped at the same time. "They do now."

That would put an incredibly large target on Honey's back.

"You don't need to worry about Honey," Crystal said in one long slur. "We have someone looking at her. Into her. We have someone looking into her. A private detective."

I was so captivated by the information Crystal was doling out in her inebriated state that I'd lifted my drink to my lips by habit. I quickly stopped myself and set the glass down just outside of my reach. "So," I said, "I heard a rumor that you did a number on Honey's windshield. Is it true?"

She laughed and nodded, stared down into her martini, noticed it was empty, and looked up. "What?"

"Where did you go after you smashed the windshield?"

Crystal's gaze narrowed as she looked at me. "Why?"

One of Crystal's bridesmaids came up to the table. "Crys, we need to get you home now. It's late and we're tired."

Crystal used both hands to steady herself in her chair. "Okay. I get it. You've had too much to drink." She pushed herself up and paused to say to me, "I'll be in touch about those flowers."

I gave her a thumb's up. "I look forward to it."

CHAPTER FIFTEEN

Sunday, November 27th

Marco had been sound asleep when I got home in the wee hours of Sunday morning, so I didn't get to share my information until I'd gotten up mid-morning. By that time, he'd walked Seedy, done his workout, showered, and had coffee waiting for me.

"I hope you had a productive evening," he said as I took that first heavenly sip.

"Oh, boy, did I ever."

He slid onto a stool next to me at the counter and listened as I recounted my evening in detail. "Someone right under Arthur's nose," he repeated. "What do you think Crystal meant by that?"

"She may have been referring to one of her brothers . . . or herself. I have no idea. I wish I could've gotten her to go into detail, but she was getting suspicious by that point."

Marco tapped his fingers on the counter, thinking. "You know who else was right under Arthur's nose? Honey Chen. And now she's set to receive a million dollars." He shook his head. "That's a motive for murder if I've ever heard one."

I disagreed. "It doesn't make sense. Honey seemed desperate for money when I interviewed her. Why would she sell her Porsche or pawn her jewelry if she's preparing to be a millionaire?"

"Maybe so no one would suspect her."

"Yes, but she gets the money only if she isn't the murderer," I replied.

"Or if she isn't caught."

"Say what you will about Honey, but I still don't think she's guilty." I took another drink of coffee. "But I have a bigger dilemma to deal with now. Crystal has agreed to let me do her flowers, but how can I continue to investigate her as a murder suspect and take her on as a customer? It doesn't seem ethical."

"I don't think you have to worry about that anymore," he said. "I got a call from Detective Corbison this morning. He told me that the murder weapon was a stainless-steel steak knife like the ones they have at Adagio's restaurant."

"Which means it wasn't one of your knives."

He smiled. "Nope. Mine have wooden handles."

"That's great news! Did he say whether he was focused on any particular suspect?"

"He said at this point they were still in the interviewing process. Corbison wouldn't comment further. He asked about our investigation, and I said we were at the same place."

I gave Marco a big hug. "Thank God you're no longer a suspect."

"So now all we have to do now is find a new home for Down the Hatch."

I released the hug. "What do you mean?"

"Technically, our investigation's over," he explained. "I'm in the clear. Now we can focus on relocating the bar. And you can take Crystal as a customer with no hesitation."

"Marco, we're right in the middle of the investigation. We can't stop now."

Boy was I right.

Monday, November 28th

My mouth dropped open. "Honey was arrested?"

I had just unlocked Bloomer's front door and turned the sign to *OPEN*. Rosa and I were about to head back to the workroom when the door opened, and a cold breeze ushered Dave Hammond into the shop. I'd clerked for Dave when I was in law school and had become a good friend of his since.

He was dressed conservatively in a light brown tweed suit with a blue shirt and tie and brown shoes. A good-looking man in his late forties, his face was on the chubby side, and his brown hair was thinning on top.

"What evidence do they have against her?"

He set his briefcase on the floor beside him. "Her fingerprints were found on the murder weapon."

"Her fingerprints? How long have the detectives been sitting on this information?"

"I don't know, but with those prints, Corbison has a solid case against her."

Lottie and Rosa excused themselves and joined Grace in the tea parlor, where I assumed they were standing just within earshot.

"I suppose the fact that Arthur McMahon made Honey his life insurance beneficiary isn't helping her any," I said to Dave.

He rubbed his hands together for warmth. "The D. A. is calling the insurance money her motive. Plus, Honey was allegedly seen near the realty office on a few security cameras downtown."

"I've viewed most of that footage, Dave. There's no way Corbison can prove that she was downtown."

"Regardless, Abby, the fingerprints are what clinched it."

"Why are you telling me this?"

"Because Honey hired me to defend her," Dave answered. "She told me you've been investigating and that she trusts you. What I'd like you and Marco to do is to keep investigating and bring me any evidence that will help her."

"She trusts me? That wasn't the impression I got from her before."

"I know. She told me. Just go listen to her story. That's all I ask. If you're still not convinced, then you don't have to take the case."

"Fair enough." I checked my watch. "It looks like I'll have time to run over to the jail to see her this morning."

"Great. I know she'll appreciate it."

"Before you go, Dave, I'd like to know if Honey was named in Arthur McMahon's will."

"That's not something I can tell you, Abby. Attorney-client privilege, remember? You'll have to ask Honey."

"If I guess correctly, could you click your tongue or something?"

"Abby."

"Okay, it was worth a shot. Is there anything you can tell me about Arthur's kids? Anything that struck you as odd?"

He was silent for a moment. "Yes, a few things. Immediately after the reading of the will, Rowell fired me."

"Wow. Was he unhappy with you?"

"I think he'd just gotten what he wanted and was done with my services. And I think there's something else you should know."

"I'm all ears, Dave."

"Two days before Arthur McMahon died, Crystal came to see me, wanting to know if her father had changed his will. When I told her that it was confidential information, she plunked down a thick envelope full of hundred-dollar bills."

"Wow," I said. "That took a lot of nerve."

"It was a lot of money, Abby. I'd say at least five thousand dollars."

"You're kidding. She must've wanted that information badly."

"She was very upset when I wouldn't accept the bribe."

"Yet, somehow, Crystal found out that information anyway."

"What do you mean?" Dave asked.

"She knew her father had an appointment to change his will. When I asked her how she knew, she said that she had her ways."

"She didn't hear it from me. I didn't accept the money. I can promise you that."

"But someone did. It could've been someone in your office. Someone who has access to your calendar or appointment book."

"We have a few interns that just started, but that's a risky move."

"I don't know," I told him. "Five thousand dollars might've seemed worth the risk. I'd look into it if I were you."

"This is why I want you to take the case," Dave replied. "This is the kind of information I need."

"I'll have to discuss all of this with Marco before we take the case, but I'll go talk to Honey right now."

"Thank you." Dave picked up his briefcase. "I have to get to court. Talk to Honey. Talk to Marco. And get back to me as soon as you can."

∾3 6∾

"Sweetie," Lottie said after Dave had gone, "we couldn't help but overhear that Honey has been arrested for murder."

Grace was standing with her, both women looking concerned. Rosa stood a little behind the two women, chewing on her lip.

"Honey is asking to see me," I explained. "She wants me to prove she didn't murder her fiancé."

"You're going to take her case, *si?*" Rosa asked.

"It's not that simple," I replied. "Honey's fingerprints were found on the murder weapon."

There was a sharp intake of breath.

"That doesn't mean she did it," I told them. "I'd like to go see her this morning so I can talk to Marco about what to do. Can you handle things without me?"

"We have two orders waiting," Rosa said. "I can do them easily."

"Go, sweetie," Lottie said.

"We shall await your report," Grace added. "It should prove very interesting."

Before heading to the jail. I stopped by Down the Hatch to speak with Marco. I found him sitting at his desk in his office.

I knocked on the door frame. "Are you busy?"

He looked up with a smile. "Not for you. What are you up to?"

"Oh, you know, the usual. Going to jail."

He raised his eyebrows. "Is that so?"

I stepped inside the office and sat in one of the slingback chairs in front of his desk. "Honey Chen was arrested for murder this morning. Dave Hammond is representing her, and he wants us to help investigate. What do you think?"

Marco pondered a moment. "First I'd like to know what you think."

"I'll have to speak with Honey first. Want to join me?"

"I have some paperwork to do. Why don't you go and we meet at noon to discuss?"

I leaned over the desk to give him a kiss. "Sounds good."

❧ ❧

Fifteen minutes later, I opened the heavy glass door and stepped inside the stark brick building that housed the county jail. I walked up to the window and gave my name to the woman in uniform standing behind the glass. Her name tag said *Potter*. I searched my memory for her first name but came up blank.

"Abby Knight!" the police officer exclaimed. "I haven't seen you in a while. Are you here on official business?"

"I came to interview a potential client. And," I leaned toward the glass partition to whisper, "I'm married now. It's Abby Knight Salvare."

"Well, congratulations! Good for you. How is your father these days?"

Most of the veteran officers on the force remembered my dad, a former police sergeant. "He's doing very well, thank you for asking."

"Who are you here to see?"

"Honey Chen."

She pulled up a list on her computer. "Honey Chen. Okay, we'll have her put in an interview room for you. You'll have to go through the security check – but you know the drill."

"I sure do."

She smiled at me and pointed toward the doorway to my right.

I walked through the metal detector, had my purse searched, and was shown down a hallway to a closet-sized interview room. The only furniture in the room was a rectangular table and four chairs. I sat down at one end to wait and five minutes later, an officer brought Honey into the room. She was shackled at the wrists and feet, but the officer removed her handcuffs before she sat down.

"Abby!" she said, nearly crying. "I'm so glad you came." She wrapped me in a hug as though we were old friends.

As she took a seat across the table from me, I could see that her eyes were red, her skin appeared ashen, and her hair lay loose and limp across her shoulders. I felt sorry for her.

"The police picked me up early this morning. It was awful! Detective Corbison questioned me for two hours, accusing me of murdering Arthur. He wouldn't listen to anything I had to say."

"Did he tell you about the evidence he has against you?"

"He said my fingerprints were on the knife. But how?"

"What else did he say?"

"The detective just kept insisting I had killed Arthur for his money. He told me he knew about my boyfriend. He knew that I had lived with Razor up to the time I was engaged to Arthur and that I went back to Razor's apartment after Arthur died, all proof that I was just using Arthur. Did you tell the detective about that?"

"Not at all."

"Then how did he know?"

The look on her face was extremely sincere and I felt the need to tell her what I'd found out. "Arthur's kids hired a private detective. They know just as much as I do about Razor and your whereabouts the night of the murder."

Her fearful expression turned angry. "I knew it. They're trying to frame me."

"Did you ask for a lawyer when he started questioning you?"

She used her fingers to wipe the tears off her face. "Not at first, but I finally did. I called Mr. Hammond. He was Arthur's lawyer. He came down right away, but he couldn't get me released. He said something about me having to go to a bail hearing." Honey grabbed my hands and squeezed them between her own. "You have to help me, Abby. I didn't kill Arthur!"

"You're going to have to help me first."

"How?"

"By being completely honest with me," I told her. "You've been keeping things from me."

Honey pulled her hands away. "Of course I have. I didn't know why you were investigating. How could I trust a complete stranger with every private detail?"

"But you trust me now?"

"Dave trusts you," Honey answered softly. "And I don't really have a choice anymore."

"I'm going to ask you a few questions. I want you to be totally honest."

"Okay."

"Did you know about Arthur's life insurance policy?"

She shook her head. "Not until I got a call from Liberty Life Insurance three days ago. I'd never even heard of Liberty Life Insurance."

"You didn't know Arthur had taken out a policy for a million dollars?"

"Please believe me, Abby, I knew nothing about it. If I'd known, I wouldn't have pawned my bracelet or my engagement ring. The only thing Arthur told me was that he'd made an appointment to see Dave Hammond about changing his will. He never mentioned an insurance policy."

"Did Arthur tell anyone else about that appointment?"

"I don't think so. He didn't want his children to know."

"I need you to be honest with me, Honey. On the night of Arthur's death, did you go downtown to his office?"

"Yes."

"Why?"

"I wanted to tell him that Crystal smashed my windshield. I was trying to call, but he wouldn't answer his cell phone or his office phone."

"Why did you have Razor drive you downtown?"

"Because I couldn't drive. I couldn't see through the windshield. That's why I called Razor. I didn't have any other options."

"You couldn't call a driver?"

"I could have, but I was nervous. I didn't feel safe."

"We're you still dating Razor while engaged to Arthur?"

"No. I broke up with Razor, but I still felt safe around him. I knew he would be there for me."

"What happened next?"

"He drove me to Arthur's office, but I didn't go inside."

"Why not?"

"When Razor pulled up in front of the building, I saw Arthur talking to Devona through the front window. I figured that was the reason why he wouldn't answer his phone. He was with her. I was so hurt, I had Razor take me home."

"Did you tell Razor why you wanted to go home?"

She shook her head. "I didn't want to talk about it. I was humiliated. Arthur and I were about to be married and there he was, alone with his former girlfriend. I told Razor I didn't feel well and wanted to go home."

"But you didn't go home."

"I meant my old home."

"And you stayed at your old apartment with Razor all night?"

"Yes. You have to believe me."

"I do believe you. It matches our timeline and what we've seen on security cameras. It's very clear that you never entered the building. How does Detective Corbison account for that?"

"I don't know."

Honey seemed so genuinely distressed, and so truly baffled by Arthur leaving her his insurance policy, that I believed she was telling the truth. But there was something that bothered me, something I'd wanted to know since I'd heard the news that Honey had a boyfriend. "Tell me about Razor."

She wiped another tear and looked at me. "What do you want to know?"

"I want to know the whole story. I want to know why he was texting you and calling you constantly."

She shook her head and gave me a puzzled look, but I wasn't buying it. "Don't lie to me. One of the waitresses told me he was harassing you. Then I saw you arguing with him in the car before we met for lunch. I saw your phone. I saw all the missed calls and messages. Tell me the truth about your relationship with Razor."

After a long sigh, she said, "I love Razor. He wasn't harassing me."

"Then explain, please."

"He wanted me to move back in. He was begging me, calling and texting constantly. He wanted to take care of me, but that's the problem. He can't take care of me. That's why I had to leave him in the first place."

"You love him, but you left him because you needed money?"

She looked away. "Yes. I needed money. I wanted a secure future. Razor promised that he would do everything he could to take care of me. He even went back to college for his master's."

"But you still left him."

She let out a tragic laugh through the tears. "I honestly thought it would be better for both of us. He has enough problems. I didn't want him to take on mine as well." She let her head drop and didn't bother to wipe the tears that fell from her eyes. She wept quietly, her shoulders shaking as she allowed her emotions to pour out.

I held her hands, trying to calm her down.

She looked at me with watery eyes. "Will you help me clear my name?"

"I'll have to discuss it with my husband."

She squeezed my hands firmly. "Please, *please* help me. I have to make things right."

"I'll get back to you as soon as I can. I promise."

She searched my eyes as if hoping I'd say more, then removed her hands to wipe her face and said quietly, "Thank you."

I watched while the matron handcuffed her again and escorted her from the room, then I texted Marco, *Got some interesting information. I'll be down at noon.*

He texted back, *See you then.*

Lottie, Grace, and Rosa were waiting for me when I got back to Bloomers.

"What do you think?" Lottie asked.

"I think the Salvare Detective Agency may have a new client."

❧ ❦

Shortly after noon, I took a seat in the last booth and waited for Marco to join me. As he sat down, Gert came up to the booth to take our orders, knowing neither one of us had the time for a long lunch.

"I'll have a turkey and Swiss on Ciabatta bread," I told her.

"Hatch burger," Marco said. "And two iced teas." He waited until Gert had left and said, "What did you learn?"

"Honey's fingerprints were found on the steak knife."

"Wow. That's going to be tough to defend."

"But not impossible. Any one of Arthur's kids could've picked up her knife and used it to kill him."

"I agree with you, but it's going to be difficult to prove."

"You agree with me?" I paused to smile at Gert, who'd just brought our drinks.

She winked at me. "Two iced teas for the boss and his squeeze."

"You're the best, Gert."

"Don't I know it." She gave another wink and left.

Marco unwrapped his straw and stuck it in the drink. "What else did Honey tell you?"

"Marco, she's a mess. She said she had no knowledge of the insurance money until someone from the life insurance company called her three days ago. And she also talked about her movements the night of the murder, that she'd had Razor drive her downtown. She said she saw Devona leave the office and was so hurt she had Razor take her back to his apartment."

"You know what? I believe her."

"You do? Why are you so agreeable today?"

Marco smiled. "After you stopped in to see me this morning, I checked with campus security and verified their alibi. Both Razor and Honey were seen entering student housing at ten twenty-five that night, which means they drove straight home after visiting Arthur's office."

"That's good news. I'll bet Corbison doesn't have that piece of information."

"Then maybe we should talk to him." Marco checked his watch. "Let's run over to the police department after lunch. I think Detective Corbison needs to know what we've found out. I have about half an hour. Okay?"

"Sounds good to me."

"And I'll call the insurance company to find out whether Honey is telling the truth. If she didn't know about the insurance money, she had no motive to kill Arthur. Did she give you the name of the company?"

"Liberty Life." Gert delivered our sandwiches, so I paused to take a bite. "Oh, and Honey also confirmed that Arthur had made an appointment with Dave to change his will."

"That's interesting," Marco munched on his burger for a moment. "If Arthur told Honey about his appointment with Dave, I wonder if he told his kids."

"She said Arthur didn't want his children to know. And I believe her."

"Why?"

"Because Crystal said the same thing, and she tried to bribe Dave Hammond for that exact information. Dave didn't accept the bribe, but somehow, she still found out. I think she bribed someone in his office. And when she learned her father had made an appointment to change his will, she may have made plans to kill him."

"Or Crystal could've mentioned it to her brothers," Marco reasoned, "which would have given either of them a motive to kill Arthur before he changed his will. We still have yet to interview Rowell, and we know next to nothing about Birch."

"Don't forget about Grant Starling."

"I suppose Arthur could've mentioned the appointment to Grant, although for what reason I don't know. I just don't see enough evidence to support the theory that Grant killed Arthur."

"After we talk to Corbison, I'll walk up the street to Adagio's to see what I can find out about Birch's movements after their family dinner."

Marco took another bite of his burger and wiped his mouth with a napkin. "Are we still going to the bowling alley tonight?"

"Yes. Rowell's bowling league is tonight." I rolled my eyes. "It's going to be a fun evening."

"But first, we talk to the detective."

CHAPTER SIXTEEN

"Well, look who it is. The dynamic duo. I've been expecting a visit from the two of you."

I pulled out one of the seats in front of Corbison's desk and sat down as Marco did the same. The detective leaned back in his chair and removed a pair of thick-framed glasses from his face, setting them on the desk in front of him. I noted the dark circles under his eyes as if he hadn't slept in days. His hair was unkempt, and his necktie was loose around the collar. There were large stacks of papers, binders, and folders piled up on the filing cabinets behind him.

"Thanks for meeting with us, Detective," Marco offered politely. "We won't take up much of your time."

"What do you need?" Corbison replied on an exhale.

"We'd like to share some information with you."

He tapped his pen on the desk. "Shoot."

"Abby went to see Honey Chen this afternoon."

The beleaguered detective put down his pen, leaned forward, and rested his elbows on the desk. He looked me in the eyes and said in a dry voice, "Now why would you want to do that?"

I answered in the same tone, trying to mask my immediate irritation. "To help you out."

Corbison stared me down. "How is that?"

"Yes. I want to make sure you're charging the right person with murder."

His glare narrowed. "You think Honey is innocent?"

I glared right back. "I'd like to know what makes you think she's guilty."

He sat still, unblinking. I did the same.

Marco leaned forward to break up the staring contest. "We have reason to believe that Honey didn't know about the million-dollar insurance policy until a few days ago."

Corbison shifted his focus to Marco. "She told you that, did she?"

"It would be easy to verify," Marco replied calmly. "We just need to call the insurance company."

"I have," Corbison revealed. "Liberty Life reached out to Honey Chen exactly three days ago, which would significantly decrease her motive . . . unless . . ." he let the sentence trail off, leaning back as if pleased with himself before continuing. "Unless Honey was informed of the policy by someone other than the insurance company, say, for example, Arthur McMahon."

I sat back, surprised. Had Honey lied to my face, or was the detective making assumptions? "Do you have proof that Arthur told her?"

"We have reason to believe he did."

Honey's story was so incredibly convincing, I hadn't really challenged any of her information, but I wasn't about to make that mistake with the detective. "What reason do you have?"

"We have reason to believe Arthur told her about the insurance policy. That's all you need to know."

Marco moved the conversation forward. "Can you tell us what other evidence you have against her?"

"Besides the murder weapon with her fingerprints on it? You want more evidence than that? Come on, Salvare. Now you're wasting my time."

"We've seen the security cam footage," Marco told him. "We watched Honey and her boyfriend drive up to the realty office, but she didn't enter the building. We also have evidence suggesting that they drove directly back to his apartment after leaving the scene."

"You don't have all the footage," Corbison corrected. "I've checked the camera from the courthouse. There's no way to prove that Honey was in the car when her boyfriend drove up to the front of the building."

"Then what's your theory?" I spouted. "How do you suppose Honey entered the office and killed her fiancée?"

"You want my theory? How about this? Her boyfriend, this so-called Razor, dropped her off in the alley so she could enter the back door with a key that Arthur had given her. From there it was just a matter of waiting for the right time. Razor then parked his car out front as some sort of ridiculous alibi while Honey did the deed. As soon as she was finished, Razor met up with her in the alley and drove back to his apartment."

"That's a stretch," I told him. "How are you going to prove that in court?"

"All we need are the fingerprints on the murder weapon."

"And a made-up story on how she entered the building."

"It fits the timeline, Abby. What more do you want from me?"

"You said you found Honey's bracelet at the crime scene, but it couldn't have been hers. She pawned it. Talk to the owner of Bingstrom's jewelers. He can verify that. You could also question Devona Esmond. Ask where her bracelet is."

Corbison rubbed the bridge of his nose. "We've already done that, too. Devona Esmond has been cleared. And so has Kenton Lang, for that matter."

"What about Rowell?" I asked. I had Marco show the detective a picture of Rowell that we'd captured from the security footage outside of Ascott's Shoe Store. "Tell me that doesn't look like him. Why would someone who looks like Rowell be walking toward the realty office after ten o'clock?"

Corbison put his glasses on and still had to squint at the image. "I can't tell who that is, besides, Rowell has five eyewitnesses who claim to have been with him at the bowling alley all night."

"They could be lying," I countered.

"Then prove it. Is there anything else you need from me?"

I was flustered, but it seemed as though Corbison had done a thorough job. I couldn't accuse him of rushing the case or painting a target on someone's back. His information matched up with ours, although he had much more information than we had. I sat back in my chair, unsure of what to do next.

"Can you prove that Honey had a key to the realty building?" Marco asked.

Corbison nodded. "It was on her keychain."

"Were her fingerprints found anywhere else in the building?"

Corbison shook his head. "It doesn't matter. They were on the murder weapon. That's all the evidence we need."

Marco ran his fingers through his hair. "Okay then. Thank you for talking to us."

❧ ☙

After we'd finished talking to Detective Corbison, Marco and I discussed our conversation on a park bench on the courtyard lawn.

"Dave wants us to take this case, Marco. What should we do?"

He sat with his arm around my shoulder for a minute, thinking. "Corbison has a strong case, but there's something about it that bothers me."

"His attitude?"

"No, the fact that Honey's fingerprints were only found on the knife, and not anywhere else in the office." He shook his head. "Even after all the evidence Corbison laid out, I still don't think Honey is guilty. And I'd still like to talk to Rowell."

"Then let's take the case, Marco."

"Okay," he said, "but don't get your hopes up. We might not be able to prove Honey's innocence."

"We haven't failed yet."

Marco leaned over and kissed my cheek. "True, and I'd really like to try that bottle of Merlot I bought from Joe."

I turned to accept more kisses, but he stopped me. "My thirty minutes are up. I have to get back to work, but we can continue tonight."

After one more quick kiss, Marco headed back to the bar and I walked up to Lincoln Street to *Adagio's Italian Restaurant.* Inside the quiet restaurant, I began by asking the hostess whether she knew the McMahon family. She said she did, so I asked if she remembered the McMahons eating there on the night of the murder. She said that was all the staff was talking about the next day. She also remembered that the server named Rob had waited on them, so I approached him and asked if he could give me five minutes.

A nice-looking guy in his forties, Rob was standing near a serving station wrapping silverware in crisp maroon napkins. There was something familiar about the sight, and I watched him perform his monotonous task for several seconds before approaching him

"You'll have to make it quick," he said. "I have a big reservation arriving soon."

"I will. Do you know the McMahon family?"

"*Everyone* knows the McMahons," he replied with a touch of sarcasm.

"In talking about the night Arthur McMahon died," I said, "do you remember seeing Birch leave the restaurant after dinner? He would be the younger son, thin, long hair?"

Rob paused to think, holding the silverware in one hand and the cloth napkin in the other. "As I recall, that particular young man had too much to drink and ended up in the restroom at the end of their dinner."

"He was drunk?"

"That's how he appeared."

"Did he leave after that?"

"I offered to call him a cab and he accepted."

"Did you see him leave?"

"No, I helped him out the back alley door, so he could pick up a cab at the mouth of the alley."

"Why the back door?"

"It's just something we do for our customers. Save them the embarrassment, you know? He was in quite a state, could hardly stand on his own. Another gentlemen and a blonde woman helped me get him outside."

"Do you know who these people were?"

"No."

"Did you see the cab waiting there?"

"No, I had to get back to my tables."

So, Birch left through the alley door, which was why he hadn't been caught on any of the downtown cameras. Would he have gone back to the realty later that night in an inebriated state? Would he have had a key to the realty building? I doubted his father would've given him one. He hadn't even invited Birch to his engagement dinner. Why would he trust him with a key?

Unless Crystal had given him a key. After all, she'd been the one to invite Birch to their dinner. Maybe she'd even given him the idea to swipe Honey's steak knife. Maybe she was the mastermind behind her dad's murder. Or maybe my thoughts were running away with me.

When I got back to Bloomers, I called Marco and told him what I'd learned at *Adagio's*."

"If you think it's possible that Birch had a key," Marco said, "then we'd need to verify that info."

"Rowell would know," I said.

"We can ask him about it tonight."

❧ ❦

Shortly before eight o'clock that evening, we hopped into the Prius and headed to the east side of town to Arman's Arcade and Bowling Center.

"We've never gone bowling before," Marco said, as he turned onto the main road. "Why is that?"

I shuddered dramatically. "I can't stand the place," I told him. "My dad used to bring me and my brothers to Arman's every weekend."

"How have you never told me this before?"

"I don't know. Maybe I've blocked it from my memory. My brothers were really good, and they used to tease me because I couldn't keep up with them. I hated it. Plus, the bowling alley was dark and dingy, the bathroom was disgusting, and my shoes always stuck to the floor. Why? Do you like to bowl?"

Marco laughed. "No. I'm terrible at it. I was more of an arcade guy."

We continued to talk for the next ten minutes until we reached Arman's, then we walked inside to find

225

a clean, newly remodeled, brightly lit space. We walked past a little pizza shop with black tables and shiny chrome stools, then the arcade room where Marco stopped to check out the games, and finally ended up in the bowling center. To our right, against the back wall, was a very long bar with red padded stools. Beyond the bar was an area of high-topped tables

To our left were the bowling lanes. They had added quite a few lanes since I'd been there, with modern lighting, new plush seating, and large, flat panel screens above the lanes which automatically kept track of the score. I was impressed with the updated establishment. It was fairly busy for a Monday night, with most of the bar full of patrons and almost all of the lanes full.

"How are we ever going to find Rowell?" I asked, scanning the lanes.

"Let's go sit at a high-top table. We can search from there."

We took seats at one of the tables and ordered beers. As we waited for our order, I surveyed the bowlers. "Is that Rowell?" I asked, pointing. "Third lane from the right. He's the large guy, brown curly hair, wearing a green bowling shirt and tan pants."

Marco stared at the man for a minute. "That's definitely him."

"Here are your drinks," a young man said, setting our beer mugs down in front of us.

Marco retrieved his wallet and flashed his private eye license. "How late do the bowlers play?" Marco asked him.

"Most play until ten p.m.," he replied. "A lot of them hang out at the bar afterward."

"Do you know Rowell McMahon?" Marco asked.

The young man made a face. "Yeah, I know him. He's here every Monday night."

"Does Rowell hang out at the bar after the game?"

"Yeah. He stays late, drinks a lot, and never leaves a tip."

I took a sip of beer, smiling at our shared contempt. "Obviously you don't think much of him."

He put his hands up. "I didn't say that."

Seeing the young man look hesitant, I added, "It's okay. We don't either."

"I don't have anything against Rowell," the young man said. "He's just a big blowhard, always sounding off like he's such a know-it-all. It gets old, you know?"

"I get it," I said.

The young man looked back over at the bar. "Anything else you need?"

"That'll do it," Marco said, handing him a ten-dollar bill. "Thanks."

His eyes grew big. "Thank *you!*"

As he strode away, I asked Marco, "So how do we approach this know-it-all blowhard?"

Marco focused on Rowell and took a long drink. We watched as the big man threw his bowling ball down the lane. He moved his head as if he could somehow control the ball with sheer will. After knocking down all ten pins, he spun around and pumped his fist, celebrating with his teammates enthusiastically.

"I say we wait until Rowell is at the bar and surprise him," Marco said.

"What makes you think he'll talk to us?"

"Look at him. He's having a good time drinking with friends. He might be a little thrown off to see us, but if we don't confront him about anything too serious, we could possibly get some information out of him."

"I don't think we'll get much."

"Then we need to focus on the important questions, like his whereabouts on the night of the murder."

"And I want to know what Rowell has to say about the security cam footage. I know it's him in that video. I want to see his face when he sees that clip. Do you have it?"

He patted his pocket. "I have it saved on my phone. But we don't want to go in hot. We'll have to make it seem like we're not here to see him."

"Like we're on a date?"

"Yes, like we just happened to run into him."

"I don't think he'll buy it."

"Then let's make it a real date. We have a lot of time to kill, and it's not so dark and dingy in here anymore."

"This coming from the man who works in the darkest, dingiest place on the square."

"Hey, it might be dark, but it's not dingy."

"I still leave with sticky shoes."

Marco put his arm around me. "Point taken. So, how about we finish these beers and then check out the arcade?"

"It's a date."

After about fifteen minutes, I was over the arcade. The disharmony of horrible, high-pitched, digital music and sound effects echoed throughout the room, giving me an instant migraine. Kids were running amuck, change jingling in every pocket as they ran past. And the smell of shoe disinfectant and greasy pepperoni was enough to send me straight over the edge.

"I'm sorry," I told Marco as I guided him out the doors. "I just learned that I am *not* an arcade girl."

"It's okay," he said. "I was out of tokens anyway."

I checked my watch as we headed back to the lanes. "We still have well over an hour until the league games are done."

"Why don't we bowl a few games?"

I rolled my eyes.

"Come on, Abby. You said you used to come here all the time. Maybe you could teach me a few things."

I folded my arms, thinking of an excuse.

"Besides, if Rowell sees us bowling, he'll be even more convinced that we're not here to question him."

I let out a defeated breath. "Fine. You can bowl. I'll watch."

We walked over to the shoe counter and got bowling shoes, then we were given a lane at the very end of the alley. Even though the place was full of people, we had almost two lanes to ourselves, which was nice. I was used to the old days when we would all be crammed next to each other, desperately searching for a ball that wasn't too heavy. I sat back on the comfy leather seats as Marco sat at one of the two main terminals to enter his information.

Marco entered my name as player one, but he used my nickname. He entered himself as player number two and looked back at me. "Have you picked out a ball yet, Sunshine?"

I sighed, trying to find a reason to be annoyed at his persistence, but instead, I gave in and picked out a pretty pink six-pound ball. The finger holes fit perfectly, and the weight felt good in my hands.

"My little bowler," Marco said. "Let's see what you got."

I stood about three feet back from the toe line, trying to block the memories of my brothers heckling me from behind my back. I took in a deep breath and let it out as I strode forward, drawing my arm back and sending it forward gracefully. Or, at least what I thought was graceful. The ball came to an abrupt halt as it smacked the back of my outer thigh.

"Ouch," Marco said as he came up to check on me. "Did that hurt?"

I grabbed my leg as the tingling torture coursed throughout my body. "Of course it hurt."

"Maybe this wasn't such a good idea."

"No. It's okay. I'll get the hang of it." I hadn't noticed that my ball had bounced off my thigh, veered directly into the gutter, and was stuck in the middle of the lane.

"I'll get the attendant," Marco said. "Try to walk it off."

The pain had dulled by the time I had the ball back in my hands. This time, as I lifted the ball behind me, I angled my legs so that I didn't injure myself again, and suddenly I had the old feeling back. The pink ball glistened as it slid down the oiled lane and cracked just right of the main pin. Unfortunately, one pin remained. On my second attempt, I managed to catch just enough of the final pin to knock it down. I turned around to see my husband nodding as if he were impressed.

Marco took his turn next, sending his bowling ball hurtling down the middle of the lane only to have it veer off to the right and sink into the gutter.

"Your form is all wrong." I stepped up behind Marco and guided his arm into the correct position. I gently kicked his heel into place and then changed out his fifteen-pounder for a slightly lighter ball. "Now try it."

He followed my advice and released the ball smoothly, watching as it veered off into the gutter once again. "See, I'm terrible."

We spent the next hour working on Marco's form. After a short while, he was throwing the ball evenly, and not getting any gutter balls. Finally, on the very last frame, Marco threw the ball with just enough curve and force to knock down all ten pins.

"Maybe I should've been a bowling instructor," I teased him.

Marco looked back at me with a smile but stopped as he spotted something over my shoulder. I turned to see Rowell McMahon standing with his arms folded across his massive chest at the back of our lane.

He did not look happy.

CHAPTER SEVENTEEN

"Hi there, Rowell," Marco said. "Good to see you."

Rowell ignored him and frowned, one eyebrow raising suspiciously at me. "Are you following me?"

I gave him a surprised look. "*Following* you?"

"We're having a date night," Marco told him.

"Uh-huh. So you're not here to question me about my father's death?"

"Why would you think that?" I asked.

"I talked to Grant Starling," Rowell replied. "I know you're investigating."

"Actually," I said, "we did want to talk to you at some point, but since you're here, we can talk right now."

"I'm busy right now."

"Then let's set up an appointment to talk," Marco suggested. "We won't take up much of your time."

"Sorry," he said in a bored voice. "I've got a jam-packed schedule."

"We'll work around it," Marco countered. "We're very flexible."

Rowell sized him up for a moment. "Tell you what, Salvare," he said brazenly. "I saw your little strike there. You a bowler?"

Marco shrugged. "Not exactly."

"How about we have a little contest? If you can beat me at a game, you can take all the time you want."

"How about we just set up an appointment to talk?" Marco suggested. "No more games."

Rowell laughed again. "Come on. One game."

"Not happening."

"How about one frame?"

"No."

"Okay, how about this? One roll. You knock down more pins than me, you can ask me anything you want."

"Rowell," I said, "you're on."

He looked at me sideways. "I wasn't talking to you."

"What's wrong? Are you afraid of losing to a woman?"

His belly bounced as he let out a snarling laugh. "I don't lose to anyone. You really think you can beat me?"

"Only one way to find out. Let's go."

As I stood up, Marco said to me quietly, "What are you doing?"

"I've got this," I whispered as I stepped up to our lane.

Rowell followed. He carried with him a specially designed bag. From it, he pulled a fancy, glossy black ball with golden-trimmed finger holes. He set his ball in the return gate and looked up at the flat-screen TV that still displayed our names. "Who's this player two? Who's Sunshine?"

"That's me. You play under Marco's name, so you're up first."

Rowell wiped his palm with a dry cloth then set it down and gripped the ball firmly. His large frame blocked the entire lane as he squared up his shoulders. He pulled his arm back and let loose with a mighty force. Marco and I had to change seats to see around him. We watched as the ball sailed down the lane and cracked the pins loudly, sending them sailing in all directions.

Rowell turned around and shot me a crafty smile. "That's a strike," he said coolly as he took his seat across from us. "Your turn."

I stepped up to the lane, clutching the ball at my chest with both hands, and closed my eyes.

"You only got one shot at this," Rowell called from behind me. "Don't mess it up."

I breathed in and out slowly, Rowell's mocking tone a haunting reminder of my teenage brothers. I opened my eyes and pulled the ball back as I strode ahead, leaned my body to the side as I let the ball swing forward, and released it. I even remembered a move my dad had taught me, a final twist at the release point, giving the ball just enough spin to strike at the perfect angle.

I stepped back with my fingers crossed. The ball approached slightly off course, but at the last second swung back and attacked the pins perfectly. I jumped up in excitement as all ten pins fell.

Marco clapped as I joined them back at our seats. "Good job, Sunshine."

Rowell shook his head. "Still didn't beat me."

"Then we'll go again," I said confidently.

"Tell you what," Rowell said. "I'll give you five minutes right now, and then you two have to leave me alone."

After Marco and I agreed, the three of us took seats at a high-top table and ordered beers.

"You're good," Rowell said. "I wouldn't have believed it."

"And now it's payback time," I told him, pulling my notebook and pen out of my purse.

"Five minutes," he reminded me.

I glanced at Marco. "You want to start?"

He waited until the waiter had set down our beers then said to Rowell, "Do you know anyone who would want to harm your father? Any enemies? Anyone jealous of his success?"

"I can't even begin to list his enemies," Rowell responded. "But I can tell you that my father and Grant Starling didn't get along. My father was a savvy businessman. He owned a lot of real estate, knew a lot of influential people. Grant didn't have that same knack. And Grant always wanted control of the realty. Maybe he got tired of waiting."

Rowell was giving Grant a motive. I wrote it down.

"Where did you go after you left Adagio's?" Marco asked.

"I came here. We've got league games every Monday."

Marco waited until I was finished writing then asked, "How late did you stay?"

"My usual time," Rowell answered. "Around eleven or so."

"How long does it take to get to the realty office from here?" I asked.

Rowell thought for a moment. "About ten . . ." He stopped mid-answer and gave me a sly smile. "It doesn't matter because I didn't go back to the office that night. Nice try."

"Maybe we should check the realty office's security video," Marco said, pretending he didn't know that it wasn't operational.

Rowell took a drink of his beer. "You go right ahead. Check that video."

He didn't seem the least bit bothered by the idea. My guess was that he knew the camera wasn't working. I wondered what else he knew that he wasn't sharing. "We have information that someone used a key to get in the back door. Can you tell us who else might have a key to the realty building?"

"You sure do have a lot of inside information about this case," Rowell said. "It must be nice having friends on the force."

Marco ignored him and pulled out his cell phone. "We have someone on video tape who looks just like you walking toward the realty office about ten-thirty on the night of the murder. Take a look."

Rowell took the phone and studied the image Marco had taken from the security footage. "That's not me," he said, handing it back. "I was right here."

"Do you have anyone who can verify that?" I asked.

He pushed his glass away. "Your five minutes are up."

I gave him a hard look. Rowell met my gaze steadily but wouldn't answer my question. "So that's a no," I said, writing it down.

"Ask anyone you want. I was right here all night." With a final glare, he got off his chair and walked back over to the group of men he'd been bowling with. We watched him chat with them for a few minutes, then he left.

Marco watched him leave, then said, "What do you think? Was Rowell credible?"

"I kept watching his eyes, Marco. They never shifted away when he was answering, but I still don't know how I feel about him."

"Okay, what do we know about Rowell?" Marco asked.

I began to list on my fingers. "Number one. We know he could've picked up Honey's steak knife while he was at the restaurant that evening. Two. We know he had a motive – money and property. And three, he could have left here early to go to the realty office, giving him the opportunity."

Marco slid off the stool. "Wait right here."

I watched him walk over to a high-top table and speak to the five guys sitting there. I could see them nodding their heads in answer to whatever he was saying, then he thanked them and came back. "His buddies verified Rowell's story. They said he was here with them until midnight."

"Were they credible?"

"They didn't even hesitate to think about my question. I'm guessing Rowell gave them a heads-up."

"So he stays on top of our suspect list?"

"He stays."

I took one last sip of beer. "What do you say we head home?"

Tuesday, November 29th

There was a buzz of excitement in the air as we went about our morning routine that day. The big cooler was operational, the fluorescent lights were new and bright, we had a stock of fresh flowers, and Crystal was coming to select her wedding flowers. My fingers were crossed that she remembered setting the date.

Around nine-thirty I heard, "Good morning, Abigail," and looked around to see my mother come through the purple curtain into the workroom. "I've brought more plaques. Hello, Rosa." She put a shopping bag on the floor and smiled. "May I say how pretty Bloomers looks today?"

I gave her a hug. "Thanks, Mom. We're back in business."

"That's wonderful!"

I kept glancing at the curtain, waiting for Lottie to announce that Crystal had arrived.

"What do you keep looking at?" Mom asked.

"Crystal McMahon is supposed to be here for a wedding consultation at ten o'clock."

My mom checked her watch. "You've got fifteen minutes. Relax."

Easier said than done. What if Crystal didn't even remember our conversation? Or maybe once she'd sobered up, she'd reconsidered.

"*Respira,* Abby," Rosa said.

I shrugged. "I don't know what that means."

"It means to breathe," she answered.

My mom dug through her bag and removed a plaque. "Here you go. I made this one for you."

I read it aloud: "Be strong; be fearless; be beautiful. And believe that anything is possible when you have the right people there to support you." I blinked tears out of my eyes. "It's perfect, Mom."

"Let's hang it up," Lottie said. "It would look great behind the cash counter. There's a hammer and box of nails in the cabinet back here.

Accompanied by Lottie and my mom, I took the plaque out to the shop and held it against the wall behind the counter.

"It even has a yellow background," Mom said.

As Lottie hammered a nail into the wall, Mom glanced around to make sure the pair of customers in the shop wasn't too close, then asked in a whisper, "Any new developments in the murder investigation?"

"I think we've narrowed it down to Arthur's kids," I answered quietly.

"Including Crystal?"

"We can't rule her out yet," I said, "which leaves me in a sticky situation. I don't want to question her about the murder for fear that she'll get angry and take her business elsewhere."

"And if she is the killer?" Mom asked,

I had no answer.

"Just concentrate on the wedding flowers and let Marco interview Crystal if necessary," Mom suggested.

"Good idea." I caught sight of Crystal walking past the bay window. "Here she is now."

Lottie immediately began to move the arrangements around in the window to look busy, and my mom pretended to shop the selection of gifts in the big oak glass cabinet. Crystal walked in, glanced around, saw me standing behind the counter, and announced loudly, "Here I am."

Customers in the coffee and tea parlor looked around.

I gathered up the two big wedding planners and said, "Let's go into the parlor."

We sat in the back near the coffee counter, where I opened one of the large books and swiveled it for her to see. "Let's look at some ideas I found for you."

Crystal held up a finger and pulled her phone out of her purse, reading something on the screen that appeared to be a text. She replied and then put down her phone with an annoyed sigh. "Birch is driving me crazy."

"How so?"

She rolled her eyes. "He's upset about the private detective we hired. I told you about that, didn't I?"

I was trying to follow my mother's advice, so I said, "I don't believe you did. If you take a look at this page, you'll see several different arrangements for –"

Another text dinged. She picked up her phone and spoke out loud as she typed. "If you don't have anything to hide, you don't have to worry." She put down her phone, shaking her head. "You have to wonder why he's so nervous. Right?"

Of course I thought she was right! But once again, I didn't want to say anything. I cleared my throat, smiled, and nodded. I turned the page for her and pointed to a very pricey selection. "Here's another idea I thought you'd want to see."

"And then there's Rowell," she continued, barely glancing down at the book. "Oh. My. God. All he cares about is money. He calls the estate manager every day."

I tried to focus on the task at hand, but inside my head, questions were buzzing. Was Crystal telling the truth? Was Rowell truly desperate for money? Was he in debt or just greedy? And had his desperation been enough to make him kill his father? "What did you say your colors were?"

"Navy and cream." Crystal's phone dinged once again. "Oh, for crying out loud!" She picked it up and read the long text. She typed in a reply and shook her head. "Now Birch is worried because the camera inside the realty office was broken."

"Why does that worry him?"

"Because Detective Corbison questioned him about it. Birch thinks the detective believes one of us disabled the camera."

"Does Birch have a key to the office?"

"Both my brothers do." She sat back, "Why do you look so surprised?"

"It's . . . it's just that . . ." I stammered, searching for a reason "Birch wasn't involved in the realty business, was he?"

"No, but he used to do small repair jobs around the office."

There went my theory about Birch. "I can see how having a key would make your brothers look guilty," I said. "Does anyone else have a key?"

"Grant Starling," she replied.

"But you don't?"

"I never went into the building when my dad wasn't there." Crystal cocked her head and looked at me quizzically. "Birch told me you're a private eye. Is that true?"

"I'm a part-time private eye."

"You were asking him questions about my dad's murder, too. Are you investigating us?"

Oops. I thought I was being careful. "My husband and I *were* investigating because he was a suspect and we wanted to clear him, which we did."

"Then you're not investigating anymore?"

How was I to get around that one? "I'm focusing on my flower shop business right now." Which, at that very moment, was the truth.

She offered a sly smile. "That's too bad because I was going to tell you who I think killed my dad."

I wanted to cry.

"Aren't you the least bit curious?"

My curiosity was killing me, but I held back because it felt like she had something up her sleeve.

"Okay, listen," she started anyway, "I put the clues together just like a detective. And you know what I came up with?"

I was prepared for her to tell me Honey was the guilty one. Instead, she leaned in and said in a whisper, "I think it was one of my brothers."

I forcibly kept my mouth from dropping open. Was she actually pointing her finger at her brothers? It took all my strength to say very calmly, "Why do you think that?"

"Because they both have a key to the office, and they would've known about the security camera. And if you think about it, either one of them could've grabbed a steak knife from the restaurant."

Including you! I wanted to say, but instead, I asked, "Why would either one want your father dead?"

"Well, duh. Isn't it always about money?"

What was her game? "Why are you telling me this?"

Crystal glanced around the room to be sure no one was eavesdropping. "If one of my brothers is guilty, then we won't have to split the inheritance three ways." And then she laughed.

Was she pulling my leg? Or was she so money-hungry that she was willing to throw her brothers under the bus? My gut feeling about her was all over the place.

"So where are we on these wedding flowers?" she asked, as though our previous conversation was already forgotten. She flipped through pages in the open wedding planner and began to point out the arrangements she liked. I drew in a deep breath and started writing down her selections.

Half an hour later, Crystal closed the planner and smiled. "I think that should do it."

"You've made excellent choices," I told her.

"Thanks. I think so, too. And you'll have everything ready by Saturday morning?"

"Guaranteed."

"Perfect." Crystal stood and grabbed her purse from the back of her chair. She pulled out an envelope full of money and set it on the counter. "Here is a generous deposit to get you started. And just in case you change your mind about investigating my father's murder, Rowell has an office at the business center on Washington Street, and Birch is usually at the auto shop on Lincoln."

"You really think one of them did it?"

"Let's just say, I'll pay you double for your floral services if you can prove one of them did." She gave me a wink and walked out of the parlor.

CHAPTER EIGHTEEN

"She dropped all these hints about one of her brothers being the murderer, then she offered to pay me double if it's true. She's playing me, Marco."

I'd met my husband at noon, taking seats in our favorite booth in the back corner, Marco with a beer and me with a glass of iced tea. We'd given Gert our orders before I began filling Marco in.

He finished his sip of beer and put his glass down. "Why would she be playing you?"

"Maybe to keep herself from being a suspect?"

"Let's work it out," he replied.

Okay," I said. "One theory is that Crystal actually believes that one of her brothers is guilty."

"Based on what?"

"Based on the broken camera, the key, and the money motive. You know, when I first met her, I overheard her joking with Rowell that she thought Birch had done it. Maybe it wasn't a joke." I took a sip of tea, thinking. "But like I said, maybe Crystal has an ulterior motive for telling me all of that. Either way, she's using me. She offered to double my fee if we found out that one of her brothers is guilty. She wants her dad's money, as much as she can get, and she obviously doesn't care what happens to her brothers."

"Well, the good news is that you got her business."

"Yes, but I feel like I made a deal with the devil."

"The wedding will be here before you know it. Just focus on that for the time being."

"Once I place an order for the wedding flowers, there won't be anything else to do until Friday, and then it'll be all hands on deck. I'm even going to ask Jillian to come in to help. But in the meantime, I think we need to interview Birch McMahon. I'm very interested to hear what he has to say about his movements after he left Adagio's."

I paused as Gert brought our lunches to us.

"Thanks," Marco said to her, then picked up his sandwich. "Any ideas on how to get Birch to talk to us?"

"I could tell him about the eye-witness who saw him leave through the back door."

Marco thought for a moment. "That might get him talking."

"Crystal said he hangs out at the auto shop on Lincoln. I know you'll be busy, so why I don't go see him after work tonight?"

"As long as it's not another date."

❧ ❦

By the time I got back to Bloomers, more orders had come in, so Rosa set to work on them while I sat at the computer to place a huge order for Crystal's wedding flowers. At two o'clock, just as I was finishing up a birthday bouquet, Grace came back to the workroom carrying two cups of hot chamomile tea.

"I thought you could use a break," she said and set the cups on the table.

"Thanks, Grace." I put down my rose clippers and picked up a cup to take a drink.

244

Grace pulled back the curtain to leave and immediately stepped back. "Oh, good heavens."

"What is it?" I asked in alarm.

"That horrible Patrice Englund. I can see her across the street. She's coming this way and she doesn't look happy."

"She came all the way here from Dora's Discount Center?" Rosa asked.

"That's not good." I put down the teacup and headed out to the sales floor. "Lottie?"

Lottie stood near the register, watching out the window with her arms crossed. "I see her."

Grace, Rosa, and I formed a semi-circle behind Lottie as Patrice entered. She flung the door open and slammed it behind her, and as she did, the bell above the door once again came unfastened and fell directly on top of her head. She stopped cold, conjuring a contorted, utterly baffled look on her face as the bell landed on the floor with a loud, merry, jingle.

The four of us tried to hide our smiles, but Rosa busted first, letting out a sharp laughing snort, which caused Patrice's face to flush hotly. She wore her customary red, this time a red jacket with blue jeans, her dyed-blond hair pulled back tightly behind her head. She pointed her finger at Lottie, squinted her eyes, and snarled, "You."

"We don't want any trouble, Patrice," I interrupted. "Whatever you have to say, say it to me."

"And *you!*" she cried, causing customers in the coffee and tea parlor to look our way. "You stole my business!"

"What are you talking about?" I asked her.

"You know exactly what I'm talking about," she shouted. "Crystal McMahon's wedding!"

"I can't help it if Crystal prefers quality arrangements for her special day," I replied calmly.

"You undercut me! How could you stoop so low?"

"You shouldn't talk about undercutting, Patrice," Lottie said. "Your prices are set to deliberately undercut our business."

"It's a discount center," Patrice hissed. "What do you expect?"

"A little civility," Grace replied. "As William of Wykeham said, 'Manners maketh man.' You'd be wise to remember that."

"Well, I'm going to counter your prices," Patrice snarled. "We'll see who Crystal chooses then!"

"She's already made her choice," I said. "She's even selected her flowers."

Patrice closed her hands into fists at her sides. "You'll regret this. Your little shop can't begin to compete with mine. I'll show you."

"And I'll show you the door," Lottie said. She stepped up to the yellow frame door and opened it. "Don't let the bell hit you on the way out."

Patrice looked from me to Grace to Rosa and finally to Lottie. She turned stiffly and marched out the door without a backward glance.

"Well," I said, "that was . . . fun."

"Did you see her face when the bell dropped on her head?" Rosa chortled.

"It won't be funny when she hires a lawyer," I countered. "And what happens if she keeps lowering her prices?"

"I wouldn't worry about Patrice," Lottie said. "She can't cut her prices any farther than she has already, or she won't make a profit."

"The quality of her flowers is poor," Rosa said. "She can't fool people more than once."

"We shall persevere," Grace said. "We have a wonderful reputation."

I laughed. "She's going to put herself out of business trying to put *us* out of business."

There was a moment of silence, each thinking our own thoughts. I picked the bell up from the floor and handed it to Lottie. Then we all moved at once, Grace to the parlor, Lottie to the cash counter, and Rosa and I back to the workroom. And so our afternoon continued.

Shortly before closing, Jillian came through the curtain carrying her guitar case. "Guess what?" she said, setting the case on the floor and sliding onto a wooden stool.

"I don't know. What?" I responded.

"I've written a song that I think people at Down the Hatch will love. Want to hear it?"

"Do I have a choice?"

"Nope." She slid off the stool, opened the guitar case, and removed the shiny brown instrument. She climbed back onto the stool and rested the guitar on her knees, where she began to strum it and sing.

Home is never far away.
Home is where you want to stay.
Home is one great place to play.
It's where you'll find me day to day.
Down the Hatch is like a home.
Never far away you'll roam.

I sat there listening in complete and utter astonishment. Jillian had come a long way. She strummed the strings gently and with better precision. The tone of her voice was warm, and her pitch was nearly perfected. I found myself smiling and tapping my toe as she continued.

So pour a beer and taste the foam.
You'll be happy till you're dead in your tomb.

She gave the guitar one last strum and looked at me with a big smile. "Well?"

My smile dissolved. I had no words to express my confusion. I glanced at Rosa who raised her eyebrows. I searched for something positive to say but nothing was coming to me. I finally said, "Tomb doesn't rhyme with foam."

"I know, but I couldn't think of anything else. Plus, it's about the message."

"*Death?* Why would you want to sing about death?"

Jillian frowned and began to pack away her guitar. "The entire song is about life except for the *last line*. Why do you have to focus on that?"

"Because it's the last line! It's what people will remember. The song was wonderful up until that point. I'm sorry, Jillian, but you'll have to come up with a better ending. Marco is not going to let you play that at the bar."

"But the ending is the hardest part!" With a huff, she slid off the stool and stormed out.

"Well," Rosa said, "that was . . ."

"A song about drinking yourself to death," I said.

Rosa went back to arranging the lilies. "The melody was nice."

I spent the rest of the afternoon in the back room working on orders with Rosa. The coffee and tea parlor was hopping; we had customers in the shop all morning; and a flock of orders had come in for a funeral, keeping all four of us busy.

Everything was going well. Business had picked up. Marco and I were close to solving the case. I felt good for the first time since we'd come home from Key West – and suddenly that started to worry me. I thought back to my meeting with Crystal and a knot formed in my stomach. Something felt off. Marco and I had narrowed down our suspect list to Arthur's children, which I had been so sure about from the very beginning, so why was I starting to doubt myself?

Could it be agoraphobia? Had my mom been right all along? Or was it the packet of cash Crystal had given me that felt more like a bribe than a deposit? I'd gone back and forth in my mind for almost two hours. Did she really think one of her brothers was a murderer or was she playing me for a fool? There was no doubt in my mind that Rowell was a top suspect, but was Birch capable of killing his father?

There was only one way to find out.

I looked at the clock. Bloomers closed in one hour. I grabbed my coat and purse and asked Rosa to finish up the last two orders.

"Where are you going?" she asked.

"I have one last interview," I told her. "I'll be back in time to close up shop."

◆8 8◆

The auto body shop was seven blocks up Lincoln Street, so it didn't take long to make the drive there. I parked in the lot alongside the shop and went inside through an open bay door. At the rear of the shop, I could see Birch standing in front of a vintage Chevy Corvair, its hood raised.

"Birch," I called, as I walked toward him.

He looked over the hood with a smile and stared for a moment before recognizing me. His smile froze and his eyebrows lowered. "Abby. What are you doing here?"

"I came to see you. Your sister said you worked here."

Birch came around the driver's side, holding a large solid steel wrench in his hand. "I don't work here. I'm the new owner."

"You bought the place?"

He walked toward me slowly. His long, straggly hair was loose on his shoulder, and there was grease on

249

his hands and clothes. "I love working on cars. What can I say?"

I looked around and noticed that the shop was empty. "I don't know if you've heard or not," I said, "but Honey Chen was arrested for your father's murder yesterday."

"Then why are you here?" He took a step closer. "To humiliate me again?"

I backed up. "Stay right there."

He stopped in place and dropped his head, chuckling to himself. "Why? Now you think I'm a murderer?" He set the wrench down in a large, red toolbox, and sat on a stool at his workbench. "Please leave, Abby. One embarrassment is enough."

"I didn't mean to humiliate you or embarrass you. I'm sorry."

"Then what do you want?"

"I just want to ask you a few questions."

He looked at me with narrowed eyes. "Why?"

"We're still investigating," I replied. "We'd like to eliminate you as a suspect."

"I've been cleared by the police, so what could you possibly have to ask me?"

"I want to know where you went after you left Adagio's."

"I went home."

"Do you have anyone who can verify that?"

"I don't know. Probably not."

"I spoke with a waiter at the restaurant. He said you left out the back door."

"I took a cab home."

"But there's no proof," I said.

"Then call the cab company. Or even better, ask Grant Starling. He was there."

My eyes widened in surprise. "Grant Starling was at Adagio's?"

"Sitting at the bar with his wife," Birch replied. "After my family left the restaurant, I sat at the bar with them and had a few drinks. A few too many, to be honest."

"Then Grant and his wife were still at Adagio's when you left," I clarified.

"Yes. They helped me out to the cab."

"Did they go back inside?"

He shrugged. "I have no idea."

"Okay, Birch," I said. "That's all I needed. Thanks for your cooperation."

"Yeah." He stood up and walked back to the Chevy. "Whatever."

❧ ☙

By the time I got back to Bloomers, it was nearly closing time. Since there were no customers, I told the ladies to go home and that I'd close up. I turned off the lights and went into the workroom to shut off the computer. Then I phoned my husband.

"Grant didn't tell us the whole truth," I told him. "He said he had dinner with a business client and then watched television with his wife the night of the murder."

"He wasn't lying."

"Yes, he was. Birch said that Grant and his wife helped him out to the cab, which means he wasn't at dinner with a business client."

"How would Birch know the difference? Maybe he assumed the client was his wife."

"But why wouldn't Grant have mentioned Adagio's?" I replied.

Marco cleared his throat. "I don't know."

"That makes him look very guilty, Marco."

"Or very worried that he'll look guilty."

"Marco, come on. Grant lied about being downtown the night of the murder. We didn't see him on the security camera from Adagio's, which means he and his wife left out the back door with Birch."

"Why didn't we see him enter the restaurant?"

"Because we weren't watching for Grant. I'll bet if we search that footage, we'll see him."

"What about the fingerprints on the murder weapon? How would he have gotten Honey's steak knife?"

"I don't know, but he had a key to the building. He could've easily come in through the back door. Devona said that she thought Grant Starling was in his office that night. Don't you want to know what he was to say about all this?"

"Why don't I ask him? He should be here any minute."

"What are you talking about?"

"I got a text message from Grant saying that he had the perfect property for my bar. I'm waiting for him now."

"Are you kidding me? You can't meet him alone. Tell me where you are. I'll meet you there."

"Abby, it's all the way across town."

"Please, Marco. Just wait for me there. I'll meet you as soon as I close up the shop. What's the address?"

"Twenty-two eighteen Baker Street."

"I'll see you shortly."

I pulled my purse off the back of the computer chair and slid my phone inside. There was no way I was going to let Marco meet that man by himself, not after he lied to both of us about being downtown the night of the murder. I raced out front with keys in hand, and there stood Grant Starling blocking the exit.

CHAPTER NINETEEN

Grant stood in the doorway, his jacket collar pulled up around his neck. I hadn't heard him enter because we hadn't yet fixed the bell above the door. He moved closer and I instantly stepped back toward the purple curtain, ready to flee.

"What are you doing here?" I asked. I tried to sound casual, but the words came out shaky and uncertain.

Grant gave me a cagey smile. "What do you think I'm doing here?" He took a step closer.

I took another step back, wondering whether I could make it to the back door before Grant could grab me. Then I watched as he pulled open his jacket.

"Stop right there."

He retrieved a wallet from an inside pocket. "I'd like a dozen roses, please."

I stood frozen in place, his words not making sense.

"Red roses, if you have them."

I simply stared at him, my body still in fight-or-flight mode. Grant stood at the register patiently watching me, his credit card at the ready.

I swallowed. "You . . . you want flowers?"

"Of course. Why else would I be here?"

I tried once again to sound casual, but my voice came out strained. "You said roses?"

"Yes, and I'm sorry. I can see you're closing, but it's kind of an emergency."

"I thought you were meeting Marco."

Grant looked at me in surprise. "What?"

"You didn't text Marco and ask him to meet you at Baker Street?"

"No, I didn't, Abby. What's going on?"

"Marco told me that you texted him. You wanted to show him a property."

"I couldn't have texted him. I lost my phone today. And believe me, my wife is going to kill me when she finds out. The phone was a birthday present. That's why I need flowers. To smooth things over."

"But someone texted Marco from your phone."

"I can assure you that it wasn't me."

I pulled up my text message from Marco and showed the address to Grant. "Someone sent this to him."

He tapped on the screen. "I know where that is. That's one of the properties I inherited from Arthur. It's just south of the New Chapel University campus. I don't know why Marco would want to set up a bar out there. It's kind of deserted."

"One of the properties you inherited? I thought Rowell got the properties."

Grant nodded. "He got all the properties downtown. The good ones. I got everything else."

"Wait a second, Grant. When did you lose your phone?"

"I had it this morning when I came into the office. I lost it sometime after that."

"Did anyone else come to the office today?"

Grant shook his head, but stopped and said, "Just Rowell."

With a feeling of dread, I set the phone on the counter. Rowell had sent the message. Marco was in danger.

&3 8&

When Marco didn't answer his phone, I left Grant standing at the counter and ran out the front door. I fumbled through my purse, searching for my keys, only to realize that I'd been holding them in my other hand. I tried to call Marco again with no luck. I tried a third time, leaving a rushed message explaining the situation. When I reached my car, I unlocked the door with shaking hands and slid inside, slamming the keys into the ignition. I put the car in *Drive* and pulled into the street without looking.

A car swerved around me and laid on the horn, bringing me to an instant stop, physically and mentally. What was I doing? What was my plan? I couldn't very well rush into a strange building and put myself in danger, too, although that was my first instinct. Instead, I checked my mirrors and drove on, making sure I was stopped safely at a traffic light before making my next call.

"Reilly, thank God you answered. Marco is in trouble. He's somewhere on Baker Street. An abandoned building south of the campus. Let me look up the address."

"Woah there. Calm down and start again. Where's Marco?"

"Hold on. I'm looking it up now. Twenty-two eighteen Baker Street."

"What kind of trouble?"

"He's in danger, Reilly. He's not answering his phone. I'm on my way there right now. Can you meet me?"

"I'll head that way, but I need an explanation. What's going on?"

My voice was high and rushed. "Rowell McMahon killed his father and now he's after Marco. How far away are you?"

"I'm fifteen minutes out. Are you sure about this?"

"I'm positive. Please hurry."

"Abby, calm down and talk to me. How do you know Rowell killed Arthur?"

The light turned green, and I proceeded forward. The traffic through town was heavier than normal, causing my hands to grip the wheel in frustration every time I had to stop. My thoughts were racing and my heart was pounding, but Reilly's words eventually registered. How did I know that Rowell was the killer? How could I explain it?

"Rowell planned it all out," I finally said. "He must've been planning it for days, just after he learned of Arthur's decision to change his will. Marco was right, and now he's walking into a trap."

"Slow down," Reilly said in a calming voice. "Tell me how you know he's the killer."

I inhaled deeply and tried to slow down my thoughts. "Because we have the evidence. We know he left the restaurant that night and went to the bowling alley. That was his alibi, but he didn't stay there all night."

"Do you have proof?"

"We have someone matching his description on security cam the night of the murder. He has a key to the realty building. He entered the back door and waited for his father to be alone."

"I meant proof that he's the killer."

"I can't explain it right now."

"What about the murder weapon?" Reilly asked. "How can you explain Honey's fingerprints on the knife?"

I searched my mind for an answer. How did Rowell get Honey's steak knife without leaving his own prints? He had to have been wearing gloves or using a handkerchief or some kind of napkin when he grabbed it.

And then it came to me.

"Rowell used a napkin, Reilly."

"A napkin? How do you know?"

"I saw a maroon cloth napkin on Rowell's office desk. It was the same napkin they use at Adagio's. I knew it looked familiar, but I didn't put it together until now. Rowell used the cloth napkin from the restaurant to swipe Honey's knife from the table."

"How do you know Rowell is planning to harm Marco?"

"I just know, Reilly. How long until you can meet me?"

"I'm about ten minutes out."

With Reilly still on the phone, I pulled up in front of the one-story red brick building at 2218 Baker Street. It looked like it could have been a diner at one point, but now it was run down, with most of the windows boarded up.

"I see Marco's car. He's parked in the alley between two buildings."

"Do you see any other cars?" Reilly asked.

"No. No cars. No people. Nothing."

A cold breeze blew down the sidewalk as I exited the car, rustling the empty branches and leaves on the street. I approached Marco's Prius parked in an alley on the side of the building, so I walked up the alley and looked inside. The car was empty.

"He's already inside the building. I'm going in."

"Don't enter that building," Reilly demanded. "Do you hear me, Abby? I've called for backup. You wait until we show up."

"I need to call Marco again. I have to let you go."

"Abby, did you hear me? Do *not* go into that building alone."

"I heard you. Just please hurry."

I ended the call and tried Marco's number, and again, no response.

I paced back and forth on the sidewalk, scanning my surroundings. Next door was a building that looked like it could've been a drugstore, with a storefront full of windows. Across the street was an old butcher shop, and further down was a pizza parlor that looked like it had been closed for decades. The area had been completely deserted. The sidewalks were cracked and overgrown with weeds.

I approached Marco's car in the alley and checked for signs of a struggle. At the driver's side door, I could see his footprints in the gravel, but there was no indication of foul play. The footprints led to the sidewalk, and from there I lost his trail. I could only assume Marco had gone inside without provocation.

The windows in the diner were covered over with faded newspaper. I listened at the door but could only hear the occasional gust of cold wind blowing through the large oak trees behind me. My adrenaline was still pumping, but my skin began to tingle against the cold air. I checked my phone. Nothing. I called Marco. No answer.

"Marco," I called through the glass pane. "Are you in there?"

I listened for a long moment. In the distance, I could hear the bells start to ring out at the railroad crossing a few blocks away. Then my phone signaled an incoming message. It was Marco's ringtone and my heart nearly stopped when I recognized it. I read the message quickly. Then I read it again.

When will you be here, Sunshine?

Did he not just hear my calls? I typed back a quick response. *I'm here. Where are you?*

I'm across the street. Grant sent the wrong address.

Except it wasn't Grant who had sent it. I quickly typed a response: *Marco, get out of there. It's a trap.*

I watched my phone, waiting for his answer. I called him again, waiting still. Another burst of wind sent shivers up my arms, and my inner radar went on high alert. Why wasn't Marco responding? Was it even Marco that was writing the messages?

I made my way across the street, studying the building in front of me. The once-white facade was faded and peeling. The trim around the large windows had cracked and the glass front door was crusted with grime. A large sign above the windows read MEAT MART in faded lettering.

I stood in front of the plate glass window just steps from the front door and cupped my hands around the dirty glass. The lights were off, but I could see a long white counter topping a glass-fronted display case. A bulky register sat at one end of the counter, with debris from a drooping ceiling scattered around the checkered floor. Behind the register was a door with a small rectangular window leading to a back room.

Another text came through. *Come on in. The door is open.*

I caught a brief flash of movement through the glass, but when I peered in, I saw nothing. In the distance, the signal at the railroad crossing blared out its alarm. The train was approaching, and still no cops in sight.

Then I looked down at the phone in my hand while another message was being written.

Sunshine, I'm waiting.

Then I knew for certain that Rowell had Marco's phone. That was not how my husband talked. Rowell was leading me inside. He was waiting for me, but where was Marco?

"Marco?" I called loudly. "Can you hear me?" I waited for an answer, but none came. "Marco," I shouted. "Where are you?"

My phone dinged again. *I'm inside. Phone is broken.*

It was clear that Rowell was trying to trap me, which meant Marco was incapacitated – or worse. My stomach dropped. Desperate, I glanced around for the police, then ran to the door and pounded on it. "Rowell! I know you're in there! The police are on their way. Let Marco go before it's too late."

I listened hard. The sound of the train was now pulsing steadily, sending a rhythmic echo throughout the empty streets around me, but no response from inside. I raised my hand to pound on the door again but stopped. I heard a loud bang come from around the side of the building. Had my threat worked? I walked to the corner and peeked around slowly. "Marco?" I called loudly. "Are you there?"

No one answered and nothing looked out of the ordinary.

I slipped my phone into my purse and continued up the alley. At the rear corner of the building, I peered around to see a metal door flanked by a row of dumpsters. I walked up to the door and tugged on the handle, but the door wouldn't budge.

I cupped my hands around my eyes and looked through a small glass window into what appeared to be a meat processing room with different stations for hanging and cutting meat. Old, rusty, metal hooks hung from the ceiling, while rows of sinks and basins lined the far wall. The only light came from the opposite corner, shining through a rectangular window in the door separating the processing room from the sales floor.

Before I could step back, the door flew open with a crash, sending me sprawling backward onto the gravel in the alley. Rowell's massive figure appeared above me, lunging for me before I had time to scramble away. I struggled to get loose, but his massive arms surrounded me. "You won't get away with this," I gasped.

"The hell I won't."

I fought violently, but I was no match for Rowell's strength. He dragged me inside and slammed the heavy door shut behind us. He gave me a hard shove, and I fell onto my hands and knees, shooting pain radiating up my arms. I took in my surroundings as quickly as I could, looking for a way to escape.

Before I could get to my feet, Rowell grabbed my arm and dragged me across the hard, dusty linoleum floor. I had little time to think. There was nothing near enough to grab, no sharp objects or pieces of debris to use as self-defense. I held onto one of the aluminum table legs but the table just scraped against the floor until my grip gave out.

As we passed into another room, I clung to the doorframe, holding on as tightly as I could, but one powerful tug pulled my fingers loose. I tried to kick free as Rowell spun me around and forced me through a wide doorway, but another mighty push had me back on my hands and knees.

I heard Rowell's heavy breathing behind me. He then spoke in a low growl, "I'll be back for you."

The door closed. I heard a latch. And then there was nothing but darkness and silence.

CHAPTER TWENTY

I lay on my back as I caught my breath, feeling the pain in my knees and hands, my chest heaving up and down. The room was completely dark and eerily quiet. My fingers tingled as I reached into my purse for my phone. Luckily, my purse had been secured around my neck, so I hadn't lost it in the struggle. I turned the phone's flashlight on and shined it toward the door.

I immediately recognized the locking mechanism, very similar to the lock on the inside of Bloomer's flower coolers. I shined the light on the walls and felt a twinge of panic as I realized I was inside an old, airtight meat locker. Luckily, the freezer was no longer operational, but that wasn't the worst of my problems.

I heard moaning behind me and shined the light quickly, revealing a sight that turned my stomach upside down. Marco lay on his side in a puddle of dark red blood. I scrambled over to him, shining the light on his face. His eyes were closed, mouth was open, with a gaping wound on his forehead.

"Marco," I said in a shaking voice. "Marco, can you hear me?"

He responded with a slight groan. Thank God he was alive.

I shined the light in his eyes, and they fluttered briefly. "Marco, wake up."

He didn't answer. With eyes closed, he lay still. I felt his pulse. It was still strong. The wound on his forehead wasn't deep, but it was bleeding profusely. The area around the wound was already bruised and swollen, causing my panic level to increase significantly. It looked as though Rowell had used a heavy object to knock Marco out. He must've surprised him as he did me because Marco wouldn't have gone down without a fight.

I dug in my purse for a package of tissues, pulling several out with trembling fingers. I pressed the tissues against Marco's wound, hoping to staunch the bleeding. Then I tried calling 911 but had no signal.

I sat down next to my husband, holding his hand and reassuring him that everything would be fine. But deep down I knew we were in trouble. Rowell had this all planned out –
first using Grant's phone to lead us to an abandoned property, then leaving us locked up in the freezer to suffocate. And once our bodies were found, Grant would take the fall, and Rowell would be in the clear.

But would Rowell leave anything to chance? Would he leave us alive? Probably not now. He said he'd be back for me, maybe thinking that Marco was already dead. I'd made a mistake by telling Rowell the police were on their way because all that did was force his hand. Now he didn't have a choice but to make sure we were dead before the police arrived.

I couldn't let that happen. I had to come up with a plan of my own. I looked around, realizing that the only way out was to get around Rowell once he opened the door. But how would I get Rowell to come inside the freezer? How could I convince him? What would it take to manipulate a know-it-all blowhard?

Marco lifted his head and groaned. I shined my light so I could see his face and he squinted up at me. "Abby?"

I held his hand, squeezing it tightly. "I'm here, Marco. Try not to move."

"What happened?" He shut his eyes and lay his head back on the floor.

"Marco," I said softly. "Marco, listen to me. Rowell has us trapped in a freezer. He's going to be back any minute."

"Rowell?" he asked as though confused.

"Marco, the police are on their way. I just have to let them know where we are. When Rowell comes back, I'm going to try to get around him and get out of this meat locker. I think I can make it to the back door before he catches me."

"Wait for the police," Marco said. "Try to stall him."

"The police are searching the wrong building," I explained. "I don't have a choice. When Rowell comes back, I'm making a run for it."

He gave a brief nod as though he understood.

"But I'm worried about you. I'm afraid to leave you alone with Rowell."

"Don't worry about me. Just get out." With that Marco rested his head and closed his eyes.

I checked his wound again and found that the bleeding had not stopped. I needed an ambulance. I tried to dial 911 again, but it was no use. I hurried to the metal door and examined the frame. It was sealed tightly, the lock engaged from the outside, leaving me no way to free us. I held my phone up toward the ceiling and found a faint signal. I tried Reilly, and when he answered, I was practically crying.

"I can hardly . . . you, Abby," Reilly responded, his words breaking up.

"Reilly," I shouted. "We're across the street. Rowell has us trapped and Marco needs an ambulance."

"Abby?" I heard him call. "Can you hear me? Officers are at the scene. I'm almost there."

I shouted louder. "Reilly!"

Suddenly the freezer door was flung open in front of me, causing me to back up in fright as Rowell's portly figure loomed over me.

He held out his hand. "Give me your phone."

I backed up until I reached Marco, feeling his legs behind me. "If you're smart," I said, trying to sound brave, "you'll leave now before the police get here."

His chiding laugh echoed ominously inside the empty freezer. "The police are already here. But as you know, they're not looking in the right spot."

"Then you don't have much time," I told him. "You better leave before they start searching all the buildings."

He took a step inside the freezer door frame. "I have plenty of time."

"They're not just searching for me," I warned him. "I told Sergeant Reilly all about you, and about your plan to frame Honey with her steak knife."

"You spoke with your good old friend Sergeant Reilly." He laughed again. "Must be really nice having friends on the force. Unfortunately, you have no proof that I killed anyone."

"I do have proof. I saw the napkin on your desk. The cloth napkin you used to wrap up her knife. We caught you on a security camera. I figured you out, Rowell. The police will be looking for you now. Killing us won't stop that. You better leave while you can."

He stepped further inside the freezer, careful not to leave space for me to escape. "Throw me the phone," he demanded again.

"You're not getting this phone from me."

He grinned salaciously. "Wanna bet?"

"You're going to have to take it from me."

He took another step. "If you insist."

I held my phone up, turned the flashlight on, and aimed it straight into Rowell's eyes.

He held out his hand to block the light. "Now you're really starting to piss me off."

"Then you know how I feel every time I have to look at your face."

His nostrils flared and he stepped further inside the freezer, still shielding his eyes. "Give me your phone right now."

"Or what?"

"Or your friend Reilly is going to find your lifeless corpse hanging from a meat hook."

I only needed him to take one more step and I could make my move. Just one more step and I would make a run for it.

"That's big talk, Rowell," I chided, "but I shouldn't be surprised. There's nothing little about you."

"Throw the phone!"

"Except maybe your pathetic bowling score."

Rowell rushed deeper into the freezer, baring his teeth, growling in a mad rage. He lunged for me, but I was ready. I stepped aside quickly and made a run for it.

Rowell spun his large body and just barely grabbed the strap of my purse, pulling me backward. I strained at the tension around my neck and tried to push the strap around my head, but Rowell was strong. He tightened his grip on the purse strap and pulled me closer.

"Abby," I heard Marco yell. "Run!"

I turned my head to see Marco reach out his hand and take hold of Rowell's ankle. Rowell let go of me to focus his attention on Marco, and I ran. I was out of the freezer in a moment, making my way down a short hall and into the processing room. I ran straight for the back door only to find it blocked, barred from the inside. I tried the door, but it wouldn't budge. Then I heard the freezer door slam shut with a loud bang.

I searched the room, looking for another way out. The aluminum processing stations were laid out in even, long rows snaking throughout the large room. The only other exit was in the opposite corner, the sales room I'd seen from outside with the deli counter and register. From there I could exit the building, but there was one problem. The door was right next to the hallway where I'd just escaped, and as soon as I started for the door, I heard Rowell's hard footsteps approaching.

I slid down onto my hands and knees, only barely feeling the pain. I could hear Rowell stop once he entered the processing room. His breathing was heavy, as if Marco had given him a good fight. My hero had saved me once again, and now it was up to me to return the favor. My only option was to stay low, be quiet, and keep moving, avoiding Rowell until I was close enough to the door to make my escape.

Rowell's breathing had steadied. Each footstep fell heavily as he made his way across the room toward me. "Abby Knight Salvare." He spoke each word slowly, hatred radiating off every syllable. "You think you figured me out?"

I crawled around the table nearest to me, moving carefully so as not to make a sound.

"The only evidence you have against me is a blurry photo and a napkin. That's not going to stand up in court. It doesn't matter what you told the police now. Once you and Marco are gone, your case goes with it."

I watched him from under one of the processing tables as he approached the back exit. I crawled further away and rounded the corner of the next table.

"Come on out. There's no place to hide." Rowell gave the metal table nearest the exit a hard shove. "You can't escape. I've made all the necessary arrangements, taken all of the greatest precautions." He walked up to the table and lifted it with ease, searching. "Why do you think I sent you to the wrong address? You think I'd give you the chance to mess up my plan?"

Rowell took several loud steps forward. I could hear him scoot another aluminum table away from its position, still searching. I made my way around the next table, trying to get closer to the front door, only to come to a dead end.

I glanced back to see one of Rowell's pant legs from under the tables as he approached. My only move was to climb across a metal shelf under the table standing in my way, but there were several old pans and rusty tools blocking the path.

"I've already won," he continued. "This won't be like our little bowling match. There won't be any ties this time. Do you want to know why? Because I always win."

But Rowell hadn't won. Not yet. I pulled my phone from my pocket and typed a quick message to Reilly, hoping that he would receive it in time.

"When Crystal told me what my dad was planning to do, I had no choice. Honey was a gold digger. She didn't deserve the money."

I carefully removed the items from the shelf that was blocking my path forward, as Rowell continued talking between heaving breaths.

"I had to deal with that horrible excuse of a father my whole life. I went to all the right schools, followed his every instruction, and even then, he didn't trust me. He gave Grant the business. And he would've given Honey the entire trust just to spite me."

I crawled on top of the shelf, the aluminum sheet bending under my weight. Still, I moved forward, placing each hand and knee down with heightened precision.

"So you see? It won't matter what you told the police. All of the evidence in your death will point to Grant, just like all of the evidence in my father's death points to Honey."

The sheet bent sharply, causing a twang to echo throughout the room.

"I hear you," he sang out sadistically. Another loud sound ground out behind me as Rowell pushed away another table. But I had made it to the other side, out of his view.

I was one row away from the exit. I had made it through the room, and now I only had to get around one last table. Then Rowell stopped talking, making it harder to decipher his position. I started to crawl forward, then froze in place. Rowell's legs were directly across from me. He was standing in front of my only escape.

I reached over to quietly pick up a rusty metal spoon on the floor, then threw it in the opposite direction, holding my breath.

Rowell moved toward the sound. "I always win, Abby. It's no different than bowling, really. You and Marco are the only remaining pins to knock down."

I turned toward the door, moving quickly but quietly.

"Honey doesn't get my dad's money," he continued bragging loudly. "Grant doesn't get my dad's business," he yelled, and with a tone that curdled my blood, he screamed, "And you can't stop me!"

I scooted across the floor faster, the doorway just inches away. I heard a table scrape against the floor behind me as I turned the door handle.

Then I heard the table upend and Rowell's ferocious growl. "Now I've got you."

Before he could act, I dashed through the door and scrambled over the deli counter. I fell over onto the checkered floor below. The front door was only a few feet away. As I reached the door, I noticed a padlock had been fastened to the frame. I ran to the window and pounded on the glass. Rowell came from behind and grabbed me, dragging me back with his thick arm around my throat.

"I told you I've taken care of everything. You're trapped. You lost."

I tugged at his arm, unable to speak.

From outside the door, I heard, "New Chapel Police. Back away from the door."

Instantly, he let go and backed up, staring at the door in utter confusion. "No," he shouted frantically. "That's not possible. How did they know you were here?"

I backed up and rubbed my throat, staring at him. "You don't win this time, Rowell. There is one thing you failed to do." I backed away further and reached into my pocket, watching Rowell's jowls drop in utter defeat. I held up the device for him to see. "You never got my phone."

The door came down with a battering ram. Officers flooded the scene, guns drawn, flashlights on. "Show your hands!" one of the officers shouted.

Rowell's hands shot up, the flashlights revealing a wide brow dripping with sweat and an expression of pure terror as the police surrounded him. His arms were pulled behind his back and handcuffs snapped on his wrists.

"I guess it is kind of nice having friends on the force," I said to Rowell as Sergeant Sean Reilly entered last.

Rowell breathed in and out forcefully, staring at me with eyes wide and nostrils flaring. He kept his eyes on me as the police forced him through the front door, never saying a word.

"Are you alright?" Reilly asked as he entered the building.

"I am now, but Marco's hurt. Follow me."

❧ ❦

I sat with my legs hanging out of the passenger seat of Reilly's squad car. He'd put a wool blanket around me and found a pair of gloves and a knit cap to keep me warm. I told him as much as I could remember in the moment, but my mind was on my husband, who was being treated by paramedics in an ambulance nearby.

"I told you not to go inside," Reilly said. "Why don't you ever listen to me?"

"I didn't go inside."

He put his hands on his hips. "Uh-huh."

"Not willfully."

"Sure."

I held my hand up. "I swear."

"Speaking of that, you'll probably have to go to court. Rowell is denying he had anything to do with his father's death."

"He'll never admit to it." I looked over at the squad car where Rowell sat in the back seat. I could just make out his face behind the glass. The whites of his eyes were focused on me, piercing and angry. I stared back, wanting to sneer, but I didn't. We hadn't won yet. I knew that putting him away for life wouldn't be easy. Rowell would make sure of that.

"He's claiming that he was trying to help you tonight," Reilly continued. "He says that Grant told him his plans to kill you and Marco. That's why he showed up here."

"It's obviously a lie."

"I know that, but as of right now, it's your word against his."

"Rowell's story will fall apart," I said, "Just give it time."

"I have no doubt Rowell will be charged with attempted murder but proving his involvement in Arthur's death will be much harder without a confession."

"He confessed it to me. And I'll testify to that."

271

An officer came by and handed Reilly two coffee cups. He gave one to me. "I thought you might need this. It's going to be a long night."

I took the coffee and looked up at him. "You know something, Sean. I'm thankful to have you as a friend."

He took a sip of his steaming drink and shook his head. "Don't get all mushy on me. Thanksgiving is over."

An EMT walked up to let me know that Marco wanted to see me. I thanked Reilly again, even though he pretended not to appreciate it, and made my way over to the ambulance. Marco was resting on a stretcher with a thick bandage wrapped tightly around his forehead. Even in his state, he still looked sexy in his torn shirt and five o'clock shadow. I was also thankful that Marco was going to be okay.

I sat next to him in the ambulance and held his hand. "How are you feeling?"

"My head's going to hurt once these meds wear off, and my ego is a bit bruised. I can't believe I was duped."

"See, I told you not to meet Grant alone."

Marco squeezed my hand. "Very funny, but I was right about Grant."

"You were right about Rowell, too, yet somehow you were duped by both."

"I guess my intuition isn't as strong as yours."

"Intuition? You don't need intuition to tell you that a run-down meat market in an abandoned area might not be the best place for a bar. Didn't you notice something wasn't right?"

"Okay, fine. I wasn't thinking. It's not like me to wander mindlessly into a dangerous situation."

"Thank you."

"That's your job."

I punched him playfully. "Trust me, I would much rather have you save me. It's way less stressful."

"And usually less painful." He touched the gauze wrapped around his forehead. "I never even saw him coming."

I put my arms around my husband. "When I saw you laying there, I thought you were –" I couldn't finish over the lump in my throat.

"I know, Sunshine, and I'm sorry." He pulled me in for a long kiss. I sat with him in the ambulance while the paramedics checked his vitals and bandaged his other minor wounds.

"I'm still heated about Grant Starling," I told Marco once we were alone. "I can't believe he didn't tell us he was at Adagio's with his wife."

"How would Birch know that Grant was with his wife?"

"I don't know. He said that Grant and his wife helped him to the cab. And the waiter at the restaurant confirmed that. He said that Birch was too drunk to walk on his own. He said a man and a blonde woman helped Birch out the back door."

"Oh." Marco put his arm around me. "Now it makes sense."

"What do you mean?"

"Grant's wife," Marco said, thinking.

"What about her?"

"She's not blonde."

❧ ☙

After a while, Sergeant Reilly joined us. "We're going to need a statement from you, Marco, but I want you to spend the night at the hospital. Get some rest and meet me at the station when you're released. You and Abby can both give your statements then."

"I thought we were required to give our statements before we left the scene," I told him.

"Just be happy you have a friend on the force. Goodnight, you two."

CHAPTER TWENTY-ONE

Crystal McMahon's wedding was a huge success. When I'd said I'd need all hands on deck, I hadn't exaggerated. Rosa and Lottie helped out when they could, but Bloomers was finally bustling with winter orders. I'd recruited my mom to help out after she was done teaching for the day, and Jillian too, when she wasn't at her guitar lessons. Marco's mother was happy to help when she could, and even Tara was put to work on the weekend. Thank goodness our coolers were up and running, and the bell above the door was finally secured back in place.

Crystal was an absolute pain in the butt to work with, but it was worth it to see how happy she was with the outcome, not to mention our sizeable profit. The wedding venue was filled to the brim with flowers of every kind, all of them different shades of pastel purple, with cream, gold, and navy accents. Up and down the rows of seats we attached large bouquets of white lilies, all facing the aisle. Behind the altar were large, golden planters filled with lavender lilacs and dark navy peonies, accented with white birch twigs.

The women held a similar bouquet, and for the boutonnieres, the men had a lavender rose wrapped in dark navy lace. The head table featured a centerpiece of roses, spray roses, ranunculus, eucalyptus, dusty miller, and veronicas. Needless to say, Crystal was overjoyed with our work.

She'd even invited me and Marco to attend the reception where I was able to make amends with Birch for my little lunch date scheme. I made friends with some of New Chapel's elite who'd been invited to the reception, and I was able to slip my business card to several interested potential clients.

Marco and I were finally introduced to the groom, a handsome man in his mid-thirties with sparkling eyes, tanned skin, and very little to say – a perfect match for his bride. Jillian was there with her husband, but she spent most of the evening standing near the live band, studying the guitar player. As we were leaving, Crystal had spotted me and ushered me into a corner of the room. What she'd told me next was a game changer.

Saturday, December 10th

One week later, Rafe and I were crouched behind the bar at Down the Hatch. Francesca was seated in the last booth with my mom, and my dad sat at the end of the booth in his wheelchair. The bartender Chris and my favorite server Gert were standing next to the front door, patiently waiting. The entire establishment was dark except for the early afternoon sun streaming in through the front windows, and no one was saying a word.

We heard the keys hit the front lock and I could barely contain my excitement. Marco swung open the door and switched on the lights, at which time we all jumped out and shouted in unison, "Surprise!"

And boy was he surprised. He jumped back, pulling his fists up in Army Ranger combat mode. But he immediately caught himself and relaxed. He smiled as he took in all the familiar faces. Gert and Chris ushered him into the room where Rafe and I were waiting behind the bar.

Marco glanced at me and his smile widened. He pointed at me with a knowing look, the detective in him never at rest. "I knew you were up to something," he said. "What's this all about?"

"We have something very important to share with you," I told him, letting Rafe take the lead.

Rafe came around the bar and put his arm around his brother's shoulder. "Down the Hatch is staying right here."

"You're kidding."

"Congratulations, brother. You get to keep the bar!"

"You kept this from me?" Marco wrapped his brother in a manly hug, clapping his back. "You know how much I hate that."

Rafe laughed and patted Marco's back in return. "It was the least I could do."

Marco turned to me. "And you knew about this? Since when?"

"Since Crystal's reception."

"That was a week ago."

"I wanted to make sure everything was in order before getting your hopes up."

"Care to explain?"

I checked my watch. "Crystal should be here any minute. I'll let her explain."

After a while, Down the Hatch was filled with revelers. Everyone from Devona Esmond to Sergeant Reilly had shown up to congratulate Marco. Even Kenton Lang sat in a shadowy corner of the bar with the collar of his long, green army jacket pulled up to his cheeks. Lottie, Grace, and Rosa came through to offer their well wishes before heading back to Bloomers. Dave Hammond was there, along with several of his associates who were very happy they would still be able to walk over to the bar after work.

Marco tapped a spoon against a glass to gain everyone's attention. "Welcome, everyone," he said, standing behind the long, polished, wood bar, with me at his side. "Belly up to the bar and we'll pour you some champagne so we can toast to our good fortune."

As they lined up, Reilly came up to us, his street clothing a nice contrast to his usual police uniform. He seemed a little shorter and bulkier with his worn sneakers and heavy winter coat, and without his police hat, I could see more white hair showing around his ears. He nudged my arm and leaned across the bar. "How're you doing, kid?"

"Hey, Sean. I'm doing much, *much* better, now."

Reilly looked around the long room with a smile. "The bar wouldn't have been the same in a new home. This place has a certain charisma."

I looked up at the fisherman's netting hanging above our heads and the blue plastic carp above the row of booths. "Is that another word for old and outdated?"

"You know the locals love it," he said. "But that's not what I'd like to talk about."

I poured him a drink. "Please tell me you have news about Rowell McMahon."

He smiled and nodded while I handed him the glass. "As you already know, he's been charged with murder. They've also added a charge of attempted murder for what he did to you and Marco."

"I would hope so."

"His arraignment is next Wednesday. They'll set a trial date then."

"Has he confessed to murdering his dad?"

"Nope. He's still saying Honey Chen did it."

"He confessed to me," I said. "I hope the prosecutors call me in to testify."

"I'm sure they will."

"What's the word?" Marco asked as he finished pouring drinks.

"We were just talking about Rowell," I said. "He's got two charges against him – Murder and attempted murder." I turned to Reilly. "You know, Detective Corbison really missed the mark again. He was certain Honey was the killer. Is he going to drop the charges against her now?"

"He will," Reilly assured. "I believe she's out on bail."

"She is," I said. "She stopped at Bloomers yesterday to tell me, so I invited her here today."

"Be honest," Reilly said to me. "Didn't you have your suspicions about her?"

I shrugged. "At first I did."

"What changed your mind?"

"I don't know. She seemed genuinely distressed, and she was the only person who showed any grief over the loss of Arthur McMahon."

"Are we talking about your investigation?" Dave Hammond said, joining our little group. "You both did a great job. Huge success."

Reilly laughed and sipped his champagne. "I wouldn't classify being trapped in a meat locker as a *huge* success."

"Trapped where?"

"It's a long story, Dave," I said.

"I'd like to hear it someday," he replied. "And by the way, I found out that it was an intern in my office who leaked the information about Arthur's will to Crystal McMahon. The money was simply too tempting. Unfortunately, I had to let her go. Thank you for letting me know."

"All part of the job," I told him. "Maybe you can clear something up for me now."

"I can try."

"Crystal assured me that Marco wasn't going to be evicted," I explained. "She didn't go into the specific circumstances, but I assume it has everything to do with Rowell."

"I can't tell you the specifics either," Dave replied, "but Arthur McMahon did provide for several different scenarios regarding foul play. So, let's just say that Rowell gets nothing."

"And that means that Crystal and Birch get everything," I said.

Dave merely smiled.

"Look who's here," Marco said, pointing toward the door.

I turned to see Honey and Razor standing just inside the doorway and walked across the room to greet them. "Welcome to our party. I'm glad you both could come. Would you like a drink?"

"Yes," Honey answered, "but before we do that, I wanted to thank you again for helping me. After all the grief I gave you, I'm surprised you were still willing to help." As she talked, her eyes misted over. "I almost lost everything. Can I hug you?"

I opened my arms and she walked into them, squeezing tightly. She stepped back with a smile. "You and your husband are amazing."

"Thank you for all you've done for Honey," Razor added.

"No problem, Razor."

Surprisingly, he opened his arms for a hug, too, and just before he released me, he said into my ear, "You can call me Todd."

I laughed as he stepped back. "Thank you. But I kind of like Razor. It suits you now." I smiled at them. "So, what are your plans?"

"Honey moved back in with me," Razor said. "We'll be staying on campus until I finish my master's degree."

She smiled at him. "And I'm going to use some of the insurance money to help clean up Arthur's abandoned properties, bring the area back to life. I'm for *sure* tearing down that butcher shop, and maybe even opening up a boutique hotel in its place. It's been a longtime dream of mine."

"Good for you," I told her. "I wish you the best of luck. Please, go up to the bar and get yourself a complimentary drink."

As they walked away, I turned to see Devona talking to Marco. I walked over to them just as Devona planted a big kiss on Marco's cheek, leaving a bright pink lipstick mark.

"Should I be jealous?" I asked with a smile.

"I was just thanking your husband for clearing my name," Devona said. She shuddered. "I don't ever want to be in that situation again. That detective frightens me."

"He's not here, is he?" Kenton asked, looking around the room.

"Hey there, Kenton," Marco said. "Glad you could join us."

"Lots of strange people here," he said. "I can't stay long, but I wanted to say thanks. Happy the bar's staying and I'm happy to still have a home."

"Me, too," Devona said.

Marco handed them each a glass of champagne. "At least stay for the toast."

Over Marco's shoulder, I saw Crystal walk in and look around. "I'll be right back," I told him.

Crystal reached out for a long, over-the-top, celebratory hug, smothering me in designer cleavage and expensive perfume. "So, this is Marco's bar." She looked around as if she thought the ceiling was going to collapse. "This is what all the fuss was about?"

"People seem to like it."

Crystal pulled out a small bottle of hand sanitizer and used it while she thanked me again for the beautiful wedding flowers. "And I want to apologize for ever doubting you."

"I'm glad you were pleased."

She leaned close to say, "I didn't forget about our deal to double your fee, either."

"That's not necessary," I said.

"No, no. I made a deal, and I meant it. You made my wedding something incredible. But even more importantly, you helped me get half of Rowell's inheritance, and for that, I will be eternally grateful."

"Well, that wasn't why I did it, but –"

"Now listen, I know doubling your fee would be a good deal of money, but I may have another offer you might like even more."

Oh boy. Here we go.

Marco joined us and put his arm around me. "What kind of offer are we talking about?"

She batted her eyelashes at him. "Hello, Marco."

I pulled her back on track. "What's the offer, Crystal?"

"Birch and I have decided to sell this building and we'll let you and your husband have first dibs at it."

I stared at her in surprise. "Really?"

"Thank you," Marco replied, "but I can't afford to buy the building."

"I'll make sure you can," Crystal countered, "Between me, you, and Abby, I'm sure we can work something out."

Marco brightened. "That's very generous of you."

"Perfect," Crystal said. "Now I need something to drink." She started toward the bar but stopped and turned to me. "Speaking of that, I tried some of that bubbly you bought for me."

I inhaled sharply at the thought. I had completely forgotten about the sour champagne I had used to sneak into her bachelorette party. I tried to smile, and with suspiciously raised eyebrows, I asked, "Oh yeah? How'd you like it?"

She threw both hands on my shoulders, "Oh my God. I loved it! But my husband spit it right out. He has terrible taste."

I laughed at the irony of her statement and led her to the bar where Rafe poured her a glass of champagne. I had Rafe give me a glass of Champagne, too, and then Crystal clinked her glass to mine. "Here's to my dad."

"Here's to Arthur," I said.

We both took a drink, then Crystal downed the rest of her glass. "I've got to get going. Our flight leaves in three hours."

"Where are you going?"

"Hawaii," she said. "For the biggest, best honeymoon money can buy."

"I hope you have a great time."

She gave me a wink, but before she could leave, Marco tapped his glass again. He stepped onto a small stool behind the bar so he could speak to everyone and eventually people stopped talking and turned to him. I made my way over to sit with Francesca and Rafe. Gert and Chris stood behind the bar with Marco as he began the toast.

"As you all know, we came close to losing this place. All the tenants of this building came very close to losing their homes. I'd like to thank you all for your support in finding Down the Hatch a new home if it had come to that."

There were several good-natured boos at the mention of relocating the bar.

"I know," Marco said. "I know. That's how I felt about it, too." He looked down at me. "But Abby knew that losing this place would've been hard for me, so I appreciate her help in keeping me focused."

"And for putting my brother in jail!" Crystal cheered.

People laughed and clapped.

"Yes," Marco agreed. "That, too. And for one last thing. Abby, thank you for being my hero this time." He touched his forehead, where a thick bandage covered eight, very nasty-looking stitches. "Thank you for saving my life."

I smiled. He'd already thanked me several times, but it was kind of him to do it publicly. I raised my glass and mouthed the words, "I love you."

He did the same, then continued, "So, here's to the patrons of Down the Hatch."

Reilly raised his glass above everyone's heads. "And here's to Abby and Marco."

At that, everyone cheered and clinked glasses.

I looked around at all the happy faces. Marco, especially, was beaming. I could feel a glow on my own face as well. I'd gotten Crystal's business, and more customers were returning to Bloomers. My staff was happy. Marco's staff was happy. My parents were in good health. And I had a wonderful marriage.

I slid into the booth with my mom and dad. "Should I be worried?" I asked them.

"Worried about what?" my dad asked.

"I'll take this one, Jeffery." My mom reached over the table and grabbed my hands. "Are you worried you'll start getting that feeling again?"

"What feeling?" my dad asked.

"The feeling that something is about to go terribly wrong," I answered.

"Exactly," my mom said. "Agoraphobia. It runs in the family, you know."

My dad, the ultimate pragmatist, shifted his wheelchair closer to the table. "Something will always go wrong eventually. That's just how life works. But it's not what happens that matters, it's how you deal with it. You'll never enjoy the good times if you're always worried about the bad."

"You don't get it, Jeffrey."

He knew better than to push the subject with my mom. "Well, at least we can agree that nothing bad is going to happen today. So let's enjoy ourselves."

As my dad talked, I noticed a long, black guitar case scoot into the booth next to me, followed by my cousin Jillian's smiling face. "I'm here!" she announced, holding up the case.

I looked at my dad. "You were saying?"

"Hi, Aunt Maureen," she sang brightly. "Hi, Uncle Jeffery." She turned to me. "I can't wait for you to hear my new song."

"Jillian," I said, "now may not be the best time – "

"What better time could there be?"

"But we're celebrating Marco getting to keep his bar," I explained. "I'm sure you're not prepared to sing about that."

"Au contraire," she said. "My song is perfect. Just you wait and see." She walked to the back of the bar and took the guitar out of its case. "Attention, everyone. I'd like to play a very special song I wrote."

A murmuring went through the crowd. Marco walked over to me and said, "Is this really going to happen?"

"I promised her she could play," I reminded him.

"And I'm sorry."

Jillian strummed the strings, warming up.

I looked around at all the expectant faces, my stomach pulling itself into knots as she began to sing.

The best thing about love

285

Is that it has no end.
Believe me, my friend.
It takes you round the bend.

She paused to strum a few chords, then began again:

The worst thing about love
Is that it can break your heart.
Your world falls apart.
It spikes off the chart.

She paused again, strumming gently.

But without love
there would be no end to misery.
We all can see
That this can never be.
So trust in me
And love.

She gave the strings a final strum and stopped. She then took a bow at the impressive round of applause she received.

I wiped a tear from my eye as she joined us at the booth. "That was wonderful, Jillian."

"See?" she said. "I told you it'd be perfect."

"You were right. It was perfect."

I'd been wrong about Jillian – wrong to expect the worst. I decided right then and there to stop worrying about the future and try instead to enjoy the present. Around the room, others were talking, smiling, and laughing. The party continued. Life was good.

And for that, I was extremely thankful.

ACKNOWLEDGMENTS

I would first like to thank the readers. The Flower Shop Mysteries have continued – and will continue – because the fans and friends of this series have been so encouraging, engaging, and eager to follow our favorite characters as they develop, grow, and (of course) solve crimes. This is the first full-length book since the series was discontinued by the publisher. I cannot express enough gratitude for the fact that, because of the support from readers, I am able to see Abby and Marco through to the next phase of their lives. And just wait until you see what happens!

I would also like to thank my editor Jason Eberhardt for his expert advice and skill in writing this book. I would like to thank James V. Tsoutsouris for his legal expertise. And as always, I would like to thank my daughter Julia for her encouragement and support.

FLOWER SHOP MYSTERY SERIES

Mum's The Word
Slay It With Flowers
Dearly Depotted
Snipped In The Bud
Acts Of Violets
A Rose From The Dead
Shoots To Kill
Evil In Carnations
Sleeping With Anemone
Dirty Rotten Tendrils
Night Of The Living Dandelion
To Catch A Leaf
Nightshade On Elm Street
Seed No Evil
Throw In The Trowel
A Root Awakening
Florist Grump
Moss Hysteria
Yews With Caution

Missing Under The Mistletoe – Christmas Novella
Tulips Too Late – Spring Novella
A Frond In Need – Summer Novella
Till Death Do Us Pot – Fall Novella

GODDESS OF GREENE ST. MYSTERIES

Statue Of Limitations
A Big Fat Greek Murder
Big Trouble In Little Greektown
Gone But Not For Garden

Continue reading for chapter one –
GONE BUT NOT FOR GARDEN

The Goddess of Greene St. Mysteries
Flower Shop Mystery Crossover

GONE BUT NOT FOR GARDEN

GODDESS OF GREENE ST. MYSTERIES

KATE COLLINS

PROLOGUE

Thursday evening

Mayor Charles E. Sloan strode out onto the stage and took the microphone off its stand. He flashed his pearly white smile and waited for the crowded ballroom to finish their applause. "Thank you, everyone, and welcome to the final night of our Small Business Association fashion show. I see the association chair and coordinator of this event, Fran Decker, standing in the wings. Fran is the owner of Fabulous Fashions. All of her outfits are created by local designers and will be for sale after the show. The proceeds will go to help small businesses all across our fine community, because as you know, nothing is more important to me than keeping Sequoia small. Fran, step out and take a bow for all the hard work you've done.

He waited until the clapping stopped to say, "Folks, we have a great show lined up for you, with summer fashions from some of the best designers in town, and models whom I'm sure you'll recognize. We have Ms. Carly Blackburn, PTA president and campaign coordinator, Mrs. Hope Louvain, the wife of our esteemed Chief of Police Ed Louvain, and my beautiful wife, Eleni Sloan, who can't wait to show you the outfits she's modeling this year.

"To get things started, I'd like to introduce our emcee and fashion consultant from New Chapel, Indiana." He pointed in my direction, but the audience couldn't see me. I was standing just off-stage behind a curtain set up in the large banquet room of the Waterfront Hotel. It was my first year officiating the event. I'd done quite a few shows before but none in Sequoia, Michigan.

The mayor waited until I was beside him to introduce me, as he'd done the previous evening. Then, as he led the audience in a round of applause, he handed me the microphone and strode off-stage and into the audience.

"Good evening," I said, absolutely loving the way my voice boomed over the loudspeakers. "As Mayor Sloan said, we have a great show lined up for you. So, let's get things started."

As the clapping subsided and the upbeat music began, I glanced at the notecard in my hand. "Our first outfit, modeled by Eleni Sloan, is from designer Martinique. This fun and flirty jumpsuit comes in a gorgeous coral floral print. The lightweight organic rayon fabric is flowy and breathable--perfect for a day at the beach or dress it up with wedges for dinner! The leg slits will make you feel pretty and sexy - perfect for that special summer night out."

I watched as Eleni crossed the stage and started down the runway, smiling at the women who *oohed* and *aahed* over her outfit. She was tall and fit, with dark features emboldened by a palette of smoky makeup and thick, curly black hair. At the end of the runway, she pivoted smartly and walked back, exuding confidence. I liked confident women.

"Thank you, Eleni," I said. "And our next outfit is modeled by Hope Louvain. This tropical floral jumpsuit by artist Jane Strayer has an elegant v-neckline and is fully lined. The waist tie is removable and can be wrapped in multiple ways, tied in the front or the back. This all-in-one wonder can be dressed up with your favorite heels or, for a more casual take, paired with platform sneakers and a denim jacket."

Hope was cute and short. Her outfit suited her, but the extensions she'd clipped into her short, blonde hair didn't match. I had to hold my breath as she hobbled across the stage and down the runway, where she pivoted, faltered slightly on top of stiletto heels, and returned amid another round of applause. "Thank you, Hope," I said.

"Our third outfit, modeled by Carly Blackburn, is by designer Flora Smith, a pretty gauze dress with lace insets and pintucks. It has a plunge halter neckline, open back, and an A-line silhouette, a smart but casual dress to wear to any summer event."

I looked down at my notes as I waited for Carly to emerge from the curtain. When she didn't appear, I said into the microphone, "Sorry. There must be a snafu backstage. Are you enjoying the show so far?"

The audience applauded. I glanced to my left but still didn't see anyone waiting to walk on stage. I waited a moment, hoping Fran was simply fixing a loose strap on Carly's dress. At the side of the stage, I caught sight of the audio technician, but he merely shrugged. I blocked the bright stage lights with my hand and looked out into the audience for Charles Sloan but he, too, was gone.

I began again. "As I said, our next outfit is modeled by Carly Blackburn . . ."

And again, no one appeared.

I stood there staring down at my notecards, wondering whether I should go backstage to find out what was going on when Eleni Sloan ran out from behind the curtain. "Someone call 9-1-1. There's been an accident!"

My fingers instinctively reached for my phone. As I rushed past the curtain, I could see the models standing off to the side of one of the dressing rooms, where Carly's legs were sticking out beneath the curtain. I pulled back the flap and saw her lying on her side. No one else seemed to be calling for help, so I did.

"Hello? Yes, we need an ambulance. The Waterfront Hotel in Sequoia, Michigan. Please hurry." I listened to the instructions given by the woman over the phone and when she had finished, she asked for my name.

"Jillian Ophelia Knight Osborne."

❧ ❧

I sat down on a folding chair and tapped my fingers impatiently. The police had told me not to leave. They had grouped all of us who were involved with the show in one area next to the stage and were calling each of us individually to question us. I wasn't sure why we were being interviewed – what kind of accident could cause all this fuss?

I glanced at my watch. I wanted to be back in my hotel room by ten so I could get to bed early. I'd planned to check out by eight o'clock the next morning so I could be home by nine-thirty, when Harper's play group met. She was at the adorable age of eighteen months and although I hadn't even been gone two days, I missed her terribly.

A policeman came over and ushered me to a table, where an overweight man with a sour face was seated. He looked tired and dumpy in his wrinkled overcoat and awful brown suit.

"I'm Detective Walters," he said. "Have a seat."

I sat down across from him and folded my arms across my expensive designer top.

"Who was responsible for dispensing the water bottles to the models' dressing areas?" he asked.

"That would be me."

He wrote it down then looked straight at me. "Did you at any time open any of the water bottles?"

I stared at him, puzzled. "I opened mine. Why would I open anyone else's?"

"That's what I'm asking you."

"Believe me, I only opened mine. I put the rest in each of the three curtained dressing rooms and left, just as I did yesterday evening."

"Where did you get the water?"

"I stopped at a mini-mart about two blocks from here."

"Was it necessary to supply the models with water?"

"I wouldn't have done it otherwise."

"Is that a yes?"

This man was way too serious. "That's a yes. It's what I do at every fashion event. And that's all I have to say because I really need to get to my hotel room now."

"I'm going to have to instruct you not to leave town."

"What?" I rose in indignation. "I can't stay here. I have a baby at home."

"Who's taking care of the baby now?"

"Not that it's any of your business, but my husband, the father is."

"So the baby is in good hands."

"That's not the point."

297

"State your full name for the record."

I sat down again. "I don't understand what's going on. Why can't I leave town?"

"You were backstage before the event."

"So?" I sat forward, my fingers on my knees, and said in a confidential voice, "We're not talking about a murder here, are we?"

"That's still to be determined. Now state your name for the record."

I huffed impatiently. "Jillian Ophelia Knight Osborne." I leaned over to see what he had written. "No. That's Osborne with an *e* on the end - and no *u*."

I huffed again. The man couldn't even spell. "Can I go *now*?"

"Yes, you may go. But don't leave town."

I rose and put my purse over my shoulder. If he thought I was going to stay in Sequoia, he had another think coming. In fact, forget about staying until morning. I was going to leave tonight.

Take that, detective sour face.

Please visit www.katecollinsbooks.com to read more.

About the Author

Kate Collins is the author of the best-selling Flower Shop Mystery series. Her books have made the New York Times Bestseller list, the Barnes & Noble mass market mystery best-sellers' lists, the Independent Booksellers' best-seller's lists, as well as booksellers' lists in the U.K. and Australia. The first three books in the FSM series are now available on audiobook.

In January of 2016, Hallmark Movies & Mysteries channel aired the first Flower Shop Mystery series movie, MUM'S THE WORD, followed by SLAY IT WITH FLOWERS and DEARLY DEPOTTED. The movies star Brooke Shields, Brennan Elliott, Beau Bridges and Kate Drummond.

Kate started her career writing children's stories for magazines and eventually published historical romantic suspense novels under the pen name Linda Eberhardt and Linda O'Brien. Seven romance novels later, she switched to her true love, mysteries.

Printed in the USA
CPSIA information can be obtained
at www.ICGtesting.com
LVHW042130040823
754239LV00003B/351